TARRACO

TARRACO

Book III, The Middle Empire

CONN HALLINAN

Ballingarry Press

To my sons
Sean, Antonio, Brian and David
who have enthusiastically encouraged my writing, always;
and have given me four wonderful grandchildren.

Characters in Tarraco, in order of their appearance

Antonius Crispus, Centurion Third Century, Tenth Cohort VII Legion in Tarraco

Tiberius Cicero, Tesserarius, Third Century, Tenth Cohort, VII Legion

Gaius Porcius, Head Douviri, Tarraco

Lucius Thorius, Second Douviri, Tarraco

Julius Dasumi, Wealthy merchant

Demaratus, Signifer, First Century, First Cohort, VII Legion

Flavius Priscus, Optio, First Century, First Cohort, VII Legion

Titus Valens, Legate, VII Legion

Publius Felix, Tribune in Legio

Marcus Favonius, Praefectus Castrorum, VII Legion

Septimius Granius, Praefectus, or auxiliary cohort commander in Caeseraugusta

Alberic, Frank commander

Hildebold, Frank second in command

Brocard, Frank supply commander

Grimbald, Frank infantry commander

Leufrid, Frank cavalry commander

Coventina, Celtic woman in Tarraco

Cassius Cornelius, Decurion, commander Ala II Flavia Hispanorum Romanorum

Cleomanes, Cretan archer officer

Wallgard, Frank in charge of ships

Androdamus, Tailor

Telamon, Androdamus's son

Aristeus, Androdamus's wife

Vipsania, Leader of the women's Legion of Tarraco

Vallerius Tullius, Retired centurion

Publius Maxus, Praefectus of the auxiliary legion from Valentia

Appius Thorius, Praefectus Castroum of the Valentia auxiliary legion

Contents

Prologue

251 AD

It is 300 years since Julius Caesar conquered Gaul and made it one of Rome's wealthiest provinces, but once again the Empire's legions are fighting desperate battles in the dense forests of the north. Victories no longer signal the end of a war, instead presaging future wars. The myriad tribes Rome once so easily defeated or manipulated have banded together into great confederations that contend almost as equals on the field of battle. While the Empire strains to hold back the floodtide of Goths and Franks pouring across the Rhine and the Danube, fierce Parthian horsemen press in on Rome's eastern borders. Assailed from without by invasion, the Empire is shaken from within by inflation and political upheaval.

The year 251 AD is in the center of the "Middle Empire," that period between the conquests of Julius Caesar and the last stages of the Empire before the Vandals sack Rome in 455 AD. In the Middle Empire, Rome is still immensely powerful, but a careful listener might hear the first whispers of decline and fall.

From the reign of Caracala (211-217 AD) to the Emperor

Diocletian (284-305 AD) Rome will have 12 emperors. All but two die by violence, five by murder. Civil war becomes the norm.

As instability grows and trade declines, the Empire shifts from conquest to defending its borders, and the once all-powerful Roman economy begins to falter. For hundreds of years, Rome's economy had depended on the millions of slaves captured through war. But by the Middle Empire those days are a distant memory: Rome's last successful war of conquest was the Emperor Trajan's second Dacian War in 106 AD. The era of cheap slaves is over and, as slaves grow increasingly expensive, the system's inefficiency and instability accelerate.

As political crisis grips the center, centrifugal forces spin off provinces in the east and north, creating independent Empires in Britannia and Gaul, and Palmyra east of the Levantine coast. But Hispania—Rome's oldest and arguably richest province—remains loyal. It was here that Rome first confronted an enemy as powerful as itself: Carthage. It was here that the Empire began. It was here that Caesar defeated Pompey in the civil war that ends the Republic. And it was here that the western Empire makes its last stand.

In 251 AD, Hispania was a land of vast mineral wealth, and for a time, the Empire's major source of fish, olive oil, and grain. It was an early flashpoint between Christianity and the Roman state. And it produced two of Rome's greatest emperors, Trajan and Hadrian.

Book I, "Hispania." follows three principal characters. Centurion Marcus Favonius, the youngest son of a politically ambitious family, is fleeing the enmity of the Praetorian Guard. He is accompanied by his second-in-command, Flavius Priscus, a street fighter from the tough slums of Rome. And Demaratus, the centurion's third in command, a Greek, former sailor, and a man with a keen sense of history and an outsider's view of the Empire he serves. The three evade assassination and establish themselves in Spain's VII Legion.

In Book II, "Mauretania," the three lead an expedition to what is now modern Morocco to rescue Romans seized by Mauri slave traders. The expedition is a success, and Marcus finds love, but falls afoul of a powerful merchant in Hispania.

Book III, "Tarraco," is based on a Frankish invasion of Hispania.

The VII Legion Hispania Gemina Pia is one of the most interesting units in the Roman Army, and the centerpiece for these books. The VII was an unusual legion, made up of native Hispanians and, with a few exceptions, served on its home territory. The Romans normally assigned legions to areas where they had no local ties or roots. Rome wanted its legions' first loyalty to be to Rome. The VII, the oldest serving legion in the Roman Army, had an unerring knack for picking the winning side in a civil war.

The VII Hispania Gemina Pia disappeared from the written record sometime in the Fourth Century. It was never officially disbanded, but when the Visigoths overran Hispania (469-478 AD) there is no mention of the VII Legion.

I

Centurion Antonius Crispus, hastatus posterior, Third Century, 10th Cohort of the VII Legion Hispania Gemina Pia, stood at the center of the Via Domitia leading into Tarraco. Short, stocky, and bandy legged, he was old for his title, the sign of a man who had come up through the ranks. Beside him stood a tesserarius, his third in command, as much a boy as a man. Behind them at the gate through which the two officers had come was a crowd of merchants and city officials. To the north, a great army moved inexorably toward the city. The late afternoon sun flashed off the weapons and shields, and two blocks of cavalry flanked the vanguard. Behind the wall of shields, an enormous cloud of dust kicked up by horses and wagons filled the sky. It was early spring, but the day had turned hot and the sun sat molten, high in the west. The man beside him fidgeted. "Sir? Your orders?" asked the tesserarius.

Antonius turned to look at his junior officer. He wished he had his optio, Domitius Celer, at his side, but Domitius was busy organizing the century. Tiberius Cicero was a bright young man who had yet to draw a sword in anger. He was scared but doing his best to conceal it. That was fine with Antonius. Any man who could look at the army marching on Tarraco and not be scared was a fool, and foolish men were much more likely to get you killed than fearful ones.

"What do you say we march out and teach those barbarians a lesson, Tiberius?" said the centurion.

"Sir?"

Antonius stopped, reminding himself that part of his job was training youngsters like Tiberius for command. He stifled a smile and kept his face dead serious, although he sighed to himself. The Third Century—a mere 80 men—could no more resist the army descending on Tarraco than he, Antonius, could hold the sun in its place. The old centurion had made the remark in an effort to ease his young tesserarius's tension, but Tiberius was too young and too scared to get the joke.

"Tiberius Cicero, an officer's duty is to the Empire and his men. What would happen if the Third Century marched out to fight that army over there?"

The tesserarius swallowed but said nothing.

"We would all die, Tiberius. Would that help the Empire? "

Tiberius fidgeted some more, looking increasingly unhappy. Antonius again resisted the urge to tease him. "It would not, tesserarius. We would have our honor, but the city would fall."

"Umm. Isn't it going to fall anyhow, sir?" asked Tiberius.

"Yes," answered the centurion. "That's my point."

The tesserarius was silent for a moment. "How did an army that big get to Barcino without anyone alerting us, sir?" he finally asked.

"Good question, lad. I think we should ask it of our comrades in Narbo by whom that army out there had to pass," replied Antonius.

"Do you think the Franks took Narbo?" asked Tiberius.

"Not likely. If they had, there would have been a stream of refugees coming south, and as much as those fellows of ours up north don't approve of us here in Hispania, we would have gotten word. No, I expect they let that army march right past them and didn't say a word," said the Centurion.

"Why would they do that, sir?"

"You're full of good questions today, Tiberius. I suspect the answer is politics. The only thing more confusing than politics are the people who practice it. I try to avoid both and just do my duty," replied Antonius.

"What is our duty, sir?" asked Tiberius.

Antonius turned to look at the human avalanche descending on Tarraco. "Our duty, tesserarius, is to be a thorn in that army's side," he answered quietly. "Did you send the riders out?"

"Yes, sir. Two, by different roads, to Legio," answered Tiberius.

"Good. The VII Legion will come," said Antonius. "The trick, tesserarius, will be staying alive long enough to be here when they arrive."

Turning back toward the gate he eyed the crowd of merchants and politicians distastefully. "Our first job will be to deal with that lot," he growled.

Gaius Porcius, the First Duoviri, or leading magistrate for the city, separated himself from the crowd and came forward. Antonius eyed him warily. Gaius was a small, slight man, with a limp. To Antonius's way of thinking, Gaius was not, all in all, a bad sort. He was a veteran of the XI Legion Claudia Pia Fidelis, although as a clerk he had never done any actual fighting. He was not particularly corrupt, or at least not any more than most, certainly not as much as his junior co-duoviri, Lucius Thorius. Lucius would steal the coins out of a corpse's mouth. He was a heavy, florid man, who favored expensive togas, gold bracelets, and expensive rings. He followed Gaius at a discreet distance.

"What do you intend, Centurion?" asked Gaius.

"I have sent an alert to the VII Legion in Legio, Gaius."

Lucius shouldered his way into the conversation. "But surely you will not try to defend the city with your small force, Centurion? If you did, the Franks would put us all to the sword when they took the city, just like our own army does," he said.

"I was not under the impression that a junior duoviri issued orders to the army," Antonius replied coldly.

"He has a point, Antonius," put in Gaius. "We both know that the entire cohort, let alone a single century, could not defend Tarraco against that army."

"I have no intention of surrendering, even if that army out there would accept it," said Antonius.

"You endanger us all," hissed Lucius.

"And you speak treason, duoviri," replied Antonius. "Do you know what the punishment for treason is?"

"Gentlemen, gentlemen," said Gaius, "there is no time for this discussion." Turning to Lucius he said, "Antonius will do as he sees proper. Neither you nor I can issue orders to officers of the VII Legion. That is a matter for its legate. In any case, Roman soldiers do not surrender. It is an affront to the Empire." Turning back to Antonius he said, "I would ask you not to speak of treason at this time, sir. My colleague and I are responsible for the residents of the city, and we must try to ensure that they will not be ill-treated. Surely you can see we, too, have a duty as well?"

By this time several of the leading merchants and family representatives, dressed in everything from formal togas to everyday smocks and pants, had crowded forward and begun to surround the centurion and his tesserarius. Antonius knew most of them, and thought very little of any of them. Antonius had already concluded that a defense of the city would be a disaster, but he had never bothered to tell Gaius what his plan was. If he told them now, it would seem as if he was yielding under pressure, and that irked him. But then again, it was his own fault for not communicating with the civilian leaders. So. he would have to bite the leather strap and tell them.

"I have no intention of defending the city, Gaius. The VII Legion is thin enough without throwing away a century," he said. "Nor will I surrender the Third Century. I have stocked and barricaded the Praetorian Tower, and I will move the Century there directly."

"If you do not surrender, they will kill us all," one heavy-faced merchant said. Antonius narrowed his eyes and tried to place the man, but he was unfamiliar.

"And you are?" asked Fabius, putting his hands on his hips.

"Julius Dasumi," the man replied in a tone suggesting that the centurion should know who he was.

Dasumi. Yes, that explained the tone. The man probably had more wealth than all the rest of Tarraco's merchants combined. Julius Dasumi. The army gossip was that, when his sister had been taken by Mauri slave traders last year, he had been less than enthusiastic about getting her back. It took the First Cohort of the VII Legion to do that. The story was that when she got back to Corduba, she had run him out of town with the backing of Marcus Favonius, head centurion of the First Cohort, and acting commander of the Mauretania expedition. Word was the man's sister and Marcus were lovers. It was a thoroughly delicious tale.

Antonius looked him up and down slowly. "Maybe we should get your sister up from Corduba to scatter that lot out there."

Julius flushed. "You will regret that comment, centurion."

"Oh, will I?" answered Antonius softly.

"Gentlemen, the enemy approaches and we bicker," protested Gaius. Turning to Julius Dasumi, he said sharply, "Step back, sir. You impede our discussion."

Antonius was impressed. He didn't think Gaius had it in him to give orders to the head of the wealthiest family in Hispania. He must have done more than clerk for the XI Claudia. Julius Dasumi reluctantly stepped back, shooting the centurion a poisonous look. "I had best watch my back," thought Antonius to himself.

The Franks were within a mile of the city, and a group of them had separated themselves from the van and were trotting forward. They were unarmored and carried round, wooden shields. Several had long spears, and one had a large silver torq around his neck. Antonius glanced back at the Franks and then signaled Tiberius, who strode back toward the gate, gathering soldiers to him.

Turning back to Gaius, he said, "Duoviri, I leave the matter of negotiations to you. I will retire with my century to the tower. May the gods protect you and our city."

Gaius nodded and waved a group of men forward who quickly gathered around him. Antonius, with one last look at the Franks, pushed his way through the crowd and followed his tesserarius.

The city, founded by the great Scipio, father of the man who brought Hannibal to his knees, was open to the enemy.

Clodius Oppius of the Ala Victrix auxiliary cavalry kept his horse at a slow lope. Two other mounts trailed behind him. His friend Macro had the easier ride. Clodius was ordered to head south to just above Saguntum before taking the road that turned northwest to Caesaraugusta. Macro had only to head north to Ilerda, then west following the Iberus River to Legio. He would get there days ahead of Clodius.

Macro's easy ride put Clodius in a foul mood. He would ride twice as far as Macro and all for nothing. It would be Macro who brought the news of the Franks. And it was Macro who would reap the glory. Stupid army! This is what always happened: a bunch of thickheaded soldiers gave orders that made no sense, and the cavalry had to pay the price. He set himself in for the ride. It was a long way to Legio.

Macro Aelius, late member of the Ala Victrix auxiliary cavalry, lay crumpled in the middle of the road. A spreading stain of blood glistened on the polished stones around him. Half a dozen riders looked down at the body.

"He didn't put up much of a fight," one of them commented.

Another shrugged. "He was carrying a message. No shield, no spear, what do you expect?"

"I heard this VII Legion is a bunch of women and children," answered the first man. "This proves it."

"This proves nothing, except you're not much of a swordsman. You had to stab him four times before you killed him," the other man said.

"The important thing is that the VII Legion is not going to know what's up," said a third man. "I don't know if they are women and children, but they aren't very bright if they didn't figure we would seal off the roads going north."

The first man leaned down and prodded the body on the road with a lance. Getting no reaction, he turned and trotted back toward Tarraco. The others followed in his wake.

II

Praefectus Castrorum Marcus Favonius rode by himself, his staff trailing behind him. He hadn't said he wanted to be alone, but his men picked up on his mood and kept their distance. The day was early, and spring had finally arrived in Hispania's northern mountains. The fields were a rich green, and trees were just coming into bud. Mountains crowded in on the arrow-straight road with its stones polished by carts and hooves. The civilian traffic moved aside when it saw his officer's uniforms, his staff,and the banner of the VII Legion. But in spite of the lovely day, Marcus was gloomy.

His elevation from Primus Pilus, or First Centurion, to third in command of the VII Legion Hispania had put a certain distance between himself and his staff, and Marcus found that disconcerting. Like any good officer, he had always led his men from the front. But a Praefectus Castrorum is not a line officer. You don't put your commanders into the middle of a melee where some lucky barbarian could cut them down. So rather than fighting alongside his men, he sent them into battle. He was no longer a warrior but a chooser of the slain.

Was it that that was depressing him, or Aelia? He had seen her off at first light from the port of Brigantium and he was now making his way back to the VII Legion's base at Legio. Whenever he considered Aelia, his mind went off on tangents. Marcus did not mind tangents. He loved to daydream and had discovered that it was actually an effective way of working through problems. He had "day dreamed" the solution to defeating the Mauri in Mauretania, which is why he was now third in command of Hispania's only regular legion.

But thinking of the Mauri brought him back to Aelia, whom he had rescued from the slave raiders and brought back to Hispania. Aelia was a puzzle to him. What did this woman see in him? Marcus had no illusions about himself. He was of average height and looks, a bit overweight, and hailed from a modest equestrian family. Aelia, on the other hand, was stunningly beautiful, Patrician to the core, and probably one of the wealthiest women in Hispania.

At first, he thought her attraction to him was just gratitude, but it was now a year since the rescue and here he was seeing her off on a ship to Gedes. On their return from Mauretania, he had accompanied her to Cordoba to help her against her brother, after which they had become lovers. But when he had to leave with his cohort for Legio, she announced that after she had taken care of some business matters, she would take a ship from Gedes to Brigantium and visit him.

Marcus thought she was simply being polite since he could not imagine a woman like Aelia in a rough garrison city like

Legio, but three months later she arrived accompanied by more baggage than Marcus thought possible. His former optio and now chief of staff, Flavius Priscus, thought that it was likely more supplies than Xerxes brought with him to invade Greece. "And he was said to have a million men," said Flavius shaking his head in wonder.

Aelia took over the largest house in Legio, that by her standards was little more than a hut, and proceeded to create a court. She and her adopted sister Rachel held banquets and dinner parties, hosted entertainers, and sallied forth into the countryside to picnic. Marcus was certain that trying to recreate bright Cordoba in Hispania's far gloomier north would stir local resentment, but Aelia could charm the scales off a snake.

But only part of Aelia's magic was her grace and ability to captivate an audience. She was Patrician born, but she had a quality of the plebian about her that was no act. She could beguile a Legate and sympathize with the lot of a junior tesserarius. Marcus even began to resent her skill at getting people to do exactly what she wanted them to do.

She was one of the most intelligent people Marcus had ever encountered, and she had demonstrated remarkable courage during her captivity. In short, just the kind of person to make Marcus feel insecure. But the only time he had hinted at that insecurity she had been rather sharp with him. "Men," she said, "are so stupid. You worship beauty and wealth. Women are much smarter. Beauty is fleeting and wealth is spent, and then we die. I want to be with someone at the end whom I can stand to be in the same room with. Don't speak to me of this again, Marcus." She strode off and wouldn't talk to him for a whole day.

At first he was angry—and hurt—but he was smart enough to see the truth in it and he did find the line about being in the same room funny. So, it was finally all patched up and Marcus was careful to keep his insecurities to himself.

But here he was riding away from the woman he...what? Marcus turned that thought over in his mind. Beguiled, certainly. In love? Well, if he wasn't in love why was he so down and depressed? Maybe he really was in love and maybe he should spend less time analyzing it all.

What he really needed to do was talk with his friends and comrades Flavius and Demaratus. But could he talk to them about this? Not Flavius, who actually knew less about women than himself. And the Greek—handsome, smooth and experienced—would be amused. Still, they were his best friends in the world and, unlike the staff trailing behind him, they wouldn't be afraid to cheer him up.

Marcus sat up a little straighter. "Get a hold of yourself, Marcus Favonius. Two years ago you were on the lam. Now you are third in command of a legion. If the right emperor is in power, you might make tribune. You are consort to a rich and beautiful woman. It is a lovely spring day and I am riding on exactly the kind of horse I like: slow and stupid. Life is good. What can go wrong?"

III

Demaratus, Signifer of the First Century, First Cohort, of the VII Legion Hispania, was doing his best to keep his attention focused on his companion Flavius Priscus. Flavius was a friend and Demaratus took friendship seriously. But Flavius was also an optio and his superior officer. Always a good idea to pay attention to your superior in the Roman Army. Flavius was being particularly opaque, however, and Demaratus's attention kept sliding away to a pair of fetching young women seated two tables over at the small outdoor taverna. Both were dressed for Floralia, the flower festival that ushered in spring and asked the gods for a good harvest. In a city of any size, Floralia would be celebrated with six days of games, but in the small provincial vicus that surrounded the Roman fort at Legio, it was limited to dressing up, eating, drinking, and sex, all of which Demaratus thought was a splendid idea. The two women had been discreetly eyeing him since he and Flavius had wandered into the establishment. Their attention was hardly surprising. Demaratus was good-looking—and knew it—and he was used to women staring at him. While Flavius seemed indifferent to how he appeared,

Demaratus always took care with his uniform, and today he was freshly barbered and bathed.

"So, what do you think?" asked Flavius.

Demaratus shifted his attention from the women and searched his memory for what they had been talking about. He had lost the thread. Frowning slightly, he turned to Flavius, "I'm not sure."

The Optio looked impatient. "Look, comrade, you know about these things," said Flavius.

Know about what things? What would Flavius think he knew more about than a superior officer, friend or not? Women, of course. Flavius had been talking about women, but so circuitously that Demaratus's attention had wandered. There could be only one woman Flavius was referring to, one of the women that the First Century had rescued from the Mauri in Mauretania. A slave when the Mauri had taken her in a raid, she had befriended Aelia Dasumi, the wealthy and beautiful woman who was currently the—what? Not wife, maybe companion? —of his then centurion and now recently appointed Praefectus Castrorum, Marcus Favonius. Aelia had adopted her as a sister when the century returned to Hispania. Flavius had helped rescue the two women and had been smitten by the former slave. What was her name? Yes, Rachel.

Demaratus sighed with relief at having reconstructed the thread of the conversation, even though the woman's actual name had never come up.

Demaratus leaned forward and contemplated his cup of wine. He was treading on delicate ground. If his advice didn't work it might not go well for him, although Flavius was less vindictive than any Roman Demaratus had ever known. But an unhappy friend—and superior—could make one's life difficult.

"Have you had a conversation with her?" he finally asked.

"Well, not about that," replied Flavius. "We talked about…," he trailed off. "Things," he finally said.

"What kind of things?" probed Demaratus.

Flavius shrugged. "What difference does that make?"

"Did you talk about the price of onions or about life?"

"Why would I talk with her about onions?"

"What I meant, brother, was did you talk about personal things?" said the signifer, trying to keep the exasperation out of his voice. Flavius was not someone who contemplated life very much, although he was intelligent and honorable to a fault.

Flavius was silent for a moment, focused on refilling his wine cup. He was not a handsome man and his nose had been broken so many times it was a mid-face smear. But there was an open honesty about his face, which Demaratus had learned appealed to women, and he was powerfully built. It was the body of a Roman, of course, which was all wrong: long torso, short legs, everything not quite in proportion.

Flavius finally looked up. "I guess. I told her about how I had grown up in Rome, and, of course, about Marcus. She was interested in stories about Marcus. She told me a little about herself, but not a lot. She asks questions. What do you make of it?"

"That she finds you interesting," replied Demaratus. "That is not surprising."

Flavius shot him a suspicious look. The optio hated flattery.

Demaratus spread his hands. "Comrade, if you are to go into battle—and marriage bears more resemblance to battle than you would imagine—then you must know your strengths and weaknesses." Demaratus ticked off a list of the former: "You are interesting, on that you must take my word, brother. You have a respectable income, you are honored by your legion for your courage. You do not have a string of mistresses and a pack of bastards, and your commander and friend is the consort of her sister."

"And my weaknesses?" asked Flavius.

Demaratus was silent a long moment. The ground had shifted from delicate to treacherous. But Flavius was his friend and Demaratus was already deeply surprised about how much of himself he had revealed to a junior officer, friend or not.

"You are hesitant with women," he finally answered. "And they may interpret that to mean a lack of interest."

Flavius slumped on his stool and looked unhappy. "But suppose she said she wasn't interested in me?" he asked.

"If she wasn't interested in you, she would not ask questions or tell you anything about herself," answered Demaratus.

Flavius perked up. "So, you think there is a chance for me?"

"Certainly. She would be a lucky woman to get you. Have you talked with Marcus about this?" asked the signifer.

"By the gods, no!" said Flavius. "This is not a subject you talk to a commander about."

Demaratus silently cursed the rigid hierarchy of the Roman Army. "Comrade, Marcus is also your friend, and more than that, he is.... " Demaratus searched for a word, "Well, he is close to Aelia. In Greece it is traditional to have an intermediary in these matters."

"Couldn't you do that?" asked Flavius, surprising Demaratus. Apparently, the hierarchy was up, not down.

"If you wish me to, Flavius, of course I will act for you. And you honor me in the asking," replied Demaratus, "but in any case, I would speak with Aelia, since it would not be proper to approach Rachel."

"But Aelia and Rachel are back in Corduba," said Flavius.

The two women had come north to Legio for several weeks. It was during this time that Flavius had spent time with Rachel. But the cold northern climate and general primitiveness of the vicus had finally driven Aelia back to Corduba. What this meant about the relationship between Marcus and Aelia was unclear to Demaratus, but even if the two were drifting apart, he was certain that Aelia would be helpful in this matter.

"That is not necessarily a bad thing, comrade. Sometimes these things are best done by letter at a distance," replied Demaratus.

Flavius downed his wine in a single gulp. "So, you will help me to marry Rachel?" he asked.

"Of course," replied Demaratus, "but there is one matter you might want to consider."

"What's that?" asked Flavius.

"She is a Jewess," said Demaratus.

"So? I don't care what people believe," said Flavius sounding puzzled.

"No, I am certain you don't. But she might," said Demaratus.

"Okay, I'll believe what Jews believe, whatever that is," said Flavius. "Gods are gods. I have always thought they were pretty much the same."

"It is not that simple, brother. Jews don't believe in gods, they believe in one god."

"Atheists, are they? Okay, I will believe in one god. Makes life simpler. I figure I could always do some sacrificing on the side," said Flavius.

"It isn't just what you believe, it is what you do," said Demaratus.

Flavius narrowed his gaze. "Is this going to turn into one of your lectures that demonstrates the natural superiority of Greeks?"

"It is a lecture and you will have to listen to it, comrade, that is, if you want to marry this Rachel," replied Demaratus putting both his hands flat on the table.

Flavius crossed his arms, put on his long-suffering face, and nodded.

"Being Jewish is more than believing in one god. The Zoroasters believe the same thing and, as we know, so do the Christians," said Demaratus.

"Yeah, but Christians are just Jews who want to make everyone believe what they believe," said the optio.

Demaratus shrugged. "Maybe, but Jews are still different. First, they aren't interested in recruiting, unlike Christians, who want to make everyone Christian. They aren't evangelical," a word that drew a blank look from Flavius. " It's a religion for Jews, not for non-Jews."

"Are you saying I can't believe in Jewish?" asked Flavius.

"You can believe in anything you like, comrade, but that doesn't mean people accept you as one of their own. Being Jewish is about self-identification. The religion is a religion for Jews, not outsiders. Since the Jews no longer have a country, thanks to the Romans, it is the way they hang onto their identity."

"Now look, Demaratus, the Jews revolted and...," began Flavius, but Demaratus cut him off. "I am not making a judgment on what happened, Flavius. It is just an historical fact that complicates the matter we are discussing."

The optio did not look happy about being cut off by a junior officer, but he was more focused on "the matter" than protocol, so he said nothing.

"In order to marry Rachel, you may have to become Jewish," said Demaratus.

"Didn't I say I would believe whatever I had to believe?" said Flavius impatiently.

"As I said, it is not just what you believe, it is what you do," replied Demaratus.

"What does that mean?" asked Flavius, growing more impatient.

"The Jews believe they have a covenant with their God, and there is a ceremony that establishes that covenant," answered Demaratus.

"What is this ceremony?" said Flavius, uncrossing his arms.

Demaratus was tempted to tease Flavius at this point but resisted, realizing that is would be a disaster, both for what they were talking about and their friendship. "The Jews circumcise all males."

Flavius gave him a blank look.

"That is the act of covenant, comrade," said Demaratus. "It is not enough to believe, you must also enter into the covenant."

"So, are you saying that I might have to get some of my penis cut off?" said Flavius incredulously.

"It is not your penis, Flavius, it's just your foreskin," answered Demaratus. "Lots of people do it."

Flavius looked uncomfortable but nodded. "Anything else?"

"I will find out, brother. There are many Jews in Tarraco, and when I return to visit Coventina, I will take this up with one of their priests. I plan to go in a month. Is that too long for you?"

Flavius poured the two another cup of wine. "No, I guess not."

"If you do not object, I would like to write to Aelia Dasumi, although I will ask her to keep this between us until I find out more information in Tarraco," said Demaratus.

Flavius looked nervous. "You know this stuff better than me, Demaratus, so do what you think is right." He reached across the table and took the Greek by the arm. "I thank you for this, brother. I am in your debt."

"It is the debt of friendship, comrade, so there is no cost involved," he replied.

Demaratus had just finished what he thought was a nicely worded phrase, when Flavius stood up. "Something is up, signifer."

The Greek could never navigate these shifts in status as quickly as Flavius, in part because he had not spent most of his life in the Roman Army. Turning to look at what caused the optio to make his comment he saw tesserarius Sextus Aelius, the century's third in command, dressed in full uniform, coming up the street of the vicus at a brisk pace.

"Sextus," called out Flavius.

The man saw them, strode over, and saluted.

"What's afoot, Sextus?" asked Demaratus.

"An army of Franks has taken Barcino and Tarraco, sir. The legate has canceled all leaves and officers are instructed to return to their units," replied Sextus.

"By the gods, how is that possible? We heard nothing," asked Flavius.

The tesserarius shook his head. "I don't know, sir. A rider just came in. I don't know any details."

Flavius turned to Demaratus and commented "Well, it looks like you will be back in Tarraco in considerably less than a month."

The Greek, stiff and white-faced, made no reply.

Flavius put his arm around his shoulder. "Now, not to worry. This must have been just a raid, although how they got that far south without us knowing, only the gods know. We will bring your girl out just fine."

Demaratus nodded but said nothing. When the three officers reached the gates of the fort, he fell behind and slipped off.

IV

Titus Valens, legate of the VII Legion, pushed the dispatch toward Tribune Quintius Junius and Marcus.

Quintius was by far the oldest of the three, growing fat in his old age, his face flushed with dark pouches under his eyes. He had recently fallen in a steam bath, and his left leg was splinted and wrapped. The legate was tall, thin and gray, with sharp lines running down either side of his mouth.

As fourth in command, outranked by the legate and the tribune, Marcus waited until Quintius had read through the scroll, then quickly scanned it.

Titus was silent, leaning forward with both hands on the table. Quintius sighed and moved his leg to a more comfortable position. Marcus was the first to speak. "How old is the dispatch, sir?"

"Almost a week, Marcus. The rider had to go south almost as far as Segundum before he could head north to Caesaraugusta," answered Titus, leaning back on his stool.

Marcus frowned. "Can we assume that the western road out of Tarraco was cut?"

"It would seem so. I am certain that the Third Century would have sent a rider by the more direct route through Ilerda. Apparently he did not get through," said Titus. The legate sorted through a small stack of scrolls and pulled out another. "The commander of the I Tungrorum auxiliary cohort at Caeseraugusta says he is ordering a cavalry unit based in Ilerda to do a reconnaissance on Tarraco and find out what is going on. He will send his report as soon as he has information."

"Good man," commented Quintius.

"Yes, Septimius Granius is a solid commander. He says he is also gathering troops in case the Franks move west. However, the auxiliary units are scattered all over Hispania. To pull together a force capable of taking on this invasion will take a while," said Titus.

"How large is Frankish force? I did not see that in the dispatch," said Marcus.

"We don't know, Marcus, but it was big enough to take Barcino. The rider left before the Franks got to Tarraco, but the dispatch the century from the Tenth Cohort received estimated that the Frankish army was at least 20,000, maybe more," replied the Legate.

The tribune whistled. "Almost three times our size."

"But they may be little more than barbarian rabble," said the legate.

Marcus shook his head. "We shouldn't count on that, sir. Many of the Franks have served in the auxiliaries, and some of them are competent soldiers. I don't think they can match a regular legion, but it would be a mistake to underestimate them."

"I sometimes forget you served in northern Gaul, Marcus. What do you make of this?" asked Quintius.

Marcus looked at Titus, who nodded for him to talk.

"If these are Franks, I suspect they are from the Ripurarian tribe, who hail from north of the Rhenus. The Salians to the west are more civilized and have even helped us defend the frontier. Many Ripurarians have also served in the auxiliaries, but not so many as from the Salians. The people from north of the Rhenus are fierce. I fought them for three years, and they are not to be taken lightly."

"But what are they doing here?" asked Quintius. "And how did they get here without us knowing they were coming?"

"What they are doing here I have no idea, but I have a suspicion as to why we didn't know," put in Titus.

"Sir?" asked the tribune.

Titus sighed and pushed his hands through his short hair. He looked tired. "There are some in Gaul who would like to carve out their own empire, Quintius."

"And many in Britannia would join them," put in Marcus. "Gaul and Britannia produce much for Rome, but receive little in return, especially in these unsettled times."

Quintius nodded. "I see. In which case, causing the VII Legion trouble would be much to their liking. Through two civil wars we have stayed loyal to Rome. It is not for nothing we earned the title 'pia.' A barbarian invasion would keep us too busy within our own borders to deal with treason in Narbo and Massilia. That would explain how the Franks could arrive without warning. There was intent behind the lack of information."

"Would there be some in Hispania who think the same?" asked Marcus.

"Maybe," replied Titus. "There are close ties between the big merchant families in Narbo, Massilia, Barcino, and Tarraco. Many of those families stood with the enemies of the VII Legion in the last civil war, although that was a long time ago."

"So, the enemy has arrived in our midst and we are blind," said the tribune.

"Blind or not, the VII Legion will march," said Titus. He rose and began to pace. "If we leave immediately, it will take three weeks to reach Tarraco, and that does not take into account that we will have to gather auxiliaries on the way. We will heed your advice, Marcus, and not assume we are pitted against rabble. With the exception of the cavalry, our auxiliaries have little experience, but numbers may be important, particularly if it comes to a siege."

"Sir, may I suggest we send a message by ship to Gedes and contact the Ala II Flavia Hispanorum Romanorum for cavalry support?" said Marcus.

Quintius chuckled. "Get that fellow of yours from the Mauretania expedition? What's his name?"

"Cassius Cornelius, sir. He has been promoted from Decurion to commander of the Ala, and he is a fine cavalry officer," answered Marcus.

"I have no objection, as long as you think he can meet us at Caesaraugusta in time," answered Titus. "We are shorthanded, Marcus. Tribune Publius Felix is in Rome, and Quintius here is nursing a broken leg. As my new fourth in command, you will have to prepare the Legion to march. I will use my authority to pull together the auxiliaries, which will be no easy task. Once the provincial officials know there are invaders in their midst, no one will want to give up soldiers. This means you will have to make a lot of decisions on your own, a capacity you more than demonstrated in Mauretania."

"Yes, sir. I already have a staff assembled. May I ask our route?" said Marcus.

"Good question," put in Quintius. "The shorter route is through Augustabriga, but Clunia is a bigger city with more supplies and men."

Titus nodded. "Right. Clunia is our most likely route, although it will add a few days. We will delay that decision until the last moment. It is possible that information from the cavalry reconnaissance of Tarraco will reach us before we have to commit ourselves to a specific route. What they find may help us decide whether speed or force is called for."

The legate stopped his pacing. "Marcus, I want to leave in two days. By that time, we should be able to gather some auxiliaries from Augusta. You will keep me informed on how your organization is going."

"Sir," Marcus saluted. Leaving the Principia, his head was spinning with what it would take to mobilize the Legion: weapons, food, auxiliaries, logistics, an avalanche of things, big and small, that might make the difference in whether the VII Legion would survive the next month.

V

Alberic sat on a carved stool, his elbows on the table, hands clasped before him. His hair grazed his shoulders, loosely framing a face with angular cheekbones, highlighted by deep-set blue eyes. A light scar ran from the bridge of his nose to his right cheek. He was a tall man, by far the tallest in the room, and broad across the shoulders. A chain mail shirt hung lightly on him, bound at the waist by a wide leather belt with an ornate buckle. At his side stood a smaller man, dark-haired with a scruffy beard, dressed in similar mail, but with a hooded cloak tied across his chest. He gripped a long-bladed sword in a scabbard rich with runes.

"Bring me the centurion of your century," he said.

Fabius Porcius stood at the other side of the table. Behind him the junior douviri, Lucius Thorius, shifted restlessly.

"I have no power to order a centurion to do anything," he replied. "You must know this."

"What we know does not concern you, Roman," said the smaller man.

"You have the city, which put up no resistance. The century

you speak of is no threat to you. Why is it of any importance?" asked Fabius.

"It is a serpent at our breast, Roman," said Alberic.

"It is a serpent without fangs or poison. In any case, there is nothing I can do about it," said Fabius.

"There is a great deal you can do about it," countered Alberic. "You can tell them that if they do not surrender to us that I will begin executing residents in the plaza before the tower. I will execute them until they surrender or Tarraco runs out of residents."

"We had an agreement that if Tarraco did not resist you would protect its residents," replied Fabius.

"I break the agreement," said Alberic quietly.

Fabius stared at him for a long moment. "Frank, you are only here because those in Gaul let you pass through unmolested. Do you think they did so because they fear you? You are a cat's paw in a complex game. You hold this city, but you have conquered nothing. You can kill everyone in Tarraco, but you will pay a price for it."

"Death holds no fear for us, Roman," said Alberic.

"Do you speak for your women and children as well?" shot back Fabius.

"Maybe you will be the first to die, bookkeeper."

Fabius shrugged. "If you think to frighten me, you fail. I am a veteran of the XI Claudia. Romans know how to die. But mark me, Frank. The VII Legion will be here within a month. If you harm our citizens, their vengeance will be terrible."

"The VII Legion has not fought a war in memory. Many of our soldiers come fresh from the battlefield where they have fought Rome's wars on the northern borders. If the VII Legion comes against us, we will crush it," said Alberic. "And I would not assume you will see your legion quite so soon. My cavalry intercepted your messenger."

"All of them?" said Fabius.

"Yes, all of them, Roman," answered Alberic. Turning to two guards he said, "Now get this clerk out of here. I will deal with him later."

The two guards grabbed Fabius by his arms and shoved him toward the door.

As the door closed behind him, the man standing behind Alberic said, "So, there was more than one."

"We should have figured that was so, Hildebold," said the Frank leader.

"We covered all the roads leading out of Tarraco. I don't think anyone could get by. The man may be lying," said Hildebold.

"We did not cover the road to the south," replied Alberic. "And even if he is lying, we know the VII Legion will come. News that Tarraco is in our hands will eventually get out."

"We have three times the VII Legion's numbers, and our men are more experienced in battle," said Hildebold. "We can defeat them."

"Never underestimate the Romans, and we will have more than the VII Legion to contend with. They are certain to have auxiliaries as well," said Alberic, pushing himself up from the table. He went to sideboard and poured himself and Hildebold a goblet of wine and handed it to the smaller man. "And this clerk has a point about our women and children. We have a responsibility, Hildebold, and we do not plan to stay here in Tarraco for very long."

"The clerk is a mouse," said Hildebold dismissively.

"A mouse with teeth, comrade," said Alberic. "He is not afraid of us because he knows we are a lone army in the heart of the Empire."

"I can make him afraid," said Hildebold softly.

"Violence is not the answer to everything, Hildebold. Even if we kill him and thousands of others, those Romans soldiers in the tower are not going to give themselves up. Roman soldiers would rather die. Killing lots of civilians will not move them, and will unite the city against us," said Alberic. "He is right that we are a cat's paw in some scheme among the Romans themselves. What the Romans do not know is that we have a scheme ourselves."

Hildebold frowned. "I have some doubts about this scheme, Alberic."

The big man nodded. "We would be fools not to have doubts, but we are now committed. We are surrounded by lions, my friend. We have surprised them and they are off balance, but sooner or later they will gather and come for us. When they do, we must be gone."

"Will we have time to do it?" asked Hildebold.

"Not if this VII Legion finds us still in Tarraco. If it comes to a siege, we are lost. The Romans excel at the art of siege. We must destroy or at least badly wound this Hispania legion before it reaches Tarraco," answered Alberic. "Send a man north to Barcino. We need the ships we seized there. We must pull them together with those we seized here in Tarraco. We cannot get to where we are bound without ships."

Hildebold shook his head. "Alberic, we are not sailors. Even if we can get those ships from Barcino, who will guide them to where we want?"

"Wallgard has some knowledge of ships, and he is seizing every sailor he can lay his hands on right now," said Alberic. "It is good for you to question, my friend, but we must not allow the difficulties to discourage us."

"Alberic, most the ships in Barcino and Tarraco got away long before we took both cities. Even if we gather everything we have, we will not have enough," protested Hildebold.

"Don't you think I know this?" replied Alberic with a trace of impatience. "That is why we took Tarraco. We knew it would bring the VII Legion against us, and defeating the VII Legion is essential to our plan. If the Legion is beaten, the Romans will have to negotiate. They will have no choice. We hold the city and its residents as hostage. Our bargain will be ships for the city and its people. It will be months before Rome can mount an expedition to attack us, and they know this. Defeat the VII Legion and we will win our way free."

"There are many 'ifs' in this plan," grumbled Hildebold. "We could return the way we came and be equally safe."

"Do you think the Romans in Gaul will let us return?" asked Alberic. "We are only useful to them while we are here in Hispania. If we try to return, we will find the Gaulish legions massed against us, and we both know what the outcome of that will be. They opened the door to the south for us, but it is a one-way door."

Hildebold ran his hands through his hair. "I am not sure what the Romans in Gaul are up to. I suspect they have some scheme to enrich themselves and maybe declare one of their number emperor and march on Rome. Maybe the Romans here in Hispania stand against them. Who can follow their schemes?"

"I agree. It is hard to follow their thinking, and plot seems piled on plot," agreed Alberic. He took Hildebold by the shoulders. "Brother, there is no way back, only forward. Let's go look at this tower where the Romans have barricaded themselves and then to the harbor to see what we have in the way of transport. I need you to be of stout heart, Hildebold. Discouragement is contagious."

"Sir," protested Hildebold. "You know I stand with you."

"That I never doubted," said Alberic. "But we are poised on a sword's edge. We dare not show doubt. The Romans will smell it, and then we are lost."

Hildebold nodded. "Alright, Alberic. Let's go see these Romans."

Centurion Lucillius Oppius, commanding the Narbo guard, stared at the wax tablet for several minutes. His tesserarius, Primus Verus, waited patiently. His second-in-command, Optio Cnacus Pontius, sat quietly in a corner. Finally, Lucillius looked up at the younger man. "Anything else?"

"No, sir. The refugees said Barcino fell without a fight and that the bulk of the Franks were marching on Tarraco. None of them knew if the city had fallen, but all agreed that there was just a small garrison to defend the place."

Lucillius sighed, nodded, and pushed the tablet to one side, picking up a scroll that listed the men currently in the hospital. Primus continued to stand in front of the small desk that the centurion was working at.

"Well?" said Luccillius, finally looking up.

"Sir, I don't understand what is going on," answered the tesserarius.

Lucillius pushed his chair back and contemplated his third in command. Primus was young for his post, but that tended to be the case in the provinces. He was a local from Nemausus, a smart lad, but nonetheless a provincial with little understanding of politics.

"Barcino has fallen to the Franks. Tarraco is likely to fall next. What about that is hard to understand?" said Lucillius, trying to warn off the young officer by putting an edge to his voice.

"Yes, sir, I understand that. What I don't understand is why we let an army of Franks march right by us and do nothing but watch them. That is the part I have trouble with," replied Primus.

The centurion stood, put both his hands on the table and leaned forward. "Because those were our orders, tesserarius, and in this army we follow orders."

But the young officer would not give it up.

"Yes, sir, I helped distribute the orders. We were told that the Franks had been offered land out in Hispania's west where those Lusitanians are causing trouble. That wasn't a bunch of farmers that passed by, that was a couple of legions' worth of soldiers."

"Your point?" asked the centurion.

"Well, sir, did the Franks double-cross someone and decide

to go to war, or did someone know that they intended to attack Barcino and Tarraco in the first place?" he replied doggedly.

"That, tesserarius, is none of your business. Dismissed," said the centurion.

Primus hesitated, flushed red, saluted, and left.

"Bit hard on him, weren't you?" said the optio.

"Those kinds of questions are going to get that young man killed, and not only do I like him, but he is a good officer," replied the centurion.

"I doubt you telling him to mind his own business is going to keep him from asking questions. And he is not the only one, sir. Lots of the men saw those Franks go by, and few of them thought they were off to put in a crop somewhere," said Cnacus.

"Optio, how long have we been together?" asked Lucillius, turning to look at his second-in-command.

"Ten years, sir," replied Cnacus.

"What have we learned in 10 years, optio?"

Cnacus gave him a grin. "To follow orders and keep our mouth shut, sir. Still and all, I can't help thinking that whoever gave those orders had in mind to destroy our comrades in the VII Hispania. And that means maybe they think our new emperor—may glorious Augustus watch over him—might not be as secure on the throne as he thinks he is. And it also occurred to me that maybe those people have in mind something more along the lines of creating their own little empire right here in Gaul. In that case, getting rid of the VII Legion removes a thorn from their side."

The centurion glanced over his shoulder to make sure no one

was listening. "That is talk that could get us both killed," he said quietly.

"So will choosing the wrong side, sir," replied the optio. "I do what I am told, but I have 10 years before I get out of this army and can get my own piece of land. I would like to live long enough to see that."

"If someone hears you talking about overthrowing emperors, or treason, you will never see that day," said Lucillius.

The optio smiled. "These days, overthrowing emperors seems to be a monthly event. Frankly, sir, I don't much care. I just want to be on the winning side."

"The less we know about this, optio, the better it is for the two of us," replied the centurion.

The optio rose. "Yes, sir, I couldn't agree more. The only part that bothers me is what happens if the VII Legion doesn't get whipped? Then our comrades in Hispania are going to be asking some pretty sharp questions of us here in Narbo.

Lucillius gave him a level stare. "Then we say we were following orders, a copy of which I kept."

"Right, sir. Thank the Gods for orders, especially those we have a copy of," said Cnacus. "I am sure that if our brothers to the south ever come this way asking for an explanation, those orders will clear everything up," said the optio.

"Cnacus," replied Lucillius, "Shut up. Is that clear?"

"Yes, sir. Clear." He saluted and left the principia.

The centurion sat back down and took up the wax tablet again, skimming over its contents. He sighed. Life was getting more complex by the day.

VI

Centurion Antonius Crispus, Optio Domitius Celer, and Tesserarius Tiberius Cicero looked down at the small gathering of Franks in the center of the plaza that fronted the Praetorian Tower. The tower was surrounded by warehouses on two sides and backed against the circus. A ring of armed Franks—Domitius had counted three hundred—surrounded the tower on all sides.

"So they want to talk," said Domitius.

"Hmm. Makes one wonder why," said Antonius.

"I imagine they want us to surrender," put in Tiberius.

"I doubt that they really expect us to walk out of here," said the centurion. "Half of those men surrounding this place are wearing auxiliary armor. They know the Roman Army doesn't surrender."

"Will they put us under siege?" asked a fourth man who had joined the officers.

Domitius looked back at the speaker. "Sextilius Germanus. Welcome. The men I sent for you said they couldn't find you at headquarters. I was worried you wouldn't get here before we sealed ourselves in."

"I needed to gather some papers, sir. I was probably in the barracks when they came. I got here just before the gates came down," answered Sextilius.

"Well, we can use officers, signifer," put in Antonius. "As for a siege, I don't think so. We don't have siege equipment here in Tarraco, and I don't think that lot down there has engineers competent to build their own. As long as our food and water hold out, I think we will be fine. Of course, we can't stay here forever. If the VII Legion doesn't come within the next three weeks..." he shrugged, trailing off.

"Will you talk with them?" asked Sextilius.

The centurion slowly shook his head. "No. Let them eat silence," adding, "and something else." He signaled to two legionaries who reached down, picked up a catapult stone, and carried it to the edge of the tower. They looked over, judged the distance, and pitched the stone off the parapet. The small group below saw it coming and scattered. The stone missed hitting anyone, bounced upwards and rolled across the plaza.

The Optio chuckled. "Lively, aren't they?"

The group re-gathered and put their heads together. Shortly thereafter a man in a toga was brought down a side street and pushed toward the door of the tower.

"Now what's this?" asked Domitius.

"It's that duoviri, Fabius Procius," said Antonius. "I guess we need to hear what he has to say."

"They probably threatened him," put in Tiberius.

"Probably, but for all his clerkish way, Fabius won't scare

easily. Let's go hear what he has to say," said the centurion. "Sextilius, stay here and keep an eye on things." The group headed for the stairs, and disappeared into the tower.

The tower had a double-sided oak door bristling with iron studs, and an iron gate that covered the door. Antonius looked out at the plaza and Fabius through an arrow slit. The duoviri was standing about ten feet from the gate. The centurion had no intention of opening the door, even if the gate protected it. "Fabius," he called out, "come close to the door. We can talk through this arrow slit."

The duoviri dutifully limped forward until he was standing just below the slit. "Centurion?" he asked, looking up. "I have a message."

"What?" called back Antonius.

"The Franks say they will begin executing citizens if you don't surrender," answered Fabius.

"Do they?" replied the centurion. "And what did you say to them?"

"That you would not surrender. The leader's name is Alberic. I told him if he did execute residents, it would go much harder on him and his people when the VII Legion arrived," said Fabius.

Antonius chuckled. The more he got to know him, the more he liked this clerk. "Well," he said, "what did he say in reply?"

"His second in command, a runty little bastard, said he would start by executing me," said Fabius, adjusting his toga.

"Think he will do it?"

Fabius was silent for a moment. "I am not sure, but I think not. These Franks are not just a bunch of barbarians out on a raid. They have some sort of plan, but I haven't been able to find out what it is. One thing I know is that they seized all the ships that remained in the harbor. On the other hand, they might just cut off my head, or worse," said Fabius.

"You know we won't surrender, duoviri," replied Antonius.

"Of course not. I told them that. Since many of them appear to have served in the Army, they already know as well. That is why I think it is a bluff. If I were they, I would have made the same threat," said Fabius.

"And would you have carried it out?" asked Antonius.

Fabius considered the question for a moment. "No, not with the crowd of women and children they have with them."

"What's all that about?" asked the Centurion.

"I am not sure. It feels more like a migration than an invasion. To where I cannot say. It apparently involves ships, or else they want us to think that," answered the Duoviri, adding, "I have a request."

"What?" asked Antonius.

"Let me tell them you took the message but need to think about it. The more we keep this going, the more unlikely they are to start killing people. If they start executions, I told them, the city would rise against them. Each day we delay, that is a day closer to when the VII Legion gets here. The Franks will need all their forces to deal with the Legion. If they have to put down a revolt in the city and also fight the VII Legion they won't have enough men," said Fabius.

Fabius' analysis elevated him considerably in Antonius's eyes. "Sure, tell him whatever you want. Can you keep us informed if you find out what the Frank's plans are? We need to keep the VII Legion informed."

"I will try, but I have been told they have surrounded the city with cavalry and no one is allowed out. I am concerned about feeding our citizens. We have reserves, but not for three weeks, and not for the Franks as well as ourselves. My job will be to keep our people from starving."

"No argument," said the centurion. "But any information you can get to the VII Legion will be helpful."

"I will keep it in mind, centurion," said Fabius. "May Fortuna smile upon you." He turned and walked back to the small gathering of Franks.

"That's a good man," said Antonius to his optio. "I hope they don't cut his head off."

"Well, Roman?" asked Hildebold when Fabius returned to the group of Franks gathered at one end of the plaza.

"I gave the message. They are considering it," the Duoviri replied.

"Maybe they will consider it more seriously if we cut out your intestines and strangle you here and now," said Hildebold.

"If you are so anxious to root out the Third Century, Frank, why don't you just go and take the tower?" replied Fabius.

Hildebold whipped out a dagger and put it to Fabius' neck. "Talk to me like that again, Roman, and having your intestines cut out will be the least of your worries."

Fabius looked at him calmly. "We have twenty thousand citizens in this city. Your army and followers have probably tripled that number. We have grain reserves that will feed our residents for three, maybe four weeks at most. You can take it all, of course, and let us starve, but starving people become desperate. You can cut out my intestines, but then who is going to organize the distribution of the reserves, or help you run the city? You need me and my staff, Frank."

Alberic grinned and pushed Hildebold's knife away. "You're a bold clerk, but watch your tongue, Roman," said Alberic quietly. "I know something about how the Romans run their Empire. I can get others to help us. We may need your staff, but we do not need you. Talk like that again and I will make an example of you."

Fabius said nothing.

"This is Brocard," said Alberic indicating a slightly built Frank standing with the group. "He has a lot of experience with these matters. You will tell him where these reserves are, and you will also begin to gather together gold and silver. If you gather enough to satisfy me, I will spare sacking every house in the city. Do you understand me?"

The Duoviri nodded.

Alberic waived at several armed men and told them to stay with Brocard. "If this clerk delays things, kill him."

Two of the Franks grabbed Fabius and pushed him down a street, followed by Brocard and several more armed men.

Turning to Hildebold, Alberic said, "Let's go look at this harbor."

As the two headed down to the sea, trailed by a group of Frankish soldiers, Hildebold said, "Did you really mean what you said about looting? That will not be well received by the men."

"I am sure there will be some looting, but I do not want it to become widespread," answered Alberic. "That clerk mouse was right, Hildebold. We don't want a revolt on our hands. We are going to need everyone if we are to stop the VII Legion before it gets to Tarraco. If the city is restive, we will have to keep valuable troops here."

Hildebold said nothing, which Alberic knew meant that his prickly second in command agreed but didn't want to admit it.

Tarraco was a substantial city, but there was no traffic in the streets and it took only minutes to reach the main harbor, which was surrounded by armed men. Huge warehouses walled off the city from the harbor, and several boat-building enterprises clustered to the south of the warehouses. Long moles ran on either side of the warehouses, and a large cluster of boats was tied up to stone bolsters, some of them two deep. The two men surveyed the fleet.

"It is not enough," said Hildebold. "A sailor told us that the season is early and the winds are not yet favorable. Shipping will pick up in a few weeks," he hesitated, "or would have picked up. A number of ships escaped, so I doubt many will choose to come here."

"I agree, there are not enough ships," said Alberic. "We will need the ships from Barcino. We must also see if there are ships being built."

But the shipyards were deserted, and the few hulls laid down were in the early stages of construction. There were only two ships that looked like they might be finished in the weeks ahead. Alberic gave orders to find shipwrights to finish them.

As the two leaders walked back from the harbor Hildebold asked, "What if we cannot find enough ships?"

Alberic stopped and grabbed him by the arm. "Then we all die! By the great gods, Hildebold, we all knew this was a gamble. We may lose that gamble. But we will certainly lose if we see disaster at every turn. Our fate lies in our hands. Not enough ships? Find more and build more. The Romans gather against us? Defeat their legions. Why do you croak like a raven?"

Hildebold flushed. "Because you act as if nothing can go wrong."

Alberic laughed. "I see hope, you see despair. Which suggests that between us we might just pull this off."

The smaller man grinned back reluctantly. "I don't think I will ever understand you, Alberic, but you have led us to success so far. I will curb my tongue."

"Do not, my friend. I need the raven on my shoulder to remind us of how difficult the road ahead will be. But let us discuss, not argue. And let us make what needs to happen, happen," replied Alberic.

Hildebold nodded agreement.

"We need to talk with Grimbold and Dagobert. Grimbold will lead the infantry and Dagobert the cavalry," said Alberic as the two walked toward Tarraco's great temple plaza with the statue of the city's founder, Scipio.

"You will not lead the infantry?" asked Hildebold.

Alberic shook his head. "Grimbold is our best commander and we will need the two of us here in Tarraco. Grimbold is a fine fighter, but we will need more than warriors if we are to come through this. Even when we defeat the VII Legion we will be besieged. In the end, this will not be settled by arms but by negotiations. We will need you and me for that, Hildebold."

"I do not see myself as a negotiator," protested Hildebold.

"I agree," said Alberic with a smile. "You are the Frank who explains that we will cook Roman babies and feed them to their mothers, and I am the reasonable Frank who gives them a way out."

Hildebold snorted and shook his head. "If words were armies, Alberic, you would conquer the world."

"I don't want to conquer it, my friend, just get us a piece for ourselves," replied Alberic.

VII

Returning from the market, Coventina took back streets. She had left the house early, while her uncle was gathering a basket of small gold and silver vessels. The bulk of his wares, along with the raw material to make them, had been sent south to Valentia as soon as he had heard that the Franks had taken Barcino. She had worried about his reputation as a gold, silver, and amber merchant because it might bring the Franks to their door.

"You are not to worry, my dear," he told her. "The Duoviri has arranged it so if we give them gold and silver, they will not loot the city. I will take care of matters. You should try to get us whatever food you can find; however, because my friends tell me the city has been sealed and since the spring came late, there is not a lot of food. Nor can we expect grain shipments from Caesarea and Hippo Regius."

She worried about leaving him. He was a dear man, but much befuddled after the death of his wife. Coventina had come south from her people's home in the Cantabrian Mountains to nurse her and run her uncle's household. He had gradually turned over the entire house to her and lost himself in his trade. She kissed him and slipped out.

Her uncle might trust the Franks, she did not. She had never met a Frank—although she had seen many over the past few days—but Hispania's Celts had little use for outsiders, which included not only the invaders, but also the Romans and the Lusitanians. Well, to be honest, the Cantabri had little use for the neighboring Gallaici and Astures as well, not to mention those impossible Vaccaei, Arevaci, and Vascones. And of course, no one could stand the Cerretani.

She dressed as modestly as she could, her long red hair bound at the back and tucked under a light cape. She wore no jewelry, except the small stone bear she always kept at her breast. Coventina had been named for the powerful bear goddess that ruled the mountains, a goddess that gave courage, strength, and wisdom, but could be a demanding companion.

Coventina was tall and slim, but with powerful shoulders and legs. She was the first born into a family of five sisters and no brothers, and her mother died giving birth to her youngest sister. When her father was crippled in a border dispute with a neighboring clan, she had cared for him as well. Coventina had been forced to become an adult when she was hardly more than a girl.

Lately, her mind was a confusion, and not just because of the city's fall. She had agreed to stay with her uncle until his wife died, but he seemed to assume she would continue to keep his household. Coventina was torn. She missed her mountains and her family, but life at home was an endless drudge with little in the way of diversion. Tarraco was the first city she had lived in, and she had grown fond of its chaotic nature, the mix of people and cultures, and the pleasures of indoor plumbing, running water, and good food.

Whenever Coventina started on this line of thought she ended up circling back to her Greek, Demaratus. She thought of him as "her Greek" because that was how her uncle had started to refer to him. She had met him almost a year and a half ago when he arrived in Tarraco with a centurion and another officer, but he had left less than a week later. Most of their relationship had developed through letters the two had exchanged. When he returned from an expedition with the VII Legion to Mauretania Tingitana, he had appeared on her doorstep.

She had opened the door to a knock and there he was, as startlingly handsome and charming as when she had first met him. She did not know what to make of him or why he should be interested in her. Coventina was a practical person. Except for her stunning red hair, with highlights of garnet and rose that cascaded down her back, she knew she was no beauty. Her limbs were too long and well-muscled, her face too sharp, her nose too large. Men judged beauty as small. Large was handsome, and reserved for men. Indeed, she was amused by the fact that it was Demaratus, not she, whose features were fine and delicate, more girlish than her own.

The first few hours of their reunion were awkward, but gradually the common attraction they had shared in the scant week they had spent together reasserted itself, and she found herself falling in love. Coventina had never allowed that to happen before, and were she still in her mountains it might not have come to pass. But there was a certain unreality about living in

Tarraco, and the careful wall of rules that she had built around herself was more easily breached. She was lonelier than she had thought she was, and Demaratus was intelligent and amusing. And so handsome it made her chest hurt. Two days after he arrived, they made love.

For the two weeks of his leave, they had been inseparable. They had shopped together, cooked, and strolled through the city. He introduced her to his friend, the tailor Androdamas, and she took him out of the city into the hills to show him plants that would cure or kill, and plants that brought one closer to the spirit world. He did not know about her spirit guardian, the bear, or that among her people she was considered a woman of power. That was something she guarded carefully, even from him.

They had reached an agreement of sorts. There would be no talk of marriage until she returned to her mountains, which were the same ones that loomed over Legio. But now she was uncertain. Did she really want to return home and leave this bright city behind? Did she really want to be married to a soldier?

As she slipped from small street to small street, she thought of Demaratus. He would be coming soon, and a stab of fear shot through her. There were many Franks and he could be killed. She put the thought aside as she turned into the street that faced her uncle's.

She froze. A Frank was coming out of their house and right toward her. She thought for a moment of turning to run, but to run was to provoke pursuit. Instead, she lowered her head, pulling the cloak around her face so just her eyes showed. The man barely glanced at her, but walked swiftly to the main street that came up from the docks and turned down it.

Coventina discreetly watched him until he disappeared, put down her bags of vegetables, olive oil, and garlic, and carefully approached the house. The front door was ajar. She could feel the dread building in her, but she made herself quietly open the door and look inside. There was an odd sweet smell in the air, as if meat were being cooked on a fire. She was about to call out for her uncle when she heard low voices toward the back of the house and then a laugh. It was not her uncle's laugh.

She slipped into the main hall. The laugh was repeated. It was a sound that chilled her very being. Near the front door was a battle-axe. It was a trophy that her father had won fighting a tribe in Gaul. When he became a cripple he gave it to her. Normally it would have gone to a son, but there were no sons in Coventina's family, so the trophy had fallen to her. It was double-bladed, its handle carved with runes and studded with copper nails.

At her father's urging, she had taken it to Tarraco where it had sat by the door since she arrived. Coventina had kept its blades as sharp as a razor and, on occasion, had taken it up, swinging it back and forth. Her father had considered it "too slow" to be effective as a weapon. Her people favored a long, broad sword that lacked the power of the axe, but was quicker and more deadly for infighting.

She shrugged out of her cloak and picked up the axe, holding it with both hands, its great blade slightly behind her shoulder. As silently as she could she moved toward the voices.

They were coming from her uncle's bedroom at the back

of the house. Carefully, she slipped down the long hallway and edged up toward the door to the bedroom. The men were speaking Frankish, a language that sounded harsh to her ear. Slowly she put her head around the door.

Her uncle was motionless, spread-eagled on his bed. Two men —one tall and thin, the other shorter and stockier—stood above him, one holding a soldering iron. A small brazier filled with glowing coals was off to one side of the bed. Coventina immediately knew the source of the burning meat smell. The Franks had tortured him to find out where his gold and silver was hidden.

Almost without thinking she moved toward the men, raising the great battle-axe over her head. Either she had made a noise or the men sensed her presence, for both turned toward her. She closed the distance between them in three swift strides and brought the axe down on the stocky man. The blade struck him near his ear, then sliced down through his shoulder. He was so shocked that he made only a gasping sound before stumbling backwards onto the bed and falling to the floor.

The tall man cried out something she didn't understand and tried to grab at her. Instead of trying to raise the axe over her head again, Coventina swung the weapon back up, slicing into his thigh. He gave a shout, flung a chair at her, and backed toward the door. For a moment, Coventina considered following him, but the man on the floor was trying to get up. She turned, raised the axe over her head and brought it down in the middle of his forehead. He fell back and lay still.

Coventina turned to her uncle, but he was dead. It was not the torture that had done it. There were only a few burn marks on his feet and one on his right hand. Coventina had seen men felled this way. Some lingered in the twilight of life, others died as if the hand of an invisible god had struck them down. It was small solace, but he had not suffered much.

The man on the floor was also dead, his eyes sightless and staring, the great blade still cleaving his face. She tried pulling it loose, but his skull clung stubbornly to the blade and she left it embedded in the Frank. Instead, she picked up a sword that one of the men had dropped and followed the other man through the door. A trail of blood ran down the hallway and out the door.

He had gone for help. Stupid! She should have gone after him immediately. The man she struck first would not have been a threat. Now the one who had escaped would return with re-inforcements. She trembled at what that meant.

She forced herself to stop trembling and to think. She knew she had only moments. There was a noise in the street outside. She dropped the sword and sprinted for her bedroom. There was a window that faced the rear of the house and a workshop at the back of the yard. Closing her door softly, she crossed the room and unlatched the grill that covered the window. Slipping through it, she dropped to the small garden and ran around the side of the workshop where a tree grew that overhung the street at the back of the house. She hesitated. She would have to run down the street in broad daylight. They would catch her.

There was a secret panel at the back of the workshop where the craftsmen kept their supplies of gold safe from thieves. She pushed a tile to release the catch, and the panel clicked open. Sliding it aside she saw that it was empty and she could just fit into the space. Slipping in, she slid the panel closed and held her breath. The workshop was built so that it concealed the existence of the hiding place, but someone might notice that the back wall was much thicker than the rest of the workshop and ferret out her hiding place. She regretted not taking the sword. If they discovered her, she would be helpless, unable to strike at them or kill herself.

It was only moments before she heard men in the backyard and then in the workshop. She heard tables being turned over and things being smashed, but the noise gradually subsided. Then a voice seemed to be talking in her ear. Someone had come around the back of the workshop. He was joined by several more. She opened her mouth so that there would be no noise of her breathing. Her father had taught her the trick when he returned home from a hunt.

The conversation at the tree continued for a while, but finally the men left. Coventina was drenched in sweat, not daring to move or take a deep breath. She would wait until darkness and then try to escape. But the man whom she wounded saw her clearly. She was a marked woman.

VIII

Flavius was exhausted. Trying to get a legion mobilized in two days, particularly a legion like the VII that had spent most its time in garrison duty for the past 100 years, was almost impossible. Today he had lost his temper more times that he cared to remember. But the orders had finally been dispersed, the supplies requisitioned, leaves canceled, and the men sent to work on gathering and repairing their equipment.

For the past three hours he had been looking forward to meeting Demaratus and going to the baths. But the signifer was not at the principia going over the legion's books, nor was he in the room that he and Demaratus shared. Flavius was just about to give up and go to the baths without the Greek, when a thought struck him. He stepped back into the room and closed the door. Crossing the room, he stood for a moment in front of a chest. It was the signifer's chest and officers did not violate one another's personal property.

But Flavius was worried.

Steeling himself, he slipped the hasp off the chest and opened it. It looked in order, but Demaratus always kept his special knife in a case near the top. It was a lovely weapon and the Greek was particularly attached to it. The case was open and the knife was gone. Quickly kneeling, Flavius went through the rest of the chest. The signifer's heavy cloak was also gone.

Flavius carefully closed the chest, reinserted the hasp, and strode out of the room. Crossing through the barracks, which were alive with soldiers and officers coming and going, he crossed in front of the hospital and headed for the stables. Most of the horses were quartered outside the fort, but officers' horses were kept inside. He walked through the main entrance and into the overwhelming smell of hay, horse manure, and ammonia and headed toward the rear where Demaratus stabled his mare, Aura. It was the horse he had ridden when they left Tarraco almost two years ago to go to Corduba and take command of the Second Century. Small, beautiful, and lightning fast, Aura was not unlike her owner in many ways.

The optio dreaded what he would find. He approached the stall quietly and stood directly outside. Demaratus was gathering a small bundle and reaching for a bridle.

"Comrade," said Flavius softly.

Demaratus whirled at the sound and dropped the small bundle. "Sir," he said. "I was just going for a ride before my bath."

Flavius said nothing for a moment. Demaratus was one of the most self-controlled people he had every known, but Flavius could read the tension in his eyes and mouth. The optio slowly walked into the stall and leaned against one of its walls. "No, you weren't."

The signifer stiffened. "Are you calling me a...."

"Liar," said Flavius, finishing his sentence. "But I am also calling you my friend, and this is not the way to get to Tarraco, brother."

Demaratus said nothing. Flavius wondered for a moment if the Greek would kill him. The optio had long ago learned that Demaratus was probably the single most dangerous man in the legion. This fact had never bothered Flavius; indeed, it had saved his and Marcus's lives. When the Praetorians sent their assassins against the three of them, it was Demaratus who had killed their attackers. But he also knew that if the Greek wanted to, Flavius would be dead before he could draw his sword.

The signifer narrowed his eyes. "I also thought you were my friend, optio. In this I appear to have made a misjudgment."

Flavius arched his eyebrows. "A Greek misjudge? The thrones of the Gods tremble on Olympus."

"This is not a matter for humor, optio," replied Demaratus coldly.

Flavius pushed himself off the stall wall and, placing his palms up, stepped toward Demaratus. The Greek warily stepped back. "Comrade, I know where you are bound and I know why. I won't stand in your way. We have far too much between us for me to betray you. I thought you would know that."

For the first time Demaratus relaxed the tension in his face. "You have spent your whole life in the army, Flavius. For you it is a way of life. For me it is a job. I would never ask you choose between friendship and duty."

"There is no choice there, brother. You are my friend. Plus, Marcus and I owe you. If it hadn't been for you we'd have been meat for the Praetorians," said Flavius, "but this is not the way to get to your woman."

"Flavius, it will take the VII Legion three weeks, maybe more, to march to Tarraco. And even then, there is no guarantee we will win, or if we do, there will be anyone left alive in Tarraco. With Aura and a packhorse, I can be in Emporiae in a week," said Demaratus.

"And then?" asked Flavius.

"The Franks have already cut the roads to Tarraco. I will pick up a small boat in Emporiae and sail it south. The Franks will not be watching the sea," answered Demaratus.

Flavius nodded, "Not bad. You could be in Tarraco almost two weeks before we arrive. Do you think it would be as easy to get out by sea as in?"

Demaratus frowned. "I suppose, but I don't see what would be the point."

"If you could send out information about what these Franks are planning, that would be very helpful since we don't appear to know anything about what is going on right now. You could be the VII Legion's eyes and ears in Tarraco," answered Flavius.

The Greek frowned and then smiled. "Of course. But that a Roman would see something about the sea that a Greek would miss is distressing."

"You were just focusing on that Celt of yours, Demaratus. I was trying to keep the bigger picture in mind," said Flavius in a tone that suggested that the signifer would never hear the end of this. "Now let's go sell our new praefectus castrorum on it, shall we?"

Demaratus drew back. "If we tell Marcus and he says no, then I am lost. It would be better for me to slip away."

"The penalty for desertion is death, comrade," said Flavius.

"You and your Celt will never have a moment's rest. Let me handle this. Just you talk about the sea stuff. The only thing our commander knows less about than the sea is horses."

The two men—Flavius looking confident, Demaratus tense—left the stable and crossed over to the principia, which was jammed with officers, clerks and an assortment of headquarters staff. Marcus was effectively the VII Legion's acting commander. One tribune was down with a broken leg, the other in Rome, and the legate was too busy trying to pry auxiliaries away from local towns and cities panicked by the news of a Frankish invasion to be of much help. Marcus looked overwhelmed, although only Flavius and Demaratus could pick up the small signals that suggested their commander was under stress. His jaw had a tight, sharp line of tension, and he was methodically smoothing a small scroll that was spread out in front of him.

The two waited until there was a break in the waves of people beating on the praefectus for orders and decisions. But Flavius and Demaratus had helped put together Marcus's staff, and it was smart and efficient. Slowly the principia began to empty and, taking advantage of a momentary lull, Flavius caught Marcus's eye and nodded toward the legate's private office. Marcus indicated they should go in and wait for him to finish with the last few people clamoring for orders or favors.

Flavius wandered about the big office looking at sculptures and war trophies and glancing through the maps rolled out on a large table. Demaratus tensely rocked back and forth on his heels until he realized that he was showing emotion. He stopped all voluntary motion, but his index finger continued to hammer on his leg.

Finally, the door opened and a weary looking Marcus came through it, closing it behind him.

"Long day, sir," remarked Flavius.

"Long indeed, optio. How are your preparations coming along?" asked Marcus.

"All pretty much done, sir. It looks messy, but we will have the men on the road by day after tomorrow," said Flavius.

"Fine, fine. I haven't heard from the legate today, but I expect something this afternoon," said Marcus, running his hands through his hair and collapsing in a chair. "And you, signifer?"

"Our books were in order before this crisis, sir. I only have a few more requisitions to write. I agree with Flavius, the VII Legion will march on time," answered Demaratus.

Marcus looked up at his two subordinates. "Why do I think you did not ask to see me just to say things are on schedule?"

When the three were alone, the rigid hierarchy of the Roman Army broke down. They had fled Rome together and fought side by side in Hispania and Mauretania. In public, they acted out their roles, but in private the bonds of comradeship asserted themselves.

Flavius grinned at him. "And all this time I thought I was successfully manipulating you to follow my wishes," said the optio.

"I know, Flavius," replied Marcus with a small smile.

Flavius looked at Demaratus who was blank faced. "Sir," he said turning back to the Praefectus, "we have an idea."

"Which is?" said Marcus.

Flavius took a breath. "We think we need to get Demaratus into Tarraco before the VII Legion arrives, sir."

Marcus frowned and sat back. "Why would we do that?"

"Sir, the VII Legion doesn't know Franks," said Flavius, "we do. A lot of people are talking about routing the barbarians. We know they are not only tough, they are just as good as some of our best troops. This is not going to be easy."

"I know that, optio," said Marcus, "I have also communicated that fact to our commanders, which is why we are taking an extra day to get on the road and the legate is gathering as many auxiliaries as he can."

"Yes, sir, but we don't know what we're up against, and Demaratus here is the only man in the VII Legion who can help," said Flavius. "If something bad happens to us, the whole peninsula is wide open."

"You have become a strategist, Flavius?" said Marcus, cocking an eyebrow.

"Not exactly, sir," said Flavius reddening a little.

"You both came up with this idea?" continued Marcus.

The two men glanced at each other. "Sort of," said Flavius.

"Even if I thought this was a good idea, we don't know if there is any way we could get Demaratus into the city. And why Demaratus? He is one of my best officers," continued Marcus.

"As good an officer as he is, we can manage without him," said Flavius. "No offense intended," he added in an aside to the signifer.

"None taken, sir," answered Demaratus.

"And because he is a Greek he is the one man in the VII Legion who can get into Tarraco," continued Flavius.

Marcus stood and leaned his hands on the desk. "Hmm. By sea? I do not think Barcino is open, Demaratus."

"No, sir, I am sure it is not. But Emporiae would have small ships and I have contacts there from my days as a sailor."

"How would you go?" asked Marcus.

"I would take the road east to Augustabriga, then north toward Lugdunum Convenarum. Once you are over the mountains there is a rough road that runs due east until it strikes the Via Domitia near Rhodus. From there it is a short ride south to Emporiae," answered Demaratus.

"If the city is sealed, how would you get information out?" asked Marcus.

"The same way I got in, sir. A small fishing vessel can go south, even as far as Tortosa. I know many sailors and I am certain I can recruit men to carry intelligence. Once they get to Tortosa, there must be a road that goes west from Tortosa to Ilerda."

Marcus was pacing now. "This idea has merit, Demaratus. But it will be dangerous."

The Greek shrugged. "Maybe not as dangerous as what you are going to do. In any case, I am a careful man."

Marcus was silent for a moment. "All right. Start your preparations. I will have to get the legate's approval, but in the meantime, you can begin to put things together. And close the door when you leave," said Marcus. "Optio, please remain," he said turning to Flavius.

Demaratus looked confused for a moment, then saluted. "I will get started, sir." He left, closing the door behind him.

Marcus stared at Flavius for a long moment, long enough for Flavius to look uncomfortable. "Was he leaving anyway, Flavius?" Marcus asked softly.

The optio shrugged. "I am not sure he would actually have done it, sir, but he was strongly thinking about it."

"Would you have let him?"

Flavius paused. "I don't know, sir. I'm no friend of deserters, you know that, but Demaratus wasn't thinking of deserting; he was going to Tarraco. He just wanted to get there as quickly as he could."

"This woman of his?"

Flavius nodded. "It seems he is quite taken with her, sir."

"Will he help us or save his woman?" asked Marcus.

"Sir, this is Demaratus," replied Flavius with a hint of heat. "He has been with us every step of the way. There were a hundred times he could have pulled stakes. He didn't. And when we really needed him, he was there."

Marcus frowned. "To what do you refer, optio?"

Flavius caught himself. "Nothing in particular, sir."

"Junior officers try to manipulate senior officers, Flavius. That is what you were doing with all this spy nonsense. It's the way things work in the Army. But they don't lie. What are you referring to, optio?" persisted Marcus.

"There are some things it is best not to know, sir, just in case anyone asks you about it. You have to trust me on this one, sir," said Flavius. "We are standing where we are today because of Demaratus, sir. When we needed him, he was there. We owe him."

Marcus stared at Flavius. The two had grown up in the Army, although they came from very different classes. Flavius was a street tough straight out of the insulae of Rome, while Marcus came from a comfortable equestrian background. But they had bonded early. Flavius was utterly loyal and dependable and a lot smarter than he admitted to. Plus, he had saved Marcus's life on a number of occasions.

"All right, optio. I will leave it at that," Marcus said.

"Sir, this wasn't just about Demaratus'woman," said Flavius. "If there is anyone in this Legion who can get information out of Tarraco, it's our signifer. And he will do that, woman or no woman."

Marcus said, "I agree. You should see that he has money. He will need to buy a boat in Emporae and maybe others in Tarraco."

Flavius nodded. "Anything else, sir?"

"Yes, try not to be so transparent next time, Flavius," said Marcus with a smile.

"I wasn't, sir. You're just good."

"Be gone, shameless flatterer and make sure the VII Legion is ready to march," said Marcus, waving Flavius away. The optio saluted and left.

Marcus sat down at the desk and stared at some wax tablets. We are no longer young, he thought, but we can still be loyal to the memories of our youth, which Flavius had shared with him. There are times when friendship and love are more powerful than honor and duty. He did not want to live in a world in which that was not so.

IX

Marcus heard the footsteps in the hall before the soft knock on his door. He had been drifting in and out of sleep most the night, his mind racing with the thousands of things still undone. He was worried about the mules: there were enough for the VII Legion, but he was certain that the auxiliaries would arrive with only a few. The Roman Army could do without roads, but it could not do without mules. He had sent out parties to scour the countryside, but these wily northerners had gotten wind of the Frankish invasion and had driven their stock deep into the woods to hide them from the Army.

He was so deep into the mule problem that he didn't initially respond. The knock came again, this time harder. It was still dark outside, so this had to be some kind of emergency that the legate needed taking care of immediately. Marcus sighed. Titus Valens was a competent commander, but a demanding one. He seemed oblivious to the fact that there were no functioning tribunes—not that tribunes really "functioned" in a way that made much difference to the everyday life of the legion—but virtually everything had fallen on Marcus's shoulders, and the legate thought his praefectus castrorums could do the work of three.

"Yes?" Marcus called out, but there was no verbal response, just a louder knock.

Cursing, he threw off his blanket, climbed off his couch, strode across the room and flung open his door. "Yes?" he repeated in an annoyed tone.

The man at the door shrank back. Marcus had seen him around headquarters over the past few days but had no idea what his name was. He was some sort of junior clerk.

"Praefectus Castrorum Marcus Favonius, please come to the praetorium. Something has happened to our legate, Titus Valens," the man said, stumbling over the words. He looked scared.

"What has happened?" said Marcus, reaching for a cloak that hung from a peg near the door.

The man shook his head. "I don't know, sir. He fell. I don't know if he is dead or alive."

Marcus shrugged into the cloak—Legio's early mornings, even in spring, had a bitter edge to them—and stepped into the hallway. "Have the doctor and the tribune been alerted?" he asked.

"Yes, sir. I saw the doctor on his way as I came to get you," the man replied.

Marcus broke into a trot, then slowed to a brisk walk. Visions of disaster ran through his head. If the legate were sick, who would command the Legion? Marcus liked Tribune Quintus Junius, who in his youth had been a formidable battle commander, but he was old and tired now, nursing a broken leg. He was also drunk most of the time. Marcus put the thought out of his mind and concentrated on getting to the praetorium as quickly as he could without running. This was not a time to show panic.

Titus had a large office and apartment in the praetorium. He had never married, so the Spartan praetorium was all he needed. The door to the office was open, as was the side door that led into the inner apartment. Marcus walked briskly across the office, noting the pile of scrolls, letters, wax tablets and maps scattered over the top of the staff table. Some had fallen onto the floor.

The legate was lying next to his couch on his back, wrapped in a robe. The doctor, Timotheus, was bending over him with a small mirror, while holding the man's wrist in his hand. He didn't glance up when Marcus came into the room. Crossing it quickly, Marcus knelt by the legate. He could see a faint sheen of moisture on the mirror that the doctor was holding close to Titus' mouth. It was a sheen that came and went. The man was alive.

Marcus looked a question at Timotheus, who shrugged. "I don't know, sir. He is alive. As you can see, he breathes, but his pulse is very weak. I have seen men recover from things like this, but not many, and most only partially."

At that point the tribune, Quintus Junius, arrived on a chair carried by four soldiers. "What has happened?" he asked as the chair was placed on the floor.

"The legate has been struck down, Tribune. It is too early to say if he will recover," answered the doctor. "I would like to move him to the valetudinarian if I may, sir."

Quintus, who looked confused and slightly bleary-eyed, nodded. "Of course." Turning to the four men who had carried his chair, he said, "Help the doctor move the legate to where he instructs you. And Marcus, remain here."

The doctor directed the men to move Titus back to his couch and then picked it up. As the doctor kept a steadying hand on the legate, the men slowly moved the couch out of the room, through the office, and out into the dark morning.

The tribune sighed and painfully adjusted his leg. "Well, things are a little complex now, aren't they praefectus?"

"Yes, sir," answered Marcus. "Shall I continue the mobilization?"

"Sit, Marcus. We need to think this through," answered Quintus. He nodded toward a chest in the corner. "And pour me a cup of wine, if you will."

Marcus opened the chest and drew out a goblet and a small, stoppered jug. Pulling off the cork, he poured a goblet of wine and brought it to the Tribune, who downed most of it in a single long pull. Quintus silently shook the goblet for more, and Marcus refilled it.

"That's better," said Quintus taking another long drink. "Now as to your question. I think we must continue to prepare the VII Legion to march. I am sure you have matters well in hand. We must hold to our timetable if we are to relieve Tarraco."

"Yes, sir. The preparations for the VII Legion are well underway and under control," said Marcus, "But I am afraid I know little concerning the auxiliaries. Titus was taking full charge of rounding them up, and we never had an opportunity to talk about his progress."

Quintus frowned. "He told me little as well, but given that I was remaining in Legio, that is understandable." Reaching up to Marcus, the old tribune said, "Here, give me a hand. Help me over to the table. Maybe his records will tell us something."

Marcus put an arm around Quintus and helped him limp over to the table, where he lowered him into a chair. Both men started sorting through the piles of scrolls, maps and wax tablets. "Librarius," roared the tribune, and almost instantly a pale, thin-faced young man, looking slightly apprehensive, appeared.

"The legate was organizing the auxiliaries, Sossius," the tribune said, "Do you know if he has records on what the situation is?"

The clerk went over to one corner of the table where a neat stack of wax tablets was piled. "I think you will find what you are looking for here, tribune. I do know that he had hoped to work on the matter more today."

"Well, he won't be doing that," said Quintus reaching for the pile. He split the pile into two and handed a stack of tablets to Marcus. The two men were silent for a time, skimming the information.

Finally, Quintus put down the tablets, rubbed his eyes, and took another drink. "It is much as I expected. The cities don't want to give up their soldiers and are coming up with excuse after excuse why they can't come here or meet us in Clunia." Pushing one tablet toward Marcus, he said, "Here is one saying his auxiliaries are out on 'maneuvers.' Maneuvers? If they are, it is the first time in a hundred years."

"But some are coming, or at least say they will catch up to us in Clunia," said Marcus, shuffling through his pile.

Quintus snorted and drained his wine. He looked longingly at the chest, but put the goblet down. "I wouldn't bet my pay on the fall of that die," he chuckled.

"Do you wish me to concentrate on the auxiliary problem, sir?" asked Marcus.

"Praefectus, let's be honest here. I may be your superior, but you are now the acting legate of the VII Legion," said Quintus.

"Sir, you are the senior tribune in the...," started Marcus.

"Oh, rot, Marcus. I can't ride a horse and, frankly, I am just too old for command. I intended to retire in the next few months in any case. Look, I haven't commanded troops in the field for more than ten years. I can make them march in formation and deploy correctly, but we both know that has nothing to do with war," cut in the tribune.

Marcus said nothing for a moment. "I can't do this without you, sir. No local governor is going to listen to the VII Legion's fourth in command. If Titus was having trouble rounding up auxiliaries, why would they pay any attention to me?"

"Fear, son, fear. And we will stoke that fear, tell them the Franks are coming west to rape their women and enslave their children," answered Quintus.

"But won't that make them want to keep their soldiers?" asked Marcus.

"I'll handle that part of the mobilization, Marcus," said Quintus. "I will tell them that the honor of the VII Legion requires that it march to relieve Tarraco. If it doesn't have auxiliaries with it, it might be defeated, and then the entire peninsula will be open to the Franks. If they think the only thing between them and the barbarian hordes is their auxiliaries, they will send soldiers to Clunia."

Turning to Sossius, he said "I will need a number of riders and lots of clerks."

"Yes, sir," said the man.

"Marcus, you should call a meeting of the primi ordines, and you need to quickly find a centurion for the First Century," said Quintus, beginning to organize the tablets into piles. Marcus's appointment had been so recent that there had not been time to choose a centurion to lead the First Century. The centurion of the First Century, or primus pilus, headed up the primi ordines, the group of five centurions that made up the elite First Cohort.

Not only was the First Cohort double the strength of the other cohorts, it was the only unit in the legion that had seen action in more than a generation. It was the First Cohort under Marcus's command that had successfully brought the citizens enslaved by the Mauri back from Mauretania last year. Eventually he would have to pull the centurions from all the cohorts together, but right now he had to choose a commander for the First Century.

Marcus left the praetorium, his head spinning. He would have liked to appoint the older and more experienced Manlius Valeranus, centurion of the Second Century, to the post of primus pilus, but that would bypass Aulus Junius and Cerficius Nonius, centurions of the Fourth and Fifth centuries. They were both younger than Manlius, but they had seniority as centurions. Plus, both were from wealthy and powerful Hispania families.

He was heading toward the principia when Flavius intercepted him.

"What's afoot, sir? I heard something about the legate," said Flavius.

Marcus filled him in on the situation and also on the turmoil that he was having over choosing a replacement centurion for the First Century. Normally a superior officer would never ask a junior officer for advice, but Marcus trusted Flavius' judgment.

"Cerficius should get the nod, sir. He did a veteran's job with the rear guard fighting the Mauri. Manlius never expected to be a centurion, so it won't hurt his feelings. And Aulus is good friends with Cerficius, so there won't be any friction there. And Cerficius will be beholden to you sir. He comes from a powerful family down south. There are some other families in Hispania that don't much like you, begging your pardon, sir," said Flavius.

Marcus had to shake his head. Flavius had a gift for sorting through disorder and picking out the thing that would set it all straight. Marcus had fallen afoul of several powerful families when he had tacitly backed the Lusitanians in a dispute with Roman landlords in Capera.

"All right, I will talk to Cerficius. In the meantime, you inform the other two centurions to call a meeting of the primi ordines. I will tell them in the principia right after breakfast. We will need a meeting with all the centurions following that. And will need Demaratus on my staff. I am sure he will be disappointed, but I need him," said Marcus.

"Demaratus has already left, sir. But I will get the word out on the other meetings," said Flavius.

"Left? Already? Well, then I wish him well. Send Cerficius to me and tell him I am going to need recommendations to replace him and his optio in the Fifth Century," said Marcus, turning back to head for the principia.

"Sir," said Flavius, saluting. He waited until Marcus has disappeared, then walked briskly back to the barracks. Demaratus was putting together a bundle to take and had various weapons, purses, and things spread out on his couch.

"Brother, you need to leave this instant. The legate has taken ill and Marcus is acting commander of the VII Legion. He wants us both on his staff, but I told him you had already left. You need to get on the road immediately and not be seen," said Flavius.

Demaratus stared at him for a moment. "But I need to go to the stables for the horses."

"You get out of the fort and I will meet you on the road near the edge of the vicus," said Flavius. "Just don't be seen." Turning, he left and headed for the barracks. Flavius was not certain if Marcus would punish him if he found out he had been lied to, but it was a chance that Flavius would have to take. He was sure that his friendship with Marcus would survive.

At the stable the horses were ready and no one said a thing about an optio taking command of the white mare and the pack-horse. He walked them out a side entrance to the stable, keeping away from the Via Principia, the central road in the fort. The main gate was to the north, but, like all Roman forts, Legio had four gates. Flavius mounted the white mare and took the southern gate, nodding to the salute of the two guards as he passed through the town that surrounded the fort. Demaratus, wrapped in a non-descript brown cloak with a hood, was waiting off to one side near a small copse of trees. The mare, Aura, gave the signifer a whicker of recognition.

"Anyone see you?" asked Flavius.

"No," answered Demaratus, taking the bridle and calming the mare.

"All right, then, be on your way comrade. May Fortuna guide you," said Flavius.

Demaratus came around the horse and embraced Flavius. "I will not forget this, brother."

"Don't worry, I had no intention of letting you forget this, Demaratus," said Flavius with a grin. "Now be gone."

Demaratus lithely leapt into the four-horn saddle. He pulled on the packhorse with its double bundles, and the two horses cantered down the road. Flavius watched them disappear into the gray morning and then turned back toward the fort.

It was time to go to war.

X

Coventina carefully slid the panel on the workshop hiding place back a crack and listened. There were insect sounds in the tree above, but otherwise the night was silent. She waited several minutes to be sure, then pulled the panel all the way open and stepped into the space between the back wall of the workshop and the garden wall that loomed above. Her legs and arms were cramped from the small space, and she was rank with the sweat of fear, her hair tangled and oily. She desperately wanted to bathe, but that was unlikely to happen soon.

She leaned up against the cool stone of the wall. Her first instinct was to use the tree to climb over the wall, and then hide herself in the city. But they would be looking for a tall, red-haired woman, and where would she hide? She was not a native of Tarraco, and these were not her people. She had no relatives but her poor dead uncle. There were people she knew, from the market and from her uncle's business, but would they risk everything to hide her? In the end, she was a barbarian Celt from the mountains, utterly alone, with an army looking for her.

She fought back the waves of fear that rose up within her,

willing away the sting of tears. To give in to fear and self-pity would be death. She would return to the house and find a knife. Her end would be her own.

The thought warmed her and gave her purpose. Treading softly, she crept out from behind the shed and knelt down in some bushes near the entrance to the workshop. The house was silent and dark. They could be waiting for her, ready to seize her as soon as she entered, to drag her off into a world of pain and horror. She wanted to keep hiding in the bushes, or to climb back into the hiding place, but both would mean eventual capture and death.

She made herself get up and move and, using the shadows cast by the roof, she crept to the back of the house and the door that opened into the kitchen. At each point along the way she stopped and listened. Everything was silent. She froze at the sound of a shout, and almost bolted for the back wall, but then realized it was in the street and a long way from the house.

The door to the pitch-black kitchen was wide open. Taking a deep breath, she slipped into the house and flattened herself against a wall. There were no sounds, just the sharp smell of garlic and onions, the sweet odor of cooked olive oil, and corruption. She had been cutting up a rabbit before she had gone to the market, and it was beginning to go bad.

She moved carefully along the wall to a small table where the smell came from, casting her hands over the table until she located the knife she had been using. It was thin-bladed and razor sharp. It would do.

She had planned to take the knife and return to the workshop where she would cut the big artery that ran up her neck, but she hesitated. Did she really want to die? It was the way Romans did things, but what would her people think? Wasn't it better to fall in battle than by one's own hand? But how could she do battle with the Franks?

Almost without thinking, she moved toward the door into the main part of the house. She was not sure why she was doing this, except that the prospect of suicide no longer seemed quite so comforting. She ducked through the door into the main dining room and listened. There was not a sound. Then she heard a rustle and stiffened. The moon had just risen and was throwing a beam of yellow light through a window high in the dining room. The beam caught a rat sitting near the front door, washing its face and paws. She relaxed. No rat would stay in the open like that if there was anyone in the house. She stepped away from the wall, which alerted the rat to her presence. It vanished in a flash.

She made her way to her room and covered the windows with a cloak. Carefully she struck a firestone several times until it lit a small oil lamp. The sudden light was both comforting and terrifying. If the light was seen, she was dead. But the familiarity of her room, with her clothes and makeup—she noted her jewelry box was cast on the floor, empty—gave her a feeling of normalcy, as bizarre as that sentiment seemed.

She caught a glimpse of herself in a mirror and moved toward it. A dirty face, taut with tension looked back at her. She stared at it for a while and then made a decision. Using the mirror to guide her, she took the carving knife to her hair, cutting it off in great swaths. Tears rolled down her cheeks. She loved her hair. It had rescued her from plainness, making her stand out among her own people and here in Tarraco. But because it was her most identifying characteristic, it had to go.

As it fell around her feet, a rage began to build in her. Vile Franks! They murdered my uncle and they would murder me as they have killed my hair. She found herself slashing at her hair, cutting it as close as a boy's, and thinking how pleasant it would be to cut some Frank's throat. She would open him like a suckling pig, bathe in his blood. She found herself shaking with rage, her lips pulled back from her teeth. "They will pay," she whispered softly to herself. "The Cantabiri settle their debts."

The wave of rage was slowly replaced by cold calculation. The thought of suicide was pushed aside. If she were going to take her revenge on the Franks, she would have to think through what she was going to do. First, she would have to change. A tall woman in a dress, even a shorthaired one, would draw suspicion. She quickly rummaged through her clothes, but none of them would do. Taking a deep breath, and carefully shielding the oil lamp, she went into her uncle's room. The poor man was still spread-eagled on the bed. Averting her eyes, she methodically went through his clothes, choosing a pair of shorts, pants, and a work-a-day linen shirt. She took one of his belts and a light cloak with long sleeves and a hood that pulled over her head. She wrapped a piece of linen sheet around her breasts, pressing them close to her chest.

Rummaging through her uncle's belongings, she discovered one of the short swords the Romans favored—a gladis—that her father once told her had been invented in Hispania, but it was too large to conceal. Near it was a shorter blade, a sort of cross between a dagger and a sword. Her Greek had carried one. He called it a "pugio," although he favored a smaller and far more lethal dagger that his friend the tailor had given him. She slipped it under the belt and pushed it around to her side. With the cloak it was invisible.

Next, she went to a small desk and pushed in a carving on the side, opening a secret compartment. Within lay a sack of gold coins which she slipped into an inside pocket of the cloak. Then she knelt at the small hearth and scraped up some ashes. She carried them into the kitchen and put them in a small bowl. Pouring a little oil into the bowl she made a black soup that she carefully rubbed on her head. Even short, her hair was red, and while the sooty mixture was not a permanent solution, it would do until she could find some proper dye. She carefully washed her hands, and then filled a flask with water. She also took some flatbread off the counter and a cheese down from the beams over the kitchen.

There was only one thing left to do. She stole back to her room and gathered up her hair, taking it into her uncle's bedroom and piling it on his bed. The tears came again. She had come to love her uncle, and she would not leave him to the rats and the flies. He was a Cantabrian like herself, and he deserved to go properly into the West. She cut his bonds and arranged his hands on his chest, although he was already beginning to stiffen with death and she had to struggle to do it. She went back into the kitchen and selected a variety of herbs, scattering them on top of his body. Taking wood from near the hearth, she piled it under and around the bed and then took a jug of lamp oil and soaked the wood, the bed and her uncle in it. She rolled up a shirt and soaked it with oil as well, then set it near the bed.

She quietly went back into the living room and carefully closed the door to the street, bolting it. Then she went back and knelt at the bier. She closed his eyelids, and said a short prayer. "Mother of the mountains, your daughter asks you to take this good man into the West. Meet him at the dawn and guard him until he is home. None are braver or wiser than you, oh great Coventina. Please do this thing your daughter asks."

The prayer helped her master her sadness and call up her cold rage. Reaching under her shirt she gripped her bear amulet and softly chanted, "Mighty Coventina, give me the strength and the courage to revenge this blood. Let your wisdom guide my path. Let me strike our enemies. Let them pay for this deed."

Taking the small lamp she lit the rolled shirt. It flared into a steady flame that slowly began to eat its way toward the piled wood and the bed.

She rose, closing the door behind her so by the time the fire became noticeable from the street it would be too late to do anything about it.

Coventina strode through the kitchen, around the workshop and climbed the tree. She sat on a branch watching the street for a few minutes, and then dropped to the ground. Using shadows, she took back streets to move toward the harbor. She had not worked out a plan yet, but the jumble of warehouses seemed to her the best place to lie up until she planned her next move.

XI

The first signs that the Frankish invasion was generating some chaos appeared when Demaratus reached Augustobriga. The city was an important trade hub, set on the banks of a river that ran off to the northeast. Goods came up the Iberus from Ilerda and Tortosa on the east coast, then down a network of smaller tributaries that branched off from the big river. In turn, hides, gold, and grain—and, in the old days, slaves—went from west to east, eventually to Rome.

The road to Augustobriga ran through hilly country, finally dipping down to the southeast. Demaratus had ridden hard from Legio, stopping only for an occasional nap. For all her delicate features, Aura, the mare, had a core of iron, and she easily shouldered the punishing pace Demaratus set. The city—one of the few in Hispania totally surrounded by a defense wall— lay on the banks of a river, with a narrow plain opening out to the north. Beyond the plain loomed a range of mountains, purple in the distance, that guarded Hispania's northern borders.

The city was clogged with refugees, which made it easy for the signifer to blend in with the traffic, even though the stream

79

of people was going west and he was going east. He wanted to keep a low profile, pick up some food and oats for the horses, and get on the road to Caesaraugusta. It was there he would intersect the route north to Lugdunum Convenarum and then east to Rhodus. Supplies were thin and prices high, however, and at one point he was stopped by a patrol of auxiliaries.

"Where you headed, Greek?" one of them said, blocking his path through an exit gate. Three other auxiliaries flanked him.

The last thing Demaratus wanted was trouble. He had deliberately not taken the signaculum that identified him as an officer in the VII Legion. He bristled at the man's tone, but he could hardly pull rank. Even if the men—or their commander—eventually believed him, it would delay things and, worst of all, unmask him.

"I have a family in Caesaraugusta, sir, and I am trying to reach them. I have just finished a trading expedition to Augusta."

"Trader, are you," the man said. "Successful trip?"

Demaratus knew where this was going and decided to hurry the process along. He shrugged. "Not bad. Certainly enough to make a donation to those who defend us against an invader."

The boldness of his response took even the auxiliaries aback. They were clearly used to a wink and a nod and a surreptitious handful of coins. "Ahh, well, that would be appreciated, sir," said the auxiliary who had stopped him. Demaratus noted how the possibility of money had made the man polite.

Demaratus kept the bulk of his money, including all of the gold, in a sack that lay flat against his back, but he kept a small purse with a handful of silver denari attached to the front of his belt. He slipped it off, counted out eight coins, and handed it to the auxiliary. The man took it—hesitating a moment as if he might ask for more—but, seeing an officer come through the gate, slipped it into his purse.

The officer was a tesserarius, who nodded at Demaratus and told the men they would be relieved shortly so they could eat. The signifer took the opportunity to pull both his horses through the gate and cross the bridge over the river. He decided that from this point on he would avoid entering cities until he arrived at Emporiae. It would make the journey more difficult, but the more people who saw him, the greater was the possibility of discovery.

What was clear from talking to refugees was that the Franks were still in Tarraco and had effectively sealed off the city from the rest of Hispania. One man said that someone had told him that the entire Frankish nation had decamped to Hispania, and that it was protected by an army of 100,000 soldiers.

Demaratus questioned dozens of refugees, all of whom had different stories, but all seemed to agree that Hispania faced a major invasion. None of the people he talked with, however, had even seen a Frank. Demaratus doubted that the Franks had anything like 100,000 soldiers, which made it all the more urgent that he get to Tarraco as quickly as possible. While this had begun as an expedition to find Coventina, Demaratus would also do his best to find out what was actually going on in Tarraco. His beloved was inside, but his friends were outside. It would be a balancing act, but Greeks excelled at balance.

Shortly after leaving Augustobriga, Demaratus began encountering groups of auxiliaries headed toward Caesaraugusta, including an occasional cavalry turmae. He found it easier to strike up a conversation with the cavalry because of his horse. "Where was it from?" "Was it fast?" they asked, which allowed Demaratus to probe what they knew about the Franks. It was virtually nothing.

"We were just told to mount up and get on the road," said one turmae decurion who hailed from Clunia. "Word is that the VII Legion is on the march, but they are at least two weeks away."

Demaratus and the Clunia turmae were sitting in a small meadow next to a stream, watching refugees moving west and the occasional half-century of auxiliaries moving southeast toward Caesaraugusta. Demaratus passed around a wineskin and was handed a piece of rock-hard cheese in return. He took a few slices and handed it to another man.

"Know anything about Franks?" the man asked him.

Demaratus had to be careful. Knowing too much might raise suspicions. "I have traded in the north and have seen some, but I really don't know much about them. It does seem odd that they just showed up."

The man—whose name was Rufus— took a long pull on the wine skin. "Odd? That's an understatement. How could a whole army just appear? Where are the legions in Gaul?"

Demaratus shook his head. "Maybe it's just a raid, and they somehow got past the Gaulish legions."

"Maybe. All I know is that there is a call for everyone to send auxiliaries and that we're to gather in force at Caesaraugusta. I can tell you the towns and cities aren't happy about it," the man said, getting up to start putting his men back on the road. "Will you be riding with us?"

"If you don't mind," replied Demaratus, deciding that

attaching himself to the cavalry would shield him from incidents like having to hand out the bribe at Augustabriga.

The turmae of 30 men mounted and trotted down the road. Even though the road was filled with ox carts, they were all going west, so the cavalry bypassed the stream of people by keeping to single file. This forced the civilians on foot to walk on the side of the road, but, as the turmae commander pointed out, war is always a pain in the ass, and civilians ought to feel it as well.

Demaratus found Rufus an interesting man. He had served in a regular cavalry ala for many years. Retired now, he raised horses and grew grapes but found it boring, so he had agreed to command an auxiliary turmae. It was not difficult work. The auxiliaries did not train regularly, and for men like Rufus it was a way to keep in touch and pick up a little money.

"None of my men have ever been in a battle," he said, "but they are all eager to kill Franks."

"And you?" asked Demaratus. As the road had cleared a bit, the two men took to riding next to one another.

Rufus was silent for a moment. "War is a bad business, Alexon" (the name Demaratus had taken to using). "It's not all glory and heroics. These men don't understand that."

"How do you think they will react when they actually encounter it?" asked Demaratus.

Rufus grinned. "Tell me, Alexon, if you saw an elephant, what would you do?"

"Stay away from it?"

"Suppose it was bearing down on you, with huge tusks and that great trunk, bellowing like a monster?"

"Run," said Demaratus. "You can't fight an elephant."

"Oh, but you can. Elephants are tricky beasts to have on your side. They are just as likely to start stomping on their own troops as yours. I know. I have seen an elephant in a fight," replied Rufus.

"Where?" asked Demaratus.

"My ala served for a while in Numidia. Some local rich land-owner put together a game that was supposed to recreate the battle of Zama, where Scipio defeated Hannibal. A lot of the fighters were condemned criminals. If they survived they got to go free," answered Rufus. "Anyhow, a couple of the criminals apparently knew something about elephants. When the beast charged, most of the men playing Roman soldiers turned and ran. But a few others just got out of its way and stuck it with spears. The thing went berserk and ended up running right over the guys playing the Carthaginians."

Demaratus digested this story for a little while. "So what does that say about war?" he asked.

"Going into battle is like seeing a charging elephant. If you don't know what you're doing, you panic and run and the thing flattens you or the soldiers behind it kill you. But if you don't panic, if you know how to fight it, you can turn it into your ally," answered Rufus, glancing back at the men behind him. "Sometimes the men who talk the bravest run when they see the elephant, and the quiet ones stand their ground. You can't tell from the outside how men are going to react when they first encounter war. First everyone has to see the elephant, and then you know what kind of men you command."

Demaratus smiled. "So besides raising grapes and horses and fighting elephants, you are a philosopher, Rufus."

The man snorted. "Not exactly. Philosophy might lead a man into battle, but it's not much use once the swords come out."

The two men topped a small ridge and Caesaraugusta lay below them, a broad river running through the city's northern border. Demaratus could see streams of refugees coming out of the city, but also groups going in. On the city's outskirts blocks of army tents in straight lines were being set up.

Rufus whistled. "I haven't seen something like this for a long time."

"Where did you see it last?" asked Demaratus.

"We went after some Mauri in Numidia. Put together a legion of regulars, three quingeniaery of cavalry, and a half legion of auxiliaries."

"What happened?"

"Nothing. We chased those Mauri around for three months. Wore out our horses, lost some men, and never came close to catching them. Fighting the Mauri is like fighting smoke," said Rufus, his turmae spread out in a line on the ridge.

"So I have heard," said Demaratus.

Turning to his men, Rufus said, "Keep together when we get to the city. I'll try to find out where we are being quartered. I don't want you lot out drinking and whoring until we get settled, understand?"

A number of the men grinned and elbowed one another. Demaratus suspected that is exactly what they would do regardless of Rufus's orders. Auxiliary cavalry had a reputation for being wilder and more undisciplined than regular cavalry, which was saying a good deal.

Demaratus leaned over and put out his hand to the cavalry

commander. "I'll be leaving you here, Rufus. My family has a small place just north of the city. Good luck with the elephants."

"And luck to you, Alexon. May Fortuna guide your steps," replied Rufus, wringing his hand, then trotting off to rein in a few of his men who had already started off toward the city.

Demaratus decided that Rufus would be a good man to face an elephant with. He was not so sure about his men.

Turning off the road, the signifer cut across open country and headed directly toward the mountain range to the north.

XII

Four men sat astride their horses surveying the terrain that spread before them. Alberic wore a coat of mail, as did his second-in-command beside him, Hildebold. Grimbold, the Frank infantry commander, was wrapped in a great coat of gray wolfskins. Leufrid, the cavalry commander, was dressed in a simple tunic and three-quarter pants.

The four had come through a thick forest that opened out onto a broad plain flanked by mountains on the north and low rolling hills to the south. The Roman road from Ilerda ran straight across the plain to a river, crossing it by a wide bridge, then headed due east to Tarraco.

The valley formed a natural defensive barrier. To the west—the directions from which the Romans would probably come from—was a river that would anchor the defensive line. To the north, the mountains were steep, too sheer for an army to descend. The only vulnerable ground was to the south where a low line of hills guarded the flank. But as long as the river line held, there was no way for an enemy to get to the southern flank.

"It's good ground you have found us, Leufrid," said Grimbold.

"I would rather it be closer to Tarraco, but once we take the bridge down it is terrain, we can defeat anyone on," replied the cavalry commander. "The only way they can come is down the valley from the west and across this plain. They will have to cross the river."

"How deep is it?" asked Hildebold.

"Mostly waist high. These rivers are not very deep," replied the cavalry commander.

"Will that stop a legion?" asked Hildebold.

"It will if we have our infantry on the near bank," replied Grimbold. "The river will prevent them from staying in their formations and they will have to fight their way out of the river onto the land. And remember, we outnumber them."

"We don't know that for sure," said Hildebold. "We will be much larger than the VII Legion, but we don't know how many auxiliaries they will be able to gather.

Leufrid scoffed. "Auxiliaries. This province hasn't seen war in more than 200 years. We are battle-hardened from doing the Roman's fighting for them in the north. We will butcher them like pigs. That river will run blood red."

"Never underestimate the Romans," said Alberic quietly.

"We will not, Alberic," said Grimbold. "But this ground gives us the advantage. Even if we do not crush them, we will wound them so badly that they will no longer be an effective fighting force."

Alberic nodded. "I agree, this is our best ground. They may avoid us by taking the north road to Barcino, but that will delay them for many days, and I suspect that they will be under pressure to drive us out of Tarraco as quickly as possible. If they do take the north road, we will have to alter our plans."

"If they do take the north road," said Leufrid, "there are a number of places even better than this to fight. We can shift our forces to block them, particularly if our cavalry slows them down."

"Can your cavalry slow them down?" asked Hildebold.

"We have the best cavalry in the Empire," replied Leufrid. "We will harass them and pummel them. We might even stop them cold."

Hildebold arched an eyebrow but said nothing.

"What about their cavalry?" asked Alberic.

Leufrid dismissed it with a wave. "We have already encountered it. A large unit made a probe yesterday. We scattered it. A bunch of women on horses."

"That was probably not their regular cavalry," said Hildebold. "The regular cavalry will be with the VII Legion. You might not find them quite so mild mannered. I am told much of it is made up of Lusitanians, who are reputed to be fine horsemen."

"Cavalry is not about riding horses, Hildebold. It's about fighting on horseback. Maybe they can ride, but we can ride and fight. Their cavalry will not be a problem," replied Leufrid.

Alberic ended the argument by turning his horse back toward Tarraco. "Begin dismantling the bridge, Grimbold," he said over his shoulder. "And in a few days, I want to find out what they are up to at Iledra. Find out for us, Leufrid."

"My pleasure, Alberic," replied Leufrid.

Alberic's horse broke into a trot and Hildebold loped to catch up.

The two men rode in silence for a while. Finally, Hildebold commented, "What is it about cavalry commanders that annoys me?"

The Frank leader laughed. "Cavalry can always run, Hildebold, so even if they are defeated, they can just leave. Infantry cannot run. When you are on the ground, face to face with the enemy, it is different. However, Leufrid is a fine cavalry commander. He will do his job."

"I didn't say he wasn't a fine commander, Alberic, I said he was annoying," grumbled Hildebold.

Alberic grinned at him. "So speaks my crow."

Hildebold said nothing for a long moment, then said quietly, "I worry about overconfidence, Alberic. Ever since we got here the men have been talking about the VII Legion as if it were made of wax. Leufrid dismisses their cavalry as women. The Romans are not wax and they are not women."

Alberic glanced at him. "It concerns me too, brother, but confidence is not a bad thing."

"It is if it leads to carelessness," replied Hildebold.

"I trust our two commanders, Hildebold. Remember, they do not have to destroy the Romans, just bloody them, make them back off, and be ready to talk."

Hildebold nodded and changed the subject. "There is some anger among the men over the ban against looting, Alberic. And the men are particularly angry over the murder of Arcuf. They say the Romans broke the truce and hence the men should be free to loot."

Alberic frowned. "What is this matter about Arcuf? This is the first I have heard of it."

"He was killed by some woman and one of his companions was wounded," replied Hildebold.

"What were the circumstances?"

Hildebold shrugged. "They were questioning a gold merchant and some madwoman, who is apparently a relative, attacked them with an axe."

Alberic turned in the saddle and looked at his second in command. "Questioning?"

"That is what Ebrulf, the man who was wounded, said," replied Hildebold.

"Two Frankish warriors are 'questioning' a gold merchant and a woman kills one of them and wounds another? Maybe we should worry that this Roman Legion really is made up of women, since they seem capable of striking down our men. Where is this woman?"

"The woman got away, and the men are furious about it," replied Hildebold. "It is not amusing to them."

"Find her, then. Do you have a description? We will make an example of her. But if we turn to looting, the city will grow restive. We need every man we can spare to hold that river line against the Romans," said Alberic. "What is the description? I am curious."

"A tall young woman with red hair down to her waist. She attacked the men with an axe while their backs were turned," said Hildebold.

"Why do I think there is more to this story than we are being told, my friend? And is the 'anger' of the men really over this attack or is the attack a handy excuse to go on a looting spree? The gold and silver we have collected so far is enough for our purposes. Remember, we have to travel light," said Alberic. "Put out her description to all the patrols. It shouldn't be too hard to find a woman as distinctive as that. When we catch her we will execute her in the plaza in front of the Praetorian Tower. It will make a point to the Romans in the tower and to the populace. But no looting."

"There is another matter," said Hildebold.

Alberic sighed. "Yes?"

"A number of merchant families are asking how they can co-operate with us and their 'friends' in Gaul," said Hildebold.

"We must play this one carefully," said Alberic. "If these people think we are in alliance with those in Gaul who let us pass unmolested because it is a part of some scheme, that is fine with us. But we know that we are just a cat's-paw in this game. If the merchants in Tarraco think we allied with those in Gaul, we will not dissuade them. But there is danger in this for us. If we are seen as part of a Gaulish invasion, it will raise not only Hispania but also Rome against us. Let them eat hints and rumors."

"They want a meeting," said Hildebold.

"This duoviri, Fabius, is part of this?"

"No," relied Hildebold. "This group of families says he is not trustworthy."

"I knew I liked the mouse," said Alberic.

"They are wealthy, Alberic. And we can use their wealth. We should encourage them."

"Oh, we will, Hildebold, we will. And then hopefully we will leave them without any money and explaining their treason when we leave. Who leads this group?"

"The man who approached me said he represented a Julius Dasumi."

"We will meet with this Julius Dasumi when we get back to Tarraco. Arrange it, Hildebold."

The second in command nodded and the two rode in silence until they caught a glimpse of sea to the east.

"Our salvation," said Alberic.

"Or our tomb," replied Hildebold.

Julius Dasumi absently twisted a ring on his right hand while scanning the list on the scroll. He looked up at the three other men and nodded. "This mix of goods should get people to the market. The prices are too low, however."

"We need to start low, Julius," replied Decimus Domitius, a thin man with a pinched face and small, deep set eyes. "And we have to be careful. If our prices are too high there may be trouble."

"It won't be trouble for us, Decimus, but for the Franks," responded Lucius Thorius, the junior duoviri who had put the meeting together. "And I am sure they can handle it."

The comment drew smiles from everyone but Decimus.

"People are starting to go hungry," said Decimus. "And making people desperate can lead to trouble. We should keep prices low." He crossed his arms and leaned back, a truculent look on his face.

Lucius sighed. "All right, let's do it Decimus' way for the first few days and see how things go. Can we agree to that?"

"I do not," replied Julius. "I will set my prices to what I think the market will bear. If I am wrong, then all of you will make money and I will go broke." The "broke" comment was met with sidelong glances among the other three. It was more likely that the Empire would go broke before the fabulously wealthy Dasumi family did.

"Let the market choose the winner," continued Julius, dismissing the others with a wave of his wrist. The others looked unhappy but said nothing.

"Now, what of our friends in Gaul and Britannia?" said Julius directing his comments at the douviri.

Lucius pursed his lips. "There is not complete agreement between all the parties on this matter, except that the key to their plans is the destruction of the VII Legion."

"Explain the disagreements," said Julius.

"Britannia is of a mind that the Empire is breaking up. There is talk of an independent empire in the Palmyra, and we know that there are others in Mauretania who harbor such thoughts. Some in Gaul agree with that analysis," replied Lucius. "But there are others in Gaul who think the Empire will survive the current onslaught of barbarians, and that it would be better to build an army and march on Rome. Then we would have our own emperor.

There was a long silence around the table.

"I recommend caution," said Decimus. "If those in Gaul and Brittiania fail, it will go hard on their supporters. I have no desire to end my days on a cross or in the arena."

"Or worse," put in the fourth member of the group, who had sat back from the discussion up to this point.

"Gain always involves risk, Quadratus," said Julius.

"Easily said for one of your wealth and influence. The rest of us here have no friends in the Roman Senate, and our resources are not close to yours," replied Quadratus.

"Quadratus is right," said Decimus. "There must be no way to connect any of us to the plot in Gaul."

"You only talk about failure," answered Julius. "What about success? And what will we gain from that success if we hang back? Opportunists are not as well rewarded as those who are bold enough to act."

"Speak for yourself, Dasumi," said Decimus. "None here will commit themselves to plans that are nothing more than dreams at this point. We will watch how things develop. Then we will see."

"Women!" said Julius, pushing himself to his feet. "Fine. We will wait and see. But I for one have many reasons for wanting to see the heads of those who command of the VII Legion on a lance point."

With that, he strode to the door, opened it, and slammed it shut.

There was a long silence, finally broken by Quadratus. "Do not try to play both sides in this matter, Lucius. You work for us, not Dasumi. Remember that. He has a personal score to settle with this man who humiliated him in Cordoba. That is not our argument. We wish to see the bonds of Empire loosened, and it is possible those in Gaul and Britannia will accomplish that. But it is too early to tell. Revenge drives Dasumi. Profit drives us. Don't forget it."

"Of course I am with you," answered the duoviri. "I also agree that there should be nothing that ties us to the plotters in Gaul.

But Julius Dasumi is a powerful and wealthy man. We need his support and we should not court his enmity."

Decimus snorted. "Politicians! You will be the death of the Empire yet."

XIII

Coventina's plan to go to ground in the maze of warehouses near the port had come to naught. The entire area was ringed with Frankish guards. She tried a variety of streets leading to the port area, but all of them were garrisoned. As the sky went from black to gray to pink and blue, she slipped through a gate into an overgrown garden at the back of a sprawling domus that had seen better days. Hiding in the riot of plants that had taken over the garden, she watched the house carefully. A slave came out to gather herbs near what was likely the kitchen and then disappeared. For the rest of the day no one ventured out of the house.

She dozed, once snapping awake covered with sweat and trembling from a nightmare about her uncle on fire. She clutched her bear totem and willed herself calm. She made herself eat some of the dry cheese and bread and drink some water. In the late afternoon, she crept back to the gate and opened it carefully.

"You there, girl. Come here," said a voice in the street. She froze. She saw no one, how could someone see her?

"Off with that cloak, girl. Let's look at that hair of yours," another voice said.

Coventina was literally paralyzed. She could not even reach for her blade. Her breath came in short gasps.

"No, not this one. Too short and wrong color," the first voice said. "Move along."

It finally dawned on Coventina that the men were not talking to her, but that she was hearing a Frankish patrol stopping and questioning women. The patrol must be very close to the gateway into the garden. The patrol was looking for her, and her attempt to disguise her hair with ashes would never pass muster.

Carefully, she withdrew back into the garden, praying that the patrol would not notice that the gate was open. Gradually mastering her fear, she drew her sword, not that she had any illusions about how much good it would do her if she were discovered. The voices, now muffled by the undergrowth and the wall, continued.

So she was marked, and the Franks were actively looking for her. Why they were so thick around the port, she had no idea. Maybe they thought that is where she would try to hide? That made no sense. There had to be another reason why the port was so heavily guarded. In any case, it meant that her plan for hiding out in deserted warehouses was not going to work. Nor could she stay forever in the garden. Sooner or later someone would find her, and even if they didn't, her food and water would run out in a few days.

She called up a mental map of the city. There was no possibility of getting out through one of the main city gates, and now the port was blocked. The only person she could think of who might shelter her was Demaratus's Greek friend, the tailor Androdamus. His shop was south of the port and might not be so heavily patrolled. Getting there would be dangerous, but to remain where she was for much longer was suicide. She felt a wave of guilt. She was asking the man to put himself and his family in danger. But she only intended to ask for help in getting free of the city, not that he should shelter her.

As the day darkened to late afternoon, Coventina stirred, first standing and stretching out her muscles. She thrust the sword back under her belt and made her way to the gate. She spent a long time listening, but there were no sounds from the street. Carefully, she forced herself to peek out of the garden, looking up and down the street. A dog ran past, ignoring her, but she could see no one.

Her plan was to move back up into the center of the city, then swing around to the south, but she would have to cross the main street leading to the port. She considered waiting until nightfall, but thought better of it. There would certainly be a curfew, and she would be more obvious. In the day she could blend in. As she watched, three men—Romans by their look—strode past going toward the temples at the top of the city. She waited a short while, then stood in the garden gateway, again looking up and down the street. The patrol had gone. She stepped out into the street and walked briskly to a small alley that bisected the street and meandered up the hill toward the temples. She figured she was more likely to encounter a patrol on a large street than an alley, with the disadvantage that if she did stumble across one, it would be harder to escape.

She made herself walk with confidence, as if she was on some errand. A few people came out of the backs of their houses to throw water or waste into the alley, but no one gave her more than a cursory glance. Her destination was a street with a large fountain in its center. She thought there might be people around the fountain, Reaching the street, she looked both ways. There were people out, but no signs of a patrol. Taking a deep breath, she stepped out of the alley and walked toward the fountain. Once on the other side of the main street leading to the port, she could revert to alleys and keep a low profile. She hunched her shoulders to try and make herself smaller.

Coventina passed a group of men discussing food supplies, none of whom even looked her way. Two women with empty baskets came toward her, but, deep in conversation, they barely glanced at her. She reached the main street, which was largely deserted, crossed near the fountain and was just reaching the other side when a voice called out, "You, in the cloak there. Stop."

She froze as she heard steps come toward her. Keeping her head down, she glanced up and saw a young Frank striding toward her. He wore a harness over his tunic, but no armor. A long sword swung by his waist and he carried a spear in his left hand. He could not have been more than 18 or 19 years old, his beard barely worthy of the name.

Coventina considered her options. She could run, but that would automatically make her a fugitive, on top of which, he was likely faster than she. She would have to kill or maim the man. As soon as she made the decision a calmness came over her, one that nursed a flame of hatred at its core. It was a man like this who tortured and murdered her uncle and would torture and murder her.

"Now, then, who are you?" he asked in heavily accented Latin. He grabbed her by her arm and swung her around toward him. As she turned, her cloak hid her right hand, which reached inside and drew out the pugio. She kept the blade low by her side, driving her forearm up under his chin.

"Hey, what do you think you're...," the man said in a voice mixed with anger and surprise.

He never finished the sentence. Coventina drove the pugio up the left side of his rib cage, where she knew the heart was. Her father had once told her that a stab must always travel upwards. If you stabbed down, the ribs would keep the blade from entering the chest. But an upward thrust slipped right between them, and the left side was more deadly than the right. The pugio was razor sharp, sliding into the hilt. He gasped, clutching her and staggering backwards. She shoved his hands away and pulled the knife blade out. He stood for a moment, then dropped to his knees, saying something in his guttural Frankish that she could not understand.

He had a dazed look in his eyes, as if he knew he was dying but had no idea how or why. A red stain spread across his tunic. Coventina calmly stepped forward and wiped the pugio on it. He gave her a curious, almost detached look, and then pitched forward, his body twitching. She glanced up and down the street and saw people standing and staring at her. "Death to the invaders" she said, loudly enough to startle several onlookers. Slipping the pugio back inside her cloak, she turned and made herself walk sedately down the side street until she could duck into an alley. Seeing no one, she broke into a run. A commotion had begun behind her.

She ran, skipping back and forth between the streets, alleys, and warrens of insulari, until she found a partially collapsed shed. She slipped inside, pulled several boards over her and waited. There was no uproar for a while, but soon she heard the sounds of men trotting through the streets. She also heard loud shouts and some screams, as if people were being struck. A group of Franks—she could hear their language—stood in the street near her shed, and she even heard one come over and swing open the door. But the man never came in and the group left.

Coventina had no illusion that she was safe. The Franks would be back with a much more thorough search. But if she could hold out until dark, she might be able to make it to the tailor's. First, however, she would have to get rid of her cloak. Witnesses may not have seen her face, but they would remember her gray cloak.

She tore a long strip from the cloak and wound it around her head. She had seen men wearing such head apparel. Even with this headgear, however, she was still a tall Celt, although she might be mistaken for a man at first glance. She also slipped the pugio under her shirt and used another strip of the cloak as a belt. It would make the blade more difficult to get at, but she had to change her appearance.

The day was late when she left the garden. By now the light had gone soft and the sky was turning toward darkness. She looked out at the street through a crack in the shed. There were people about, but she could see no patrols. She slid out the door of the shed and into the street, almost right into the arms of a stout older woman carrying a sack.

"Pardon me," mumbled Coventina.

The woman gave her an up and down look and then grabbed her arm. "That will never do. They will catch you in a flash," she said.

"What? Please, I need to get home," said Coventina, trying to pull her arm away.

"You have no home, and they are hunting you. You may play at being a man, but if it won't fool me, it won't fool them. And after this last killing, they are outraged. They are turning the city inside out. You won't stand a chance looking like you do," the woman replied, still holding her arm.

"Who do you think I am?" protested Coventina, still trying to free her arm.

"You're that woman from the gold merchants. You killed the Frank who murdered your uncle, and I heard nearly killed another Frank that was with him, and then burned the place down. They say you killed another Frank right in the middle of the street in broad daylight. Everyone knows who you are," answered the woman. "But if we don't get you off the street, you're going to be a dead woman."

Still holding Coventina's arm, the woman pulled her toward a door in a wall around a villa. "Come with me. We will get you fixed up."

Coventina allowed herself to be dragged through the gate and into a garden that formed the back of a small villa. The woman pushed her through, closing the gate after her, giving out a big theatrical sigh.

"Now, let's look at this warrior who is terrorizing Tarraco," she said. "Thin. I thought the Amazon who was killing Franks left and right would have a bit more meat on her."

"Why do you think I am this," Coventina paused, "this Amazon who kills Franks?"

"I know you from the market. I never heard your name, but your uncle was a well-respected man, and we all felt bad about his wife. We knew you came down from the north to care for her. You were good family to him. Good family is important." The woman delivered this speech with her arms crossed, legs wide apart as if she expected Coventina to challenge her. "We also know that the story those Franks were handing out about you was nonsense."

"What are they saying?"

"That you are a mad woman who killed your uncle and then attacked two men who came to his door. You then burned the place down to cover your crimes," she replied.

"What? They lie! They dishonor my uncle and they dishonor me," Coventina cried out, clutching her throat.

"Oh, they dishonor us all, woman. No one pays that story any mind. We figured those Franks came to rob him and you killed one of them and wounded the other. By the way, my name is Vipsania," replied the woman.

"They tortured him! When I came back from the market, he was dead. That is why I attacked them. They are dogs!" Coventina almost shouted.

"Calm down and don't shout. Someone can hear in the street. Let's get inside, and what is your name?" said Vipsania.

Coventina immediately silenced herself and looked nervously toward the gate to the street. "Coventina," she whispered.

"Celt, are you? Well, I should have figured that from your height and fair skin. I have never much taken to freckles, but I suppose you can't help them, can you? I have some makeup that will cover them." All this was said while the woman pushed her toward the kitchen.

Coventina was feeling confused and suspicious, but Vipsania seemed so certain about everything she was saying that she found herself meekly going along with the woman.

Once in the kitchen, Vipsania sat Coventina down on a chair and told her to wait a moment. She disappeared and returned shortly with a mirror. "Now tell me, woman, would you fool anyone?" she asked.

Looking out of the mirror was a face streaked with grimy sweat, and a bright slash of red hair where the turban had rubbed off the ash. Whatever it was, it was hardly the face of an Amazon.

Coventina slumped. She felt demoralized, out of control, and beaten. She was bone tired, and all of the weight of the last 24 hours came crashing down on her.

"Now, now, woman," said Vipsania, patting her on the shoulder. "Most of us think what you did was brave and proper. If you can't defend your family, why the world will just fall apart, I say. And those huge barbarians, brought down by a young woman! Well, that is a fine thing and might just put a little iron in our men's spines."

"I am not trying to lead a revolt," said Coventina.

"Well, maybe you ought to," said Vipsania, taking up a cloth, dipping it in a bowl of water and using it to clean off Coventina's face. "But whatever you are doing, we need to a better job hiding your identity."

"How?" asked Coventina.

Vipsania stepped back and squinted one eye at Coventina. "Oh, I have a few ideas, woman. When I finish, your own mother wouldn't know you."

"My mother is dead," said Coventina simply.

"Yes, yes, well life is hard," said Vipsania, pushing Coventina to her feet and herding her out of the kitchen like a mother hen. "We have lots of work to do, my dear, lots of work."

The countryside that Demaratus passed through was largely deserted. He avoided Osca because he could see from a distance it was jammed with refugees moving north and soldiers moving south. Swinging around the town, he struck cross country until he hit the road headed over the mountains.

Small farms and an occasional tavern broke the monotony of the journey, but the further he got into the northern mountains, the fewer and further between were his contacts with people. This was fine with the signifer. People meant potential trouble that would slow him down. He was pushing hard, stopping only for quick naps and to water and feed his mounts. He ate in the saddle.

It was a lonely country of high peaks and deep valleys, where the wolf and the hawk still ruled, and the road was rougher than those that ran through the civilized parts of Hispania. Once he hid in a small copse of trees while a group of horsemen rode by. They did not look like auxiliary cavalry. He thought they might be local Celts, and a lone traveler with two horses might prove too tempting a target to pass up.

The mountains seem to go on forever, but he finally noticed a small stream flowing north rather then south. He had passed the mountains' divide and was now headed down to the broad plain below and the road he hoped would take him east to the coast and to either Rhodus or Emporiae.

Demaratus was nervous about the next section of the trip, because he had no idea what the invasion had produced in the way of refugees. He might find himself in a sea of people fleeing the coast. But when the rough road over the mountains connected with the road running toward Emporiae, it was mostly deserted. He passed by ox carts moving west, and twice he pulled aside to let an auxiliary cavalry unit clatter by headed east, but rather than a difficult and dangerous trip, it was smooth and uneventful.

This was in part because the Franks had passed on through, or at least that was what the few refugees told him.

"Took all the boats at Rhodus," one man at a tavern said. "Then they just left the place. I am thinking of going back in a few days."

"All the boats?" asked Demaratus.

The man's wife nodded. "Even took small stuff. Stripped the docks bare."

"Any idea why?" asked Demaratus. He had bought a pitcher of wine and some cheese and was feeding the couple, who were more than willing to talk.

The man shook his head. "Nope. I'm a butcher, I don't know much about boats. A lot of the fishermen were unhappy, but they kept it to themselves until the Franks left. Mean people those Franks."

"And they smell like pigs," sniffed his wife.

"Are the Franks in Emporiae?" asked Demaratus.

The man shrugged. "They were, don't know if they still are. I think they are headed for Barcino, maybe even Tarraco."

"Pigs can't take Tarraco," said the woman.

"They can if there are no troops in the city," said the man. "Just because they smell bad doesn't mean they fight bad."

Demaratus poured them another round and then left to gather his horses. He would have to think this through. The couple might be wrong: there might still be boats in Rhodus. It would be worthwhile to go and see, plus he could leave Aura and the other horse with someone he could trust. Emporiae was not far south of Rhodus, and even if it had a Frankish garrison, he was confident that he could get in.

He mounted again and headed east, pushing the horses hard. After a night camping in the woods, he was on the road again at first light. By late morning he struck the Via Domitia and headed south to Rhodus.

The town, tucked into a small cape north of Emporiae, hardly looked as if it had fallen to invaders. There were no guards posted on the roads, and people were moving around the city. A market near the center had drawn a large crowd.

He headed for a stable where he knew the proprietor. Demaratus did not know much about Hispania's interior, but as a former sailor he was well acquainted with her ports. Both Rhodus and Emporiae had been Greek colonies for hundreds of years before the Romans and Carthaginians showed up. Hispania's sailors still included many Greeks.

His acquaintance was not about. "He went west to buy horses," the man in charge of the stable told him. "The Franks took most of ours. We don't know when he is coming back."

Demaratus arranged for the care of his mounts, paying in gold and, taking his bag, headed for the port. There was a tavern called the Trident that he knew would be filled with sailors.

The place was packed, because with no ships there was no work. He sat quietly, watching the crowd until he saw two men he recognized. He worked his way through the press of men and toward a table where four men were drinking wine, eating olives and playing dice. Demaratus noticed there was no money on the table.

Demaratus watched the game for a bit until one of the men looked up. He narrowed his eyes and said, "That you, Demaratus?" he asked in Greek.

The signifer leaned across the table and took his hand. "It is, Nikias. And greetings to you, Aeton," he said, putting his other hand on another man's shoulder.

"Where have the Gods been keeping you, Demaratus?" asked Nikias, introducing him to the other two other men at the table.

"Northern Gaul," Demaratus replied, as the men made room for him.

"Northern Gaul?" asked Aeton. "Better you should have been residing with the shades in Hades."

"Much the same," said Demaratus with a smile. "I was shipwrecked and took up being a merchant for a while. I finally worked my way back down to Hispania only to find the Franks have been here before me."

The comment drew groans and head shakes. "There isn't a ship to be had in Rhodus, and no merchant will dare tie up, because they're afraid the Franks will seize their ships."

"Why are Franks stealing ships?" asked Demaratus.

"Who knows," said Nikias. "Ham-fisted lot, they are. Don't know one side of a boat from another, but they forced a lot of sailors to take them south. They'd have got us too, but Aeton spotted them coming and we all went to the shipyards and pretended we were carpenters."

"They never said why they wanted the boats?" asked Demaratus.

Nikias shook his head. "They were being close-mouthed about everything. Ask a question and they'd belt you one. We stopped asking."

"There are no ships at all?" said Demaratus.

The table got quiet. "What did you have in mind, Demaratus, and why?" asked Aeton.

Demaratus had prepared the story beforehand, a mix of truth and lies. He gave the men a lop-sided grin. "Well, you see I have this girl in Tarraco."

Nikias and Aeton looked at each other and laughed. "Demaratus has one girl? Apparently being a merchant on land has addled his brains," said Aeton.

Nikias leaned across the table and put his hand on Demaratus's arm. "You've been taken with a fever, have you man? We know a good doctor."

Demaratus put his hands palms up. "All right, all right. Yes, one girl, and since when is it a sickness to settle down? And who says I have to stop being a sailor just because I marry?"

The two ribbed him for a bit, which Demaratus good-naturedly put up with. When they had finished, he re-asked the question. "No boats?"

The four men looked at one another. "Well," said Nikias,

"there is one small fishing boat. One man could handle her. But she has a stoved in plank in her bow."

Demaratus pulled out a small leather purse and handed it to Nikias. In it was five gold coins, a year's wages for a crew of four. The man whistled. "This must be some girl."

"She is. And it is likely the Franks have her. I need to get into Tarraco, brothers," he said.

Nikias slipped the purse into his shirt. "We may not be real carpenters, but we can make the ship float and get you to Tarraco, Demaratus."

XIV

Marcus and the auxiliary cohort commander, Septimius Granius, stood side-by-side, watching two centuries wheeling in formation. The centuries were supposed to turn in a flanking movement, but their timing was off—or their officers gave the wrong commands—and they ended in a tangle. Septimius flinched and stole a glance at Marcus, who watched the botched maneuver stone-faced. Flavius, who stood on the other side of the acting Legate of the VII Legion, fidgeted and sighed.

"Be patient, comrades," said Marcus quietly. "We can't expect these auxiliaries to have their timing down pat."

"These men could be in battle in less than a week, sir," said Flavius, straining to keep his voice level. "And they won't be going up against amateurs."

"I am aware of that, optio. I also know that those men will be defending their homes against the Franks, and that gives the advantage to us, regardless of how clumsily they maneuver," replied Marcus.

Turning to Septimius he asked when the cohort had last trained.

"Not for a month, sir. The auxiliary had to help out with an irrigation project near Augustabriga, and the local aqueduct needed repairs. Auxiliaries in Hispania do more fixing than fighting, sir," said the commander.

Marcus smiled. "I do not count that as a bad thing, centurion. War is something we have to do, not what we wish to do. Can we get them in shape in a week?"

"Yes, sir, we can. I won't say they will ever move and fight like the VII Legion, sir, but they won't run away when the going gets tough. You are right about the Franks, sir. We have been invaded and those men out there will fight," answered Septimius. "I can vouch for them."

"What about cavalry, sir?" asked Flavius.

Septimius was surprised to hear an optio ask the question, but it was clear that Flavius was less an optio than an important aide-de-camp to the acting legate of the VII Legion. In theory, Septimius, as a centurion, indeed, the pilus prior, or head centurion of the cohorts and in command of the other five centurions, was superior to Flavius. But Flavius was regular army and the legate's aide. Septimius had a tiny flash of resentment— auxiliaries were always considered less than real soldiers—but he masked it. In any case, Flavius had called him "sir," which was something.

"Most of my cavalry is at Ilerda, but we have not had much luck in finding out what the Franks are up to. They have put out a heavy and aggressive cavalry screen that keeps us from doing any serious reconnaissance," he replied.

"Cassius will be here soon," said Flavius.

"And Cassius is?" asked Septimius.

"Cassius Cornelius, commander of the Ala II Flavia Hispano-rum Romanorum. He is bringing the Ala up from Corduba," responded Marcus, adding, "we served with him in Mauretania."

"Ah, the Lusitanian. I have heard about him," said Septimius.

"You have a problem with Lusitanians, sir?" asked Flavius.

"Of course not," snapped Septimius.

"We have encountered such views on occasion, centurion," said Marcus. "Certain provincial officials have shown a lamentable prejudice toward Lusitanians."

"I was going to say that I heard his cavalry gave the Mauri a good whipping in Mauretania. We Hispanians have a lot of respect for Mauri cavalry, and any commander who can meet them as equals on the field of battle has my respect," said Septimius stiffly.

"Sorry, sir," said Flavius. "I meant no disrespect. It is just that Cassius not only beat up on the Mauri, he saved all our bacon last year when we tangled with those Lusitanians north of Emerita. Some fat latifundia later accused him of being a traitor. I guess I am a bit touchy about the boy."

The conversation veered into supplies, logistics, and how long they should wait for reinforcements.

"We have eight cohorts here now, sir, although some of the centuries are a little short," reported Septimius. "I would guess we have between 3,600 and 3,700 men. There are two cohorts at Ilerda, about 900 men. That gives us over 4,000, plus two auxiliary cavalry quingeniaries east of Ilerda. That's another 800 to 1,000 men."

Marcus nodded. "Carthago Nova and Valentia promised they have another auxiliary legion on the march, but I expect it will be a thin one, no more than 3,500. It will be bringing engineers, however, and if it comes to a siege, we will need every engineer we can get."

"And Cassius, sir?" asked Septimius.

"We hope he can muster four quingeniaries. That will give us a core of 2,000 regular cavalry plus your auxiliaries," said Marcus. "The VII Legion is at full strength. We left Legio with 5,400. If we pull all of this together, we should have close to 13,000 infantry and 3,000 cavalry."

"A formidable force, sir," said Septimius.

Marcus nodded but said nothing. There was an awkward pause after which Septimius saluted and said, "I should see to our supplies, legate."

"A moment, centurion. Where are your tribunes and praefectus?" asked Marcus.

Septimius looked uncomfortable. "One of our tribunes is in Corduba, sir. I have sent him a message. Our other tribune was in Barcino. He has land there. I have heard nothing from him. Our praefectus was injured recently. He fell into a well."

"Fell into a well?" asked Flavius.

"Septimius shrugged. "It was night and people had been drinking. His leg is broken, and one of his shoulders is badly injured."

"Who commands your auxiliary?" asked Flavius.

"I had hoped that our tribune from Corduba would command, but he has not arrived, nor have I had any direct communication with him. I suppose we were relying on the VII Legion for command," answered the centurion.

Marcus shook his head. "I have officers who can command, but commanding auxiliaries is not the same as commanding regular troops. Officers need to know their men. You are pilus prior of the First Cohort, Septimius. You are in command of the legion until your tribune arrives. If he does not, you must be prepared to take the legion into battle. Are you prepared to do so?"

Septimius was silent for a long moment. "Yes, sir," he finally answered.

"Good man, comrade. If I may offer a piece of advice from someone who recently took control of a legion?" said Marcus.

"Of course, sir," answered Septimius. The man looked a little dazed. The vault from head centurion to commander of a legion is a big one.

"Appoint yourself a staff of people you trust. Do it before you do anything else. A centurion does a lot of things himself. A legion commander cannot do so. You have to delegate. It is the single most difficult part of the job," said Marcus. "Appoint someone to take your place in the First Cohort. It need not be the senior person. He must be the best. The rest of the cohorts will follow the First Cohort's lead. Do you have someone in mind?"

Septimius again paused before answering. "Yes, sir, I do. He is a former centurion in the VII Legion, from the Eighth Cohort."

"Good. Give Flavius his name and the names of your staff," said Marcus.

Septimius saluted. "Yes, sir. I will have the names to you within the hour."

Marcus grinned at him. "And as you will discover, comrade, the most important thing you can do is find a secretary."

Septimius smiled back. "Yes, sir, I can see that. Now if you don't mind, I will get about organizing a staff."

Marcus waved him off, and Septimius crossed the parade ground, shouting the names of several men.

"Think he can do it?" asked Flavius quietly.

"It is hard to say. Some men are excellent optios, but they do not make good centurions. Some centurions cannot take the step up to command a cohort. To command a legion...." Marcus let the sentence go unfinished.

"At least he has shown that he can take initiative. His cavalry probe may not have been very successful, but at least he made one. He is touchy but seems solid," said Flavius.

"And you did nothing to decrease his touchiness, optio," said Marcus looking at Flavius.

"Isn't it my job to ask the questions you don't want to ask?" replied Flavius.

Marcus smiled and nodded. "Yes, but you need to be gentle with these auxiliaries. A lot of them were pruning vines and herding sheep only a week ago. Suddenly they are in the middle of a war. We are going to need them."

"I know that, sir," said Flavius a bit stiffly.

"I know you know that, Flavius. I am just reminding the two of us that we are on delicate ground here. We cannot afford a setback, and the biggest one we face right now is collecting all these auxiliaries into one place, and feeding and arming them. Battle may be the easiest thing we do," said Marcus.

"Yes, sir," replied Flavius in a tone that suggested he knew that also but wouldn't point out that fact because he was a long-suffering second-in-command.

Marcus decided virtually anything he said would annoy his prickly optio. He missed Demaratus, who was actually pricklier than Flavius, which always had the effect of making his optio seem more accommodating.

Shouting broke out on the far side of the Field of Mars, and both men dropped the low-key disagreement and looked to see what was happening.

A mass of horses, four abreast, were coming onto the field.

"Well, look at that, sir. Our king of the Lusitanians has arrived," said Flavius.

In the center of the group of lead horses was a handsome young man who rode his mount as if the animal were a part of him. He said something to the men on either side of him, who broke off and began organizing the cavalry into turmae of 30 men each.

The young commander trotted forward and turned to watch the cavalry quingeniary organize itself into its 16 turmai. A signifer, his face covered with a golden mask and holding aloft the unit's banner, moved alongside of him.

"Looks like a real commander, doesn't he?" commented Flavius.

Marcus gave his optio a sidelong glance. "He is a real commander, Flavius. We must be sure to treat him like one."

Flavius gave him a wounded look. "Of course I will treat him like a real commander. Demaratus and I always did, even when he was just a kid on a wounded horse. Of course, he is still a kid, but now he's got a signifer with a fancy gold mask. We don't have that."

"Would you like to wear a gold mask, optio?" Marcus asked with a smile.

"Only if I can melt it down after I use it," replied Flavius. "What's the right thing to do here, sir? Do we go over and greet him, or wait until he notices us?"

"As my aide, you are supposed to know all those things, Flavius," said Marcus.

"How about if I make them up?" said Flavius.

"No argument from me," replied Marcus.

"Then let him get all that cavalry in neat rows, and then we walk over there and pull him off his horse," said Flavius.

"Agreed, except for the pulling him off his horse part," said Marcus.

The conversation on protocol was entirely internal to the long relationship the two men had. Had anyone else but Demaratus been around, they would never have bantered back and forth.

Like a huge flight of starlings, the cavalry had swooped onto the field and then aligned themselves in straight, orderly lines, each turmae in two lines of 15 men, its commander in the fore, surrounded by his duplicarius, or second-in-command, and sesquiplicarius, or junior officer. Cassius waited until the quingeniary had settled down and then gave a short speech that Marcus and Flavius could not hear. When it ended, the men dismounted and pulled their horses off the field in the direction of the stables. Cassius remained, surrounded by a crowd of turmae commanders, officers, and his signifer.

Marcus and Flavius strolled over to stand by the horses—just not too close. The signifer noticed them and whispered something to Cassius, who turned in his saddle and started to give a shout of recognition. Biting it off, he remembered that command required a certain formality. Dismounting, he straightened his uniform and saluted Marcus and Flavius.

Marcus returned the salute, but Flavius stepped forward and seized Cassius by both arms. "A quingeniary commander. Congratulations, Cassius. I guess I have to call you 'sir' now."

"Not at sword's point, sir," he replied with a grin, then mastered his face and turned to Marcus. "Cassius Cornelius, commander Ala II Flavia Hispanorum Romanorum, reporting, sir."

"Welcome, Cassius," said Marcus, "and my congratulations as well."

"Thank you, sir. And where is Demaratus?" he replied.

"We need to talk in private, commander," said Marcus. "I will explain things then. Can you be at the principia in an hour?"

"Yes, sir. I will just see that the men and horses get properly taken care of. I can be there sooner if you wish," replied Cassius.

"No, take an hour. You might want to clean up after such a long ride," said Marcus.

Cassius saluted and tried to look serious, the way he thought a commander should appear, but failed. He was clearly delighted to see Marcus and Flavius. He turned and led his horse away.

"Command or not, he is still the same Cassius, sir," said Flavius.

"So it would appear," replied Marcus. "I am glad to see him."

"Same here. Maybe now we can find what the Franks are up to. What do we tell him about Demaratus?" asked Flavius. "I think we can trust him to keep his mouth shut."

"So do I, and not telling him may end up with Cassius asking a lot of questions that will only draw more attention to our signifer's absence," said Marcus.

The two walked back to the principia to find a huge crowd waiting for Marcus. "I'll sort 'em out for you, sir. When Cassius shows up, shall I send him straight in?"

"Yes, and I want you with him. After the meeting, send for Septimius. I need to keep him informed," said Marcus, taking a deep breath and following Flavius into the crowd.

Marcus, Flavius, and Cassius stood around a wide table looking at a map. "So we don't know where the Franks are?" asked Cassius looking up.

"We know where they are, Cassius, we just don't know what kind of numbers we are looking at, and if they intend to fight us before we get to Tarraco. The road west from Ilerda is packed with Frankish cavalry and our auxiliaries haven't been able to break through to do a reconnaissance," answered Marcus. "We are hoping you can push your way through and see what they are up to."

"Do we have any idea of how many Franks there are, sir?" asked Cassius.

"Anywhere from 15,000 to 50,000, according to a rider who got out of Tarraco," said Flavius. "I don't believe the 50,000, but I think we can assume we will be outnumbered two or three to one."

"And the quality of these Franks?" continued Cassius. "You both have experience with them."

"It is hard to say, commander," said Marcus. "Some, maybe even many, may be former auxiliaries who will not panic at the sight of a legion. The Franks are hard fighters, but they are a long way from home, and if they are living off the land, they may soon be on short commons. They have blocked anyone getting into or out of Tarraco."

"Do we have any way of finding out what they are up to in Tarraco?" asked Cassius.

Marcus and Flavius glanced at each other. "We may soon know that information, Cassius," said Flavius.

Cassius looked quizzical.

"It is also the answer to where our favorite Greek is," continued Flavius.

Cassius widened his eyes. "Demaratus is in Tarraco? We couldn't have a better man on the inside. Was he already there?" asked Cassius.

"No, he left over a week ago," answered Flavius.

"If the roads are blocked, then how...oh, right. I sometimes forget that the signifer is a sailor," said Cassius. "Brilliant idea, sirs. May the gods protect him."

"But Demaratus is unlikely to figure out what is happening outside the city, and the aggressiveness of the Frankish cavalry suggests they are preparing a battlefield somewhere west of Tarraco," said Marcus.

"It will be my job to find out, sir. I can leave within a few hours if I can have fresh mounts," said Cassius.

"We collected horses as we came down from Legio, and we have a little over a thousand. I cannot vouch for their quality," said Marcus.

Flavius and Cassius looked deadpan. Marcus's dislike of horses and his stubborn refusal to learn anything about them or have much to do with them was well known in the legion. As acting legate he had had to ride from Legio to Caesaraugusta. A centurion marched with his troops, but by tradition a legate wore the red cape and rode. Reluctantly, Marcus did so, but on his famously slow horse, the only one Marcus had the slightest affection for. It had carried him from Tarraco to Corduba when he, Demaratus and Flavius had first arrived in Hispania, and he had ridden it to Brigantium to see Aelia off to Gedes. It was slow—a shambling trot was its top speed—and ugly. But it never bit him, kicked him, threw him off, or did any of the wicked things that horses normally inflicted on Marcus.

"We brought extra horses ourselves, sir. There will be plenty of horses. Do you know how many auxiliary cavalry are at Ilerda?" asked Cassius.

"Somewhere between 800 and 1,000, commander. You will be in command of all the cavalry, but I recommend you include the auxiliary commanders in your decisions," said Marcus.

"I have worked a lot with auxiliary cavalry, sir. You can't just ride over them. I will make sure that the auxiliary units are represented on my staff and include them in all decisions. I intend using them mainly for flank and rearguard support, sir," said Cassius.

"I leave the horses in your hands, commander. As you know, auxiliary troops are not as well trained nor can they march as far each day as the VII Legion. We leave day after tomorrow and I hope to get in to Ilerda by noon of the fifth day. I will need the intelligence by then, commander. Tarraco is three days' march from Ilerda," said Marcus, pointing out portions of the map.

"We will be Ilerda tomorrow night, and we will do our reconnaissance two days after that. I need time to organize the auxiliaries and find out what they know before we make a reconnaissance in force. We should have the information you need the day before you reach Ilerda. I will meet you along the way," said Cassius. "By the way, did you bring the Cretans?"

"We did. I told Cleomanes I thought you might want to speak with him. Carthago Nova also sent some of its Cretans along, and they arrived yesterday. The auxiliary legion from the south will not arrive until tomorrow sometime. All the Cretans were apparently once part of the same unit. It means you will have 60 archers if you want to use them," said Flavius.

"Excellent. I will look up Cleomanes right after this meeting," said Cassius. "Are we done here, sir?"

Flavius and Marcus looked at each other. "We are done, commander. Fortuna be with you. We will meet on the road to Ilerda."

Cassius saluted smartly and left.

"Things are looking up, sir," said Flavius quietly.

"Yes, but never tempt the gods, optio," warned Marcus.

"Right. I'm just glad to have the boy with us again. If there is anyone who can find out what the Franks are up to, it's Cassius and his cavalry. Well, I will get back out front and start sending them in. Shall I have Septimius jump the line?"

"Yes. He is our priority now. Have one of those tesserari take over for you. I want you in on that meeting as well, but stay in the background," said Marcus.

"Yes, sir. I'll keep my mouth shut," said Flavius, pushing aside the flap to the outer tent and the crowd of town officials, and even a few merchants waiting to see the legate.

XV

Because the Franks were seizing everything afloat and moving ships south, Demaratus had steered out to sea and away from the coastal traffic. It was unlikely that any ship could catch him in any case. The boat was narrow and swift, and with a wind behind her, she could outrun anything big enough to carry armed men.

He had sailed these waters before, but he dipped in toward the coast on occasion to get his bearings, then headed back out to sea. It was good to be back on the water. The sharp tang of salt, the quiet wash of the waves, the sense of limitless space were all things he had grown up with, and, except for the short expedition to Mauretaina, he missed in recent years. Greeks, he thought, should never be far from the sea.

He was now wrestling with the small sail, trimming it to take a good look at the main port at Tarraco. He did not like what he saw. There were guards posted on all the moles, as well as on the long arm of the breakwater that reached out toward the open sea. A huge chain blocked the entrance. He could see boats clustered in the harbor, and tied up at the quays were a large number of boats, ranging in size from a few older warships to merchant ships and small coastal vessels. So many that they were tied to one another, sometimes three deep.

Demaratus sailed past the harbor entrance, waving at the guards, who did not return the greeting, and headed south. He knew there was a small fishing port just south of the main harbor, and he hoped it was less closely watched. In war, fishermen were considered neutral, and there was a general rule against harassing or seizing them. The rule benefited all; fishermen did not care who bought their fish and everyone needed fish. With a city and an army to feed, the Franks certainly did.

He had spent half a day casting his nets and by luck landed a half load of sardines. They were packed in four big tubs amidships, some of them still gasping for air. The fish were good cover.

Demaratus maneuvered the ship toward a long wooden pier, dropping sail at the last moment and shifting to the sweeps. Several fishermen watched him bring the boat alongside the pier, and one came over and took the line the signifer tossed ashore, wrapping it around a stone bolster.

"Much luck?" the man called out, Demaratus heard a slight Attica accent in the man's question.

Demaratus shrugged and pointed to the tubs. "Half a load," he answered in Latin with a strong Greek accent.

Three other men stood up and came over. "Half a tub if you lend a hand," called out Demaratus, a generous offer. The men pulled the craft to the pier, and two dropped down into the boat to grab hold of a tub. The tubs were out of the ship and pier side before Demaratus finished securing the small craft. With the boat tied fore and aft, he leapt nimbly from her stern and walked forward.

"Axion," he said, greeting them.

The four threw out Greek names that Demaratus tried to tie to specific individuals. The man who had come over to help with the line was Theomestes, who seemed to be the leader. Demaratus thought he might be the captain or the first mate of a vessel.

"You won't keep these long," said the man. "The Franks have been seizing everyone's fish and ship to boot, though I doubt they will take your boat. Too small."

"Too small for what?" asked Demaratus casually.

One of the other men shrugged, "They aren't saying."

"Odd. I don't think of Franks as people who know port from starboard. They make the Romans look competent," said Demaratus.

The comment raised a laugh. "Well, they are up to something. They took our trading ship before we could raise anchor," the man said.

"That's because you lot were out drinking and whoring," said Theomestres. Turning to Demaratus, he said "By the time I located them all, the Franks had closed off the entrance to the harbor. It was just about the first thing they did."

While Demaratus was mulling that piece of information, one of the men nudged Theomestres. "Look what's on its way."

Coming down the pier was a clerkish-looking man backed up by two very unclerkish-looking Franks.

Demaratus crossed his arms and waited.

"Whose boat is this?" asked the man as he stopped at the tubs of fish.

"Mine. I am Axion, a fisherman out of Emporiae. These fish are for sale," answered Demaratus.

"Why didn't you come in through the main harbor?" the clerk demanded.

"It was chained," replied Demaratus.

"Is this where you normally berth?" asked the man.

Demaratus saw the question could be a trap. If the man asked other fishermen if they had ever heard of him, he knew what the answer would be. "No. I don't normally come this far south, but it occurred to me that Tarraco might be in need of fish," he replied.

"And why would that be?" asked the clerk sharply.

"Everyone knows the Franks have taken Tarraco. That makes for a lot of extra mouths to feed. I figured I could get a good price," replied Demaratus.

"Did you? Greeks always have a scheme, don't they?" replied the clerk.

Demaratus bit back his response that Franks thought the Greeks were scheming all the time because Franks were too slow to scheme. He just shrugged.

"Well, your fish are forfeit because you did not come through the main port, so you outsmarted yourself, Greek," said the clerk.

"That's a bad idea," replied Demaratus.

One of the Gauls lowered his spear and pointed it at Demaratus's chest. "Shut your mouth, Greek, before I turn you into fish food."

"If you seize everyone's fish, fishermen won't fish. You need the fish, and I need to make a living," replied Demaratus.

The armed Frank stepped forward, but the clerk stayed him. "You have a point, Greek, and I like your spirit." Demaratus almost gagged. Spirit! The signifer could slice the man's liver out before he knew he was cut. But his mission was not to get in a fight with a Frankish clerk and his bodyguards.

"Thank you, sir," replied Demaratus, keeping the edge out of his voice.

"We will give you script that will allow you to draw food from the city's stores. If you do not use all the script, you can cash it in later for gold," said the clerk in a magnanimous tone. "We are generously not seizing your boat, but we do not want you sailing off and never returning. So we will hold your load of fish to make sure you stay an honest man, a task that I recognize will be difficult for a Greek."

Demaratus kept his face expressionless, but he saw Theomestes tighten his jaw.

"It doesn't look like I have much choice," he replied.

"You do not, Greek," said the clerk. Then, turning to the other men, he said, "Here, you, pick up these tubs and deliver them to the warehouse near the repair yard. We will give you a bucket of fish in return."

As he turned to go, Demaratus stopped him. "Sir, could I get a note from you saying that I will be paid for my fish when I produce more." Demaratus decided that a real fisherman would demand that, and he had to play out the role in full.

"I will remember you," said the clerk and strode off, followed by his two guards.

"Piece of Frankish shit," grumbled Theomestes. "A bucket of fish!"

"Well, at least we can eat it," said Demaratus, grabbing one side of a tub. "I have some wine, bread and cheese aboard. Let's take them the fish and eat."

The mention of food and wine perked the other men up and they lifted the tubs to haul them down the long pier.

Trying to move around Tarraco was frustrating because there were Frankish patrols everywhere. They were stopping everyone and asking questions. Apparently, they were looking for a killer who had struck down several Franks. The signifer had managed to avoid being questioned by inserting himself into groups of passersby. He was preoccupied by what he had seen since landing in the city. He heard that they were looking for a woman, which he found a little surprising. One Frank said she was a "madwoman."

Demaratus was headed for the market near the main harbor where he hoped to make contact with his friend, the clothes merchant Androdamus. He had known the man casually for years, but had become better acquainted last year after he had rousted two drunken auxiliaries who were trying to steal the tailor's goods. In turn, Androdamus had alerted Demaratus, Marcus, and Flavius to the fact that Praetorian assassins were on their trail, allowing the signifer to ambush and kill the two men in Segundum. He had also visited Androdamus with Coventina when on leave. The thought of Coventina sent a sharp jolt through him. He would try to locate her tonight.

Demaratus considered the information he had gathered from the men who had helped with the fish. The Franks were up to something, although nobody knew what. One of the Greek sailors overheard a drunk Frank talking about going to a "new land," but his friends had hushed him. "New land?" Put that together with gathering ships and it added up to a startling conclusion: this wasn't an invasion.

The Franks were headed elsewhere. but why were they in Hispania? Why take Tarraco? That's what didn't add up. Demaratus knew he wasn't well versed enough in the politics of Gaul—or Rome for that matter—to make sense of it. He would need information, and he hoped Androdamus could supply it. He also had the name of a retired centurion with whom Marcus had struck up a friendship and who had given his commander advice on how to fight Lusitanian cavalry, advice that saved all their lives.

The clothing shop was closed. Demaratus went around the side and climbed the stairs to the second floor where Androdamus and his wife and son lived. He knocked, and after a short pause the door was opened by Androdamus's son, Telamon, the young man who had ridden all the way to Tortosa to warn him, Marcus, and Flavius about the Praetorians.

Demaratus give him a wide smile and reached out his hand, only to have Telamon grasp his arm, pull him into the house, and quickly shut the door.

"Telamon, what is...," started Demaratus, only to have the Telamon grasp his other arm. "Demaratus," he said, his voice tight with anxiety, "the Franks are hunting your woman. We hoped she would come here, but we have heard nothing."

"What are you talking about?" said Demaratus. "Why are the Franks hunting Coventina?"

"Because she has revenged herself on her uncle's killers," blurted out Telamon. "And when they tried to take her, she killed another Frank and vanished. Some say she is a sorceress, and she has turned herself into an animal and is hiding."

"Don't speak such nonsense," said Aristeus, Androdamus's wife, as she entered the room from the kitchen. "Welcome, Demaratus. I am sorry you should hear this news when you come to our home as our guest." Turning to Telamon, she scolded him. "When a guest comes to our home you greet and welcome him first."

"But mother, it is Coventina. How can you talk about guests and greetings when they are trying to kill her? Or worse."

"Because there is a way to do things, my son. And if they are worth doing, they are worth doing the right way even when things are bad," she replied, softening her tone.

Aristeus turned to Demaratus and touched his arm. "Androdamus is looking for her now, Demaratus. He will have news when he returns. Please, sit. I will bring you a glass of wine and tell you what I know."

The story came out, although much of it was rumor. Telamon kept injecting comments: "They say she killed her own uncle. They lie! They are dogs with no honor! She struck down a Frank warrior, wiped her blade on his cloak, and shouted 'Death to the invader!' Was there ever such a woman?"

Demaratus realized there was more to Telamon's admiration of Coventina than her suddenly turning Amazon. The boy had been smitten with the tall Celt when Demaratus had brought her to visit the family, and he had teased Telamon about it when Coventina and his mother had gone out shopping. The boy had turned red and stoutly denied it. Demaratus had recalled being in love with the unattainable when he was the same age and stopped the teasing. He saw that Telamon had a crush on Conventina.

"Did she really shout 'death to the invader'?" asked Demaratus.

"That is what people are saying," said Aristeus, "and I talked with a woman whose cousin says her sister-in-law saw her wipe the blood from her sword on the man's cloak. But there are so many rumors flying around that what the truth is, who knows."

"The truth is that the Franks are turning the city inside out looking for her," said a worried looking Androdamus, pushing his way through the door. He crossed the room and embraced Demaratus. "I don't know what Aristeus has told you. Apparently some Franks tried to rob her uncle, and she fought them. One was killed, the other wounded. Coventina fled. Whether she burned the house or the Franks did, no one knows. Then she killed a man two days later and vanished again. I have people in the city keeping their eyes open, but everyone is afraid that if they help her and the Franks catch them, it will be a horrible death. The Franks say they will make an example of her by torturing her to death in the Praetorian Plaza." The merchant ran his hand through his hair and shook his head. "I am sorry you had to come back to this my friend."

Demaratus said nothing, thinking. Things were coming at him too quickly. He began asking questions: "The Franks are collecting ships. Does anyone know why? Is the bulk of the Frankish army in Tarraco? If not, where is it?"

"How can you ask such questions when Coventina is in danger?" Telamon said fiercely. "That is what is important."

"Silence!" said Androdamus. "You do not speak to adults in that tone."

Demaratus put his hand on Androdamus. "It is all right," he said. Turning to Telamon he said, "I asked the questions because what the Franks are up to and what we can do about Coventina are related."

"How?" asked Telamon, his voice heavy with suspicion.

"I think the Franks are collecting ships because they intend to leave Tarraco. This is not a conquest, or even a raid. They are bound somewhere else. The ships are the key. Anything that threatens them will focus the Frank's attention on protecting the ships and away from Coventina. If the Frankish army is in Tarraco, that will be difficult. But if it is elsewhere, and we are dealing with only a garrison, then something may be possible."

Telamon was silent for a moment. "I'm sorry, sir. I didn't understand why you were asking those questions when Coventina is in such danger," he said contritely.

"I can answer some of your questions, Demaratus," said Androdamus. "The Frankish cavalry and much of the infantry left the city two days ago by the north gate. I do not know where they went, except they did not take the road to Barcino. A client of mine came down that road and saw nothing of them. The Franks stopped him outside the city, but let him through because he had four ox carts of grain. They took it all, of course."

"If they did not go north, they must have gone west toward Ilerda," said Demaratus, thinking out loud. "And if the bulk of the army is no longer in the city, it is probably laying an ambush for the VII Legion."

"Why aren't you with the VII Legion?" asked Androdamus.

"To find out information like this," answered Demaratus.

"How will you get it to the VII Legion?" asked the merchant. "The Franks have sealed the city. No one gets out, only in."

"I can sneak out," volunteered Telamon.

"You are a child!" said Aristeus. "You will do nothing of the sort."

"Mother, I am a man," started Telamon, but Demaratus silenced him.

"It is unlikely anyone could get out by land, Telamon. The sea will be our road," he said. "But you can do a great service in this."

"What?" said Telamon sullenly. He had already imagined himself slipping out of the city, fighting his way through Franks and delivering the information to the VII Legion. He had gotten as far as getting a kiss from Coventina when he was brought back into the city as a hero.

"I need to know how many men guard the ships. I need to know if the ships have guards on them. I need to know when the guards change, and if there is any time when there are fewer guards. I need to know if they get drunk," answered Demaratus.

Telamon perked up. "Why do you need all that stuff?"

Demaratus took him by the shoulders. "Telamon, this all seems like a big adventure to you. It is not. It is about life and death, and if the Franks ever find out what you are doing, they will not only kill you, they will kill your mother and your father. Do you understand me?"

The boy's eyes had widened and the color had drained from his face. He nodded silently.

Aristeus put her arms around Telamon. "Demaratus, he is a child. You cannot ask him to do this thing."

"He is a boy, which is why they will not pay attention to him. He will write nothing down and if they question him, he can say he is just looking after his father's business. Telamon has shown himself to be a levelheaded young man, Aristeus. I would not be alive today if he had not warned us about the Praetorians," said Demaratus. "I have good friends in the VII Legion. I do not intend to bury them."

"I can do this, mother. I have already been to the warehouse a dozen times. The guards hardly look at me," said Telamon.

Androdamus had remained silent throughout the exchange. He finally sighed. "Aristeus, Telamon is no longer a child." Turning to Demaratus he said, "But he is also not a man. I will let him go twice a day, no more. I will find out what you need myself. I have trusted friends and two cousins. They will help as well. You can go look for Coventina."

"Not yet," said Demaratus. "First I need to find a man."

XVI

Demaratus watched the street for any sign of movement. For two hours he had hidden patiently in an overgrown garden across from a domus on a side street. Frankish patrols had been active all day and evening, and one had planted itself a block up from the house he was watching. The signifer had seen no one come in or out of the house since he had slipped into the garden, but the wall surrounding the house made it impossible to see if there were signs of life within.

After several hours—much of it drinking—the Franks decamped. It was now only a few hours before dawn, and Demaratus would have to chance crossing the street and climbing over the wall. Once it was light, the patrols would reappear. Trotting across the road, the Signifer leapt high and grabbed the top of the wall, dislodging a small stone that fell with a rattle to the other side. He froze, but there was no reaction in the street or in the house, so he pulled himself to the top of the wall and slipped over.

The wall hid a well-cultivated garden, with a small fountain. He could not see the fountain, but he heard water tinkling in a bowl. Demaratus carefully lowered himself. The last thing he needed was a sprained ankle or broken leg. As soon as he touched the ground he crouched, slid out his knife and waited, listening for any sounds of life. Crickets chirped in the small bushes that edged the garden. and there were tiny peeping sounds near the fountain. Small frogs, Demaratus guessed. The house was dark, and most of the garden was cast in black shadows.

Slowly, Demaratus stood and quietly made his way toward the house, although it appeared he had come on a fool's errand. He had hoped that the retired centurion, Vallerius Tullius, would be home. The man had befriended Marcus when he, Demaratus, and Flavius had first arrived in Hispania, instructing Marcus how to defeat a massed cavalry attack. Even though Demaratus had never met the man, he felt a kinship with him. Without his advice, Demaratus' century would have been overrun in the battle at the meadow last year.

Demaratus hoped that the old centurion had kept his eyes and ears open and could give him information on the Frank's intentions. However, it looked like he wasn't home. The man might have moved or even be dead.

As the signifer crept toward the house, a dark shadow to his left moved. Instinctively, Demaratus stepped back and to one side. The sword thrust missed him by a hair's breadth. He closed with the unseen assailant, grabbing at where he thought the sword arm would be. A blow from a fist caught him above the eye and rocked him back, causing him to trip over a small wall of stones. Demaratus was spinning before he hit the ground, so the sword thrust that followed him to the ground buried itself in the earth.

Demaratus whipped his leg in a wide arc, catching his attacker behind the knees and tumbling him to the ground. Rather than jumping on his opponent, however, the Greek leapt to his feet and backed away.

"Vallerius Tullius of the VII Legion, Marcus needs your help again," he said in a low voice.

The man scrambled to his feet, but did not resume the attack. There was a long silence, and then he asked: "How do you stop cavalry?"

"Javelins" answered Demaratus, " I know. I was there in the meadow."

"Were you, now?" replied the voice. "Who are you?"

"Demaratus, Signifer of the First Century, First Cohort, VII Legion Hispania Gemina Pia," he answered.

There was another long silence. Finally, "The Greek?"

"The Greek," answered Demaratus. "Can we talk?"

"Step near the fountain where I can see you," the voice answered.

Demaratus did so, stumbling on a gutter hidden by the dark. He made himself relax, but kept the knife in his hand by his side. The other man stepped out of the shadows and stood across from him. Demaratus could barely see his face, but the man was short and broad, shorter than most centurions the Greek had encountered.

"The VII Legion isn't here, but you are. Explain that" said the man who still kept his distance.

"I was sent by Marcus to find out what is happening in the city and where the Frankish army is," answered Demaratus.

"No one gets into or out of this city," replied Vallerius, his voice still suspicious.

"They get in if they are fishermen. And I hope they can get out the same way."

"If you are really from the VII Legion you would have said its legate, Titus Valens, sent you," replied Vallerius.

"Titus Valens no longer commands the VII Legion, nor do its tribunes. Our legate was struck down by an illness from which he may not recover. One tribune was in Rome when the Franks struck, and Tribune Publius Felix has a broken leg. As praefectus castrorum, Marcus Favonius has taken command," replied Demaratus.

Vallerius whistled. "The Gods give us omens that speak ill for this endeavor."

"Or else they have placed a very good man in command," answered Demaratus.

The old centurion chuckled. "Looking at both sides? Now that's a Greek thing to do."

"Does it establish my credentials?" asked Demaratus.

"No, the javelins did that," answered Vallerius. "Come inside where we can talk. Through there, by the fountain."

So Demaratus had gained admittance, but not enough trust for the old centurion to turn his back on him. The Greek crossed the garden and carefully went through the darkest part of the house. He stumbled on an uneven stair, but felt his way into the house and crossed what he assumed was a kitchen.

Following him, Vallerius took a small stone and struck sparks until the wick on an oil lamp took fire. The small lamp cast flickering shadows around the kitchen. Vallerius pointed toward the door on the far side of the kitchen, and Demaratus went through. The light from the oil lamp allowed him to avoid bumping into the furnishings.

Vallerius used the oil lamp to light two more and the room came into focus. It was small and neat, with two bed couches, a small table, and chest. The Centurion pointed to one of the couches and opened the chest, taking out a jug and two cups. Setting them on the table, he uncorked the jug and poured two cups of wine. Even from a distance Demaratus could smell the sharp odor of vinegar. Vallerius Tullius clearly was still addicted to acetum, the rough fare of the Roman army.

The old centurion sat back on his couch and gave Demaratus a considered look. "Well?"

Demaratus gathered his thoughts, trying to push down the rush of adrenalin from the face off in the garden. He started by telling Vallerius that Marcus was in command. "At least I assume he is. I left just after the legate was felled."

"Well, from what I heard about the battle in the meadow and the Mauretania expedition, the VII Legion could do worse," Vallerius commented.

Demaratus nodded. "He is the man you want in charge when things go badly."

"Why are you here in my house?" asked the Centurion.

"I need help, sir," answered Demaratus. "I have seen a number of things, but I am unsure what they mean. I need to get information out to Marcus, but I am a stranger to Tarraco. The fact I am a Greek allows me a certain freedom, but I am groping in the dark. I need information, and I may need men, men who can fight."

Vallerius leaned back and took a long pull from his wine cup. "Glorious, glorious," said the centurion. "I was turning into one of my garden plants and you arrive to bring me back from the dead." Leaning forward, he put out his hand. "I am your man, signifer."

Demaratus relaxed and grasped the man's hand.

"What do you know?" asked Vallerius, pouring another cup of wine and topping off Demaratus'.

"I know that the Franks are gathering ships in the harbor. I know that they are doing so all the way to Emporiae. I assume they intend to go somewhere, but I do not know why or where," answered the Greek.

"You should also know that the Franks have moved their army out of Tarraco. I do not know exactly where, but I think it is to the west. Since they already conquered Barcino, why would they move north? I think they are going to try to ambush the VII Legion," said Vallerius.

"Why, then, the ships?" asked Demaratus.

The Centurion shrugged. "A fall back if they fail? That I do not know. I have never understood nor liked the sea. But if I were the Franks, I would not let the VII Legion reach Tarraco and besiege it." Pouring another cup of wine, Vallerius said, "No one survives a Roman siege. The Franks know this."

"So you think this is not an invasion?" asked Demaratus.

"I didn't say that," answered Vallerius. "I just said that the bulk of the Frankish army is not in Tarraco, and that the Franks know that once the VII Legion begins a siege it can only end one way."

Demaratus spun the wine cup in his hands, thinking. "I have a thought, comrade."

"Let's hear it," said Vallerius.

"We are not sure where the Frankish army is, a good guess is that it waits somewhere for the VII Legion. That is important information that Marcus needs. It will tell him to be cautious," said Demaratus.

Vallerius nodded, sipping his wine.

"But we also know that the Franks are gathering ships, and while we do not know why, or where they are bound, we know they think these ships are important," continued Demaratus.

"Unless it is a ruse," said the centurion.

"But to what purpose?" asked Demaratus. "I think your comment that the ships are fallback may be true."

"So what?" asked Vallerius.

"If the ships are important to the Franks, then they are important to us," replied Demaratus.

Vallerius frowned. "Which means?"

"Which means we must organize a way to strike at those ships," replied Demaratus.

"How?"

"I have people watching the port. Within a few days I should know how many guards are posted, when they are changed, and whether the ships themselves are guarded," answered Demaratus.

"You want to attack the ships?" asked Vallerius.

Demaratus nodded.

"That would take a lot of men," said Vallerius doubtfully.

"Maybe not," replied Demaratus. "Maybe just enough men to

get on board and set them on fire. Maybe even the threat of setting them on fire would be enough."

Vallerius was silent a moment. "I can get some men. There are a number of old legionnaires in Tarraco. But I emphasize 'old.' I am not sure we could go up against a lot of young men."

"I heard there was a century locked up in the Praetorian Tower," said Demaratus.

"There is, but it is surrounded by Franks," answered Vallerius.

"What if things happened in the city to get the Franks' attention?" asked Demaratus.

The old centurion nodded. "A few diversionary attacks. The Franks drain the guard on the tower. The lads in the tower break out and fight their way to the docks. Good thinking, signifer."

"Can we do it?" asked Demaratus.

"We might, although right now the Franks are everywhere looking for that madwoman," replied Vallerius.

Demaratus stiffened. "Madwoman?"

"Yes, some Celt who killed two Franks and wounded another. The Franks are looking everywhere for her."

"Why do you think she is mad?" asked Demaratus with an edge to his voice that the old centurion quite missed.

"Oh, lad, all Celts are mad. If you ever fought them, you would know that," answered Vallerius taking another long pull on his wine cup.

Demaratus decided to let it slide. Mentioning his relationship to Conventina would only complicate things. "Well, if they are looking for a mad Celt, they won't be paying much attention to us, will they?"

Vallerius nodded. "You may be right. How do we contact the lads in the tower?"

"You leave that to me," said Demaratus. "Can you pull together the veterans?"

"I can do that," answered Vallerius.

Demaratus leaned forward and clicked his wine cup to the old centurion's. "To victory," he said.

"Nay, lad, to glory and honor," answered Vallerius. "We may not win, but by the Gods, we will die like men."

XVII

A dense mist cloaked the ground. Arcuf narrowed his eyes, straining to see more than a few feet in front of him. His orders were to take his 12-man squad out to relieve the pickets set far up the valley to warn of a Roman approach. Camped a mile behind Arcuf, the main body of the Frankish cavalry was ready at a moment's notice to block any attempt by the Romans to scout the Frankish defenses. The Romans had already made one attempt, and the Frankish cavalry had beaten it back with ease. Arcuf did not think much of Roman cavalry. But right now, he was lost.

He stopped and listened. There was some movement up ahead, but the fog muffled his view. There were sheep and goats in these mountains. It might be a herd crossing the road. Or the pickets looking for their relief. As he sat listening, his command caught up with him, and the 12 men clustered around him.

"Hear anything?" one man asked.

"Hard to say," another answered.

Arcuf slipped out of his saddle and knelt, placing his hand on the ground. There was a slight vibration. He leaned down further and put his ear near the stones on the road. Finally, he stood. "Horses. It must be the pickets coming back. They will catch it for leaving their post," he said.

The charge seemed to come out of the nowhere, as if it had materialized from the fog itself. A line of horsemen wielding long lances struck the patrol before any could even draw a sword. Arcuf tried to mount, but a horseman drove a lance through his shoulder, knocking him onto the road. Another slashed him with a sword. A horse flashed by, and he noticed the hooves were wrapped in leather. That is why he had heard nothing! He tried to roll away from the attack, but another lancer pinned him to the ground. Within less than a minute the Frankish patrol was destroyed.

The attackers wheeled their horses and clustered over the fallen Franks. Suddenly, a mass of horsemen emerged from the fog. Cassius Cornelius, flanked by two aides, led the group. He looked down at the dead Franks. "Well done," he said. He dismounted and called out several names. Soon a group of officers surrounded him.

"Let's go over the plan again," said Cassius. "Titus?"

"I focus on their horses, sir," answered one of the men.

"You have the critical job, Titus. We can smash through them, but we need to get back out once we see what the Franks are up to. If we can keep them off their horses, we can ride right back through them. If they mount, we will be caught in a vise: their infantry and the river to the east, the mountains to the north, and some angry Franks at our backs," said Cassius.

"Yes, sir. My job is to keep the Franks on foot," answered Titus. "We'll do that."

"Julius?"

"I take the engineers down as far as the river, sir, and make sure they come back in one piece," answered another.

"Right. Pieces of engineer are no good to us," said Cassius, drawing a quiet laugh.

"Aemilius?"

"I set the archers here, and keep the rear guard in reserve, sir."

"Right. We may be coming back in a hurry, Aemilius, and I want these Franks to meet our Cretans. Your reserve will let us through and then counterattack," said Cassius.

"Any questions?" the commander asked.

The group was silent.

Cassius mounted and wheeled his horse. "Walk and keep quiet until we see the camp. This fog is thinning out. Watch for my signal. My signifer will blow a horn blast. Then let us show the Franks what Hispania's cavalry can do."

The Roman cavalry gathered into three columns a dozen men wide and began to move down the long valley just as the sky in the east turned rose. The leather-shod horses made virtually no noise, and the men were silent. The three columns moved wraith-like through the vanishing fog.

"No other pickets?" an aide whispered to Cassius.

Cassius shook his head. "Hubris is its own punishment, Sergius. They thought beating up some auxiliaries a few weeks ago would do the job. They are about to be rudely awakened."

As the fog melted with the approaching dawn, they saw a sea of tents, a half-mile ahead, sprawled before them. A vast corral lay off to the north of the camp. One of the Roman columns began edging over in its direction. Cassius could see Titus looking toward him, but it was too soon to sound a charge. A half-mile gallop would wind the horses, and they still had to get to the river and back.

There were no fires and, as far as Cassius could see, no guards. The Franks had depended on their pickets to sound an alarm.

Even at a walk, the horses covered the half-mile quickly. Cassius saw a man emerge from his tent, stretch, and look to the west. "Now," cried Cassius. His signifer put a horn to his lips and blew a high note. The columns broke into a lope. Cassius could hear cries now, and more men were stumbling out of their tents. Titus waved and led his column toward the corrals.

Suddenly, they were on the camp, the horses pouring over the outer ring of equipment and saddles and into the center of the tents, cutting down Franks as they tried to grab their weapons. Others were lanced while they struggled to free themselves from their tents. One column spread out among the tents, their job to kill, scatter, and prevent any organized resistance. Another column, with Cassius in command, headed for the river, with Julius in the rear herding his engineers.

Almost before he realized it, Cassius' column had broken free of the camp and headed down the valley. He could hear horses screaming to the north. The valley broadened out and Cassius noted landmarks. To the north, the mountains were steep, too steep for horses, too steep even for men. To the south the mountains flattened out. A camp of soldiers loomed above, but the men must have thought the Romans were their own cavalry. A few waved before disappearing under a flood of horses.

Finally, Cassius caught a reflection. The river. The valley had spread to about two miles wide. The terrain to the south was rolling hills, and way off in the east was a band of solid black: a forest, too far away to see the trees. The valley began its slope to the river. A dismantled bridge lay dead ahead, and on the other bank a vast camp.

On the near bank of the river were soldiers and workmen who also apparently mistook the Romans for their own cavalry. A few waved and then looked more sharply. Some ran for the river, flinging themselves in and swimming across. No, not swimming, wading. The water seemed to be only about chest high. A few of the solders formed a defensive circle, but there were too many horsemen, and the circle soon vanished in a swirl of lances and swords.

Cassius looked for Julius, who already had his charges dismount, surveying the river and the bridge. One was holding up an instrument and sighting along it. Titus had formed a defense perimeter, consisting of dismounted cavalry with their shields, around the engineers. A horn blast, followed by several more, began to stir the camp on the far side of the river. A wall of earth and stakes were set close to the opposite riverbank, and soldiers could be seen appearing behind them. Cassius saw the first arrow shafts begin to arch toward the cavalry.

An engineer swung a weighted line over his head and let it go. Arching over the river, it landed on the other side. The man reeled the line back, counting the markers on it. Another engineer standing nearby made notes on a tablet. The man with the line again swung it over his head, and the two men repeated the procedure.

Three other engineers were wading waist deep in the river,

probing its bottom with long poles. One reached down, brought up some river bottom and examined it.

Cassius waved at Julius, who said something to the engineer with the measure. The man nodded, tucked away his instrument, and mounted his horse. The men in the river waded ashore and followed. The guards began herding them back away from the river. Cassius took another look around. The river seemed fordable, but he did not like the look of that wall on the other side. It was time to get out of there.

He waved to the signifer who blasted his horn, and the cavalry turned and galloped back up the valley.

The cavalry camp on the west side of the river was still in chaos, with the Roman cavalry ranging up and down the tent aisles, slashing at Franks or attacking larger groups that had managed to coalesce. Horses were running amok, so at least the attack on the corral had been partly successful. It was only a matter of time, however, before the Franks caught their horses and counterattacked. And there were far more cavalry than he had ever seen. At least 4,000 men in this camp, maybe more. Twice the Roman force.

To the south, several hundred Franks had managed to retrieve their swords and shields and were beginning to fight back. To the north, Cassius could see mounted Franks, some of them running down the loose horses. Soon they would have to deal with a significant mounted force.

"Signal retreat," Cassius told the signifer, who blew several sharp notes on his horn. As Cassius's column rode back through the Frankish camp, he could see his cavalry breaking off their attacks and moving back up the valley. Eventually, the entire force was streaming to the west. Behind him, Cassius could see the Frankish cavalry going into formation.

The Romans had a long start on the Franks, but their horses were flagging. Cassius drifted back to the rear and watched the Franks in pursuit narrow the gap. There were a lot of them. He hoped Aemilius was ready.

He spurred ahead, working his way to the head of the columns. Finally, the place where the attack had started came into view, the dead Franks still scattered along the road. Aemilius had drawn up his reserves in a block to the south of the road. The Cretans were deployed to the north, with cavalrymen holding their horses in the rear.

As the column of exhausted Roman cavalry passed by the reserves, Aemilius swung his men behind them to block the road, and the Cretans moved in to cover the reserves. Cassius pulled out of the column and watched. The cavalry that had attacked the Frankish camp and scouted the river halted to rest their horses, screened by the reserves and the archers.

Soon, the Franks came boiling up the valley, but their horses had galloped for miles, and Cassius could see they were flecked with foam, exhausted. They should not have been pushed so hard. Their horses will be too tired to fight, thought Cassius, and the Roman reserves were fresh. The Frankish cavalry commander would have a lot to explaining to do to his superiors.

Startled, the Franks saw the reserves and pulled up, just as the Cretans opened fire, unhorsing men and wounding horses. That is when Aemilius hit them. The reserves poured down the valley and unleashed a storm of javelins. When the Franks recoiled, the Roman cavalry smashed into them, slashing with their swords.

The combination of fresh Roman reserves and Cretan archers broke the Frankish counterattack, and it streamed back down the valley.

Aemilius did not pursue. The Cretans mounted and headed up the valley, while the reserves closed up the rear.

"Well done, Aemilius," said Cassius as the reserve commander rode up to him. "Time we were getting home."

"Yes, sir. Did you get what you needed?" asked Aemilius.

Cassius shook his head. "It's a tough nut the Franks have set for us to crack, commander."

XVIII

Alberic, Hildebold, Grimbald, and Leufrid stood together looking at the smashed tents and scattered equipment that made up the Frankish cavalry camp. Some men picked through belongings, while others set up the tents once more. Off to one side was a long row of bodies. The wounded had been moved down to the river and ferried over to the main camp on the eastern side.

"I am sorry, sir," said Leufrid, the cavalry commander. He looked pale and drawn, a dirty bandage around one shoulder.

"How did it happen?" asked Alberic.

"There was a heavy ground fog, and they overran the pickets before they could give the alarm. They were in the middle of camp before we even knew they were there," the man answered.

"There were no guards?" asked Hildebold.

Leufrid reddened. "No."

There was a long silence, prompting Leufrid to continue.

"I thought the pickets would be plenty. We defeated them so easily the last time that I didn't think a thicker ring of pickets or camp guards was necessary." He paused. "I was wrong."

"I think this wasn't auxiliary cavalry," said Hildebold.

Leufrid said nothing.

"So, they know what we are up to," said Grimbald. "Do we know what they are up to?"

"I am organizing a reconnaissance in force, Grimbald. I will lead it. I intend to ride all the way to Ilerda if necessary," answered Leufrid. "I'll get the answer to your question."

Grimbald nodded and then turned to Alberic. "I don't think this changes anything, sir. If they come down this road, they have to come through us, and we will be ready for them. If they decide to take the northern road to Barcino, we can still head them off before they swing south to Tarraco. It will take them several days more to make the march to the north."

"The Romans excel at set-piece battles, Grimbald," said Alberic They know where we are, they know our defenses. They know the bridge is down. I don't like it when Romans have that kind of information. Given enough time, their engineers will figure a way to even the odds."

"I know that sir, but we need to fight them out in the open. We still outnumber them more than two to one. If we pull out and go back to Tarraco it will come to a siege."

"No argument, Grimbald," said the Frankish leader, "but I would pay attention to your southern flank. It is too flat and open. That is the one part of this battlefield that makes me uncomfortable."

"I will have my entire cavalry command on that flank, sir. If they come that way, our cavalry will slow them down enough for the infantry to shift its defenses," said Leufrid. "Plus, they will still have to ford the river to get to our southern flank."

"Are there fords to the south?" asked Hildebold.

"I will send a patrol out within the hour," answered Leufrid.

Alberic turned his horse and moved back toward the river, Hildebold and Grimbald followed. Leufrid remained, gathering his staff around him.

The three men were silent. A temporary wooden bridge, one that could be destroyed at a moment's notice, had been thrown across the river. The horses made their way across the makeshift construction and turned to examine the southern bank. Halfway down the earthworks was an opening with a stout log gate. The gate swung open, and the three men trotted their horses into the main Frankish camp.

"Do you have anything more for me?" asked Grimbald. "If not, I would like to call my staff together to talk about the southern flank."

"No. Keep me informed," said Alberic, and the Frankish leader and his second-in-command continued through the camp, heading down the road that led east to Tarraco. Neither said a word until they cleared the camp.

"You are silent, my friend," said Alberic.

Hildebold shrugged. "What is there to say? That the Roman women gave us a thrashing? That arrogance and plain stupidity has given our enemies important information? I said nothing because you admonished me not to demoralize our men. Now they will die with high morale."

Alberic looked over at his companion. "We are not dead, Hildebold, we are chastised, and that is not all a bad thing. We did not lose many men. The cavalry is embarrassed. Good. They will fight harder next time."

Hildebold did a poor job of masking his anger, but he held

his tongue for several seconds. Then the words came out in a flood. "Rubbish! We were defeated by cavalry the men thought were women. That will work on them. They will begin to think that maybe this VII Legion is dangerous. Maybe their cavalry is as good as our cavalry. We are a long way from home, Alberic, and those kinds of thoughts don't make men fight harder, they paralyze them."

Alberic looked over at him. "You are right about arrogance, my friend, but we still have a good army, certainly the equal of the Romans. Even if they force the river, we can always fall back on Tarraco, and if we do our job right, the Romans will not have sufficient forces to start a siege."

Hildebold pulled his horse to a halt and turned it toward his commander. "Listen to yourself, Alberic. Good army? That fool Leufrid didn't even scout to see if there were fords to the south on the river. What happens if the Romans march in an auxiliary legion and it just sits there while the VII Legion fords the river somewhere else and hits our southern flank? If Grimbald turns to defend the south, the auxiliary legion will attack from across the river and the mounted 'women' will cut off our retreat to Tarraco."

"I saw the same things, my friend," said Alberic. "Even if somehow the Romans get on our southern flank, their cavalry is not big enough to cut us off. Let's be levelheaded here. You were right about the arrogance, but Grimbald is no fool. I saw him clench his teeth when you asked about the fords. He will make sure Leufrid does his job."

Hildebold turned his horse back toward Tarraco, retreating into silence. It was so still the horses' hooves on the stones sounded unusually loud. The trees closing in around the road took some of the edge off the day's growing warmth. Arrow straight, the road sliced through the forest, ignoring the contours of the land. If Roman engineers had a god, it was a god of straight lines.

Alberic finally broke the silence. "What of this madwoman?" he asked.

"Nothing. We patrol, we search houses, we question people, and no one knows anything. Only we lost another man," said Hildebold, his voice still tight with anger.

Alberic stopped. "Another?"

"In the middle of a street in broad daylight. The witch killed him and then wiped her blade on his shirt, shouting 'Death to the invaders.'" said Hildebold.

"That is not a madwoman. That is a dangerous woman, Hildebold," said Alberic quietly.

"I know that, sir. And the men want revenge," said Hildebold.

Alberic was quiet for a moment. "Increase the tax on gold and silver and take 50 hostages."

"Shall we execute them?" asked Hildebold.

"Not yet. Put out a reward for this woman, and announce I will begin executing the hostages if she is not turned over to us."

"Will you do it?" asked Hildebold skeptically.

"Maybe. But it may not come to that. In the meantime, keep them without food and water."

"I will see to it," said Hildebold. "Any particular hostages you have in mind?"

"Not poor ones, but not wealthy ones," answered Alberic. "No one cares about the poor ones, and the wealthy ones, fearing they may be next, will use their own resources to find this woman. Find hostages who have families and some status so that there is an uproar."

"I am sure our new 'ally' Dasumi will have some suggestions," said Hildebold.

"Good idea. He is man who holds grudges, and he will use this to settle some of them," said Alberic. "How is the ship situation?"

Hildebold shrugged. "We got some from Barcino, but we are still short. Of course, if our army is defeated, we will have plenty of ships."

"The crow has not lost his voice, I see," said Alberic

"No, sir. It is, after all, my role in life," Hildebold replied.

As the road began its descent toward Tarraco, a massive aqueduct swept in from the north, paralleling it.

"They are marvels, are they not?" commented Alberic.

Hildebold reined in his horse and looked. "They need aqueducts in this dry land, sir. This place is not to my liking."

"Nor mine," said Alberic, pulling his horse alongside his second in command.

Both were silent, contemplating the geometric artistry of the perfectly straight road and sweep of the aqueduct.

"They build well," said Alberic.

"On rivers of blood," said Hildebold. "I will not miss running water or well-made roads. Both mean Romans and I am sick of them."

"No argument, my friend," said Alberic, and set his horse in motion toward Tarraco.

XIX

The oil lamp cast a flickering ring of light that lit up the half-dozen faces gathered around the table. Demaratus sat between Androdamus, the tailor, and Vallerius, the retired centurion. On the other side of the table were three deeply tanned men, two older, one just a youth.

"I would rather we do not use names. What we do not know cannot hurt us as much as what we know," said the signifer.

"Fine by me," said one of the older men. "But I need to know what we are doing."

"You are going fishing," replied Demaratus, "only once you get out to sea, you head to the cape just south of Tarraco."

"We know it," said the other older man.

"You will meet two men at the small beach just the other side of the cape. One will replace your crew member, the other will guide one of you to a path that will take you over the mountains and to the road to Ilerda," continued Demaratus.

"What is this path like?" asked the man who was obviously the captain.

"Rough, but serviceable," said Vallerius. "I use it for hunting, and I have gone all the way to the road that leads to Ilerda on it. There are springs and you will have a mule. A horse would have difficulty in parts of it, plus if you encounter Franks, a mule will be less suspicious."

"What will we be carrying?" asked the young man, speaking up for the first time.

"Nothing," replied Demaratus. "Everything we give you will be in your head. If you are taken, there will be nothing to indicate you are carrying information. You will be hunting."

"Who are these men who will meet us?" asked the captain.

"The man who will guide you and provide the mule is my old optio. He knows this ground like he knows his own garden. I don't know who the man is who will replace your crewmember. I would guess a local auxiliary," answered Vallerius.

"Do we know these men will be there?" asked the second older man.

Demaratus shrugged. "One can never be sure, but if they are not, you fish and return. You still get the gold."

"I am sure they will be there. I received a note from my friend this morning through another fisherman," added Vallerius.

Among Androdamus, Vallerius, and Demaratus, a small fleet of fishermen who could convey messages and messengers out of Tarraco had been put together. Androdamus had used his contacts in the port to recruit the fishermen. Vallerius had a network of retired legionnaires throughout Tarraco and the surrounding towns. And Demaratus had the gold he had taken from Legio. Given the growing food crisis in the city, there was no dearth of takers. Whether those messengers could make contact with the VII Legion was another matter. They would soon find out.

The young man spoke up. "How do you know that the commanders of the VII Legion will believe me, or even talk to me?"

"The VII Legion will be waiting for information from me," answered Demaratus. "And you will have a password."

"Which is?"

"Aura," said Demaratus.

"What's Aura?" asked the captain.

"The name of a horse. Ask to see Marcus Favonius, the praefectus castrorum," answered Demaratus. "Although he may be the legate now."

"What do I tell him?" asked the young man.

Demaratus took a breath and laid out what they had discovered so far: that the city's garrison was modest because the army was somewhere else, that there were no preparations for a siege, and that the Franks did not intend to stay but were gathering ships to go elsewhere. "Tell Marcus that he should try to get any warships berthed at Valentia and Carthago Nova sent north to blockade Tarraco."

Demaratus had the young man repeat the information. When he was finished, he said, "Wear a cloak with a hood. You are young and light haired. Your replacement might be older and dark-haired. So stay inconspicuous and give your replacement your cloak."

The three men rose. Demaratus handed the captain a small bag that clinked. "You will get the rest when you return," he said. The man nodded, and the three left.

"What do you think?" asked Vallerius.

"They are honest men," said Androdamus. "I have dealt with them for years. If they make a deal they will keep it."

Demaratus changed the subject. "What have you found out about the guards and the ships?"

"We have a good idea of their schedule, Demaratus," said Androdamus. "They guard the entrance to the harbor and the quays, but there are no guards on board the ships. They have gathered 108 ships, but many are small coasting vessels."

"Are the larger ships berthed together or mixed in with all the others?" asked Demaratus.

"Mostly together," answered the tailor.

"Are you thinking we might be able to fight our way through the guards and burn the big ships?" asked Vallerius.

"The thought occurred to me," said Demaratus.

Androdamus shook his head. "There are lots of Franks, my friends. At least 150 in each guard shift. And most of them are wearing armor. Unless you have many trained men, I can't see how you could get to the boats."

Vallerius rubbed his face. "We can't take on 150 soldiers. The most I can put together is about 60 men, and many of them are my age. We can fight but not for long."

"But if we had the men in the Praetorian Tower, we might pull it off," said Demaratus.

The old centurion considered the remark. "We might," he finally said, "but the timing would have to be perfect. There are guards around the tower as well."

"We need a diversion," put in Androdamus. "Something that would cause the Franks to strip some of their guards away from the tower."

"Such as?" asked Demaratus.

Androdamus spread his hands. "I am not sure, but maybe something will come to me."

"Androdamus is right. A diversion is the thing, and we might be able to pull one off without a lot of fighters. Maybe a fire. But we can't do anything unless we make a contact with the soldiers in the tower. And I have an idea about that," said Vallerius.

"What?" asked Demaratus.

"I have an old comrade who has taken up hunting with a bow. He is very good. Kills deer all the time, and I once saw him bring down a goose. We could get a message into the tower using an arrow," answered Vallerius. "It's not ideal, because it will be difficult for them to communicate with us. But if we can give them a timetable, we might be able to coordinate a diversion with an attack on the large boats in the harbor."

"All this is dependent on what happens with the VII Legion," said Demaratus. "If it is defeated, or even too badly hurt to wage a siege, whatever we try will be suicidal. An attack on the harbor only works if the VII Legion defeats the Franks and marches on Tarraco."

"What about the war ships from the south?" put in Androdamus.

"One, we don't know if there are warships in the south. Two—and take no offense at this Vallerius—Romans and ships do not work well together. And three, even with ships, if they do arrive near Tarraco, they will be overtaken. Most of the craft in the harbor are faster than a warship, with the exception of a liburna. Keep in mind that these ships will be carrying armed men, far more than on any warship. Unless the south can produce a fleet, a few Roman warships are not going to make much of a difference. They might even refuse to engage, given the risk they may be boarded and seized," said Demaratus. "Anything we do depends on the outcome of the fight between the VII Legion and the Franks."

Vallerius said nothing but nodded his assent.

"So we wait?" asked Androdamus.

"No, we have work to do. We need to keep the VII Legion as informed as possible. We need to scout out a place for a diversion, and we need to contact our comrades in the tower," answered Demaratus. "Vallerius, when can you get your archer to look into the problem?"

"Tomorrow."

"Good," said Demaratus.

Androdamus pursed his lips. "I have a thought about the diversion."

The two other men were attentive.

"Well, some of the wealthier businessmen in the city are trying to open up a market," said the tailor. "It is supposed to be an illegal market, but I know there were meetings between some of the leading families and the Franks. I suspect the 'illegal' market will be allowed to function as long as some of its profits are kicked back to the Franks."

"What families?" asked Vallerius.

Androdamus ran off a list of names that Demaratus was unfamiliar with until he mentioned "Dasumi."

The Greek frowned. "Dasumi? Julius Dasumi?"

The tailor nodded. "He is newly come to Tarraco, but the family is one of the wealthiest in Hispania. I hear he had a falling out with his sister in Corduba, but I don't know the details."

Demaratus and Vallerius laughed. "The fun is in the details, tailor," said Vallerius, "and our friend Demaratus here knows them all."

Androdamus looked puzzled. "How would you know the details of a family dispute among the wealthy, Demaratus?"

"You could say I am part of it," replied Demaratus, giving the tailor a quick history of Julius Dasumi, his sister, what happened in Mauretania, and the confrontation with Julius when they returned to Corduba.

Androdamus frowned. "He knows you, then?"

Demaratus nodded.

"That is dangerous for us," said Androdamus. "You will have to be careful he does not recognize you."

"Do you think he is engaged in treason? That he would point out our signifer to the Franks? I find that hard to believe. I think these merchants are swine, but treason is a different matter," protested Vallerius.

"Julius Dasumi wears a scar across his chest," said Demaratus. "I put it there."

"Oh," said Vallerius, "that is different. He has a blood feud with you. Then Androdamus is right. You must not be recognized."

"I have ways to disguise myself, and I will be careful. But we must look at this market and see if we can do something with it," said Demaratus.

It was a night lit only by a quarter moon, but it was not difficult to pick out the Frankish guards surrounding the Praetorian Tower. Legionnaire Lucius Clodius and his officer, Tiberius

Cicero, leaned over the battlements and counted the small fires the Frankish guards used to warm themselves.

"Fewer tonight?" said Tiberius.

"Yes, but it is also warmer. Some of them might not have lit fires," replied Lucius.

Having grown up in a small village south of Barcino, Lucius, and Tiberius had known each other all their lives. But Lucius was of peasant stock, and Tiberius was the son of a small landowner who also dealt in pottery, buying it in Barcino and peddling it in the surrounding small towns. The trade did not make a lot of money, but with the land they owned, the family was comfortable. Both men had gone into the army as legionnaires, but the money and influence secured Tiberius a promotion so he was now a tesserarius, and Lucius still a foot soldier. But Tiberius did not let his higher status go to his head and, when other officers were not around, he and Lucius reverted to their old friendship.

"Good point, but still, I have noticed a slacking of the guard," said Tiberius.

"They started with 300. I think they are down to around 200 now. Are we thinking of breaking out?" asked Lucius.

"I am not sure what we would break out to," answered Tiberius. "That would only make sense if the VII Legion was breaking down the gates."

"Do you think the VII Legion will come?" asked Lucius. He suddenly yanked Tiberius to the ground.

"Hey, what are you...," started Tiberius, halting as his gaze followed Lucius's pointing finger. An arrow shaft quivered on the frame of the catapult.

Keeping below the parapet walls, the two crawled over to the machine, and Tiberius reached up and pulled at the arrow, unsuccessfully. It was deeply embedded in the catapult.

"There is something wrapped around it," said Lucius.

Tiberius grabbed the shaft with both hands and worked the head out of the catapult. Wrapped around the shaft was a piece of papyrus bound by thin string.

The men looked at the arrow and then each other. "Are you going to open it, Tiberius?" asked Lucius, forgetting for the moment that he was talking to a superior officer—albeit the most junior in the century—and not just the friend with whom he used to steal fruit and flirt with the girls.

Tiberius hesitated. He wanted to open it, but he stopped himself. "I better take this to the centurion, Lucius. You stay here and see if any more come, but keep your head down." He rose and, crouching, ran for the stairs to the lower tower.

XX

Coventina stared at her reflection, but she barely recognized what the mirror showed. Vipsania had applied a layer of
white makeup that eliminated the freckles, and now she vaguely
resembled a corpse. Circles of shocking red rouge on each cheek
enhanced the death-head look. Her eyebrows were blackened by
a mixture of fat and coal dust, and her short red hair was covered
by a black wig that, following the Egyptian style, sported bangs
sharply cut in a line across her forehead and tightly wound curls
that hung down on the sides and back.

The dress had long sleeves— "We have to hide those spots of
yours"—with a high Greek waist just below her breasts. Vipsania
had stuffed the bosom with cloth, making her breasts swell out
alarmingly. When Coventina protested, Vipsania brushed her
off. "My dear girl, they are looking for a tall, thin redhead. We
are turning you into a busty brunette. You really must leave
this to me."

If her hair was Egyptian, her dress Greek (and her breasts
cow-like), her jewelry was, well, that was unclear. She had a
copper bracelet that wound around her left arm like a snake, a

series of variously colored glass bracelets on her right wrist, and a necklace with a huge gold-colored sun.

"Don't you think this is a little, um, attention getting?" Coventina said.

"Nonsense. The Franks will flirt with you, not arrest you. You don't hide by becoming inconspicuous, my chick, you hide by becoming someone else. You are my cousin Antonia, come to visit from Barcino, and now caught here by these barbarians," said Vipsania, stepping back to admire her work. "Now, let me see," she said, rooting about in a small chest. "Ah, just the thing." She took Coventina's right hand and slipped a garish ring carved to look like an octopus on her finger.

The Roman woman pushed and pulled on the dress and the wig and then cocked a critical eye at Coventina's neck. "My dear, what is that thing you have around your neck? It must really come off. It spoils the line of my sun necklace."

"No!" said Coventina fiercely. "No. This never leaves my neck." Then softening her tone, said "It is very important to me, Vipsania. I think it has helped to keep me alive."

Vipsania's eyes widened. "Oh, is it Celtic magic? Yes, I hear you are all magicians and sorcerers who can turn yourself into wolves and trees and such. Does it make you strong?"

Coventina bit back her flash of anger at the Roman's view of anyone who wasn't Roman. In this case, Roman chauvinism might come in handy. Leaning forward and lowering her voice, Coventina said, "My father was a man of great power who spoke with the gods of the mountains. This amulet is my connection with those gods, and through it they give me strength. I must never take it off."

"Oh, my," said Vipsania sitting back.

"But you must never tell anyone, Vipsania," continued Coventina.

"Of course not. Never a word. I won't say a thing to the girls."

"The girls?" asked Coventina.

"Yes, my friends. My comrades. You know, that is what our soldiers call one another, 'comrade.' And they will soon be here, and we can talk about what we are going to do to chase these Franks out of our beautiful city."

"Chase the Franks?" said Coventina with a strained smile. "I am not sure a group of women can chase an army, Vipsania."

"Well, that is where you come in, dear. You are our Amazon! And now, I find out a magic one. Oh, don't worry, I won't say a word about all those mountain gods and things," Vipsania said, "Now come along, the girls, I mean comrades, should be along any time."

Coventina felt a surge of panic. She had no intention of leading a resistance movement against the Franks. What could a handful of women do in any case? On the other hand, the only thing that was keeping her alive at the moment was Vipsania. The woman had taken an enormous risk by hiding Coventina, so she could hardly dismiss the woman's fantasies. But these fantasies could get them killed.

Vipsania pushed her along into the atrium and then bustled around, laying out olives, wine cups, jugs of wine, and small honey cakes, all the time keeping up a stream of comments on the Franks, Amazons, Celts, and men, of whom she took a dim view. "They did nothing," she sniffed. "Let these big, hairy barbarians—they smell awful, my dear—come in without a fight.

Really, men are useless unless they have a good woman to tell them how to do things right."

"You aren't married?" asked Coventina, hoping to change the subject.

"I was, my pet, but he died of the plague almost 10 years ago. Sad, really, He was a good man, if a bit weak. I helped stiffen him, of course," she said, patting some pillows into place.

"Vipsania, your friends? Do they know they are going to lead a revolt against the Franks?" asked Coventina.

There was a knock at the door. "No, no, no. They think they are coming over to drink wine and gossip. Won't they be surprised?" said Vipsania brightly and headed for the door. It was the first time Coventina became aware that there were no slaves about. Vipsania was not wealthy, but certainly well off enough to have a household slave or two, but Coventina had seen none.

Vipsania threw open the door and embraced the two women standing outside. They all kissed, and Vipsania herded them into the atrium and introduced Coventina. "This is Valeria and Paccia. This is a good friend, girls. I will tell you all about her when everyone gets here." Valeria was thin and looked like a stork with too much make-up, but she gave Coventina a friendly, if somewhat curious, smile. Paccia was short and stout and beamed a lot. She clapped her hands. "Vipsania always has mysteries," she said with a giggle. Coventina was starting to feel dizzy.

In quick succession, the other women arrived. Cornelia was an older woman, conservatively dressed and reserved, Annia plain and rather nondescript. Poppaea was younger than the rest, and talked from the moment she came in, sometimes to herself ("Poppaea, you mustn't eat those honey cakes, and only two cups of wine").

All of them were polite, discreetly examining Coventina. Vipsania ran about filling wine cups, putting out fresh cakes, and obviously relishing the tension. Finally, Cornelia coughed delicately and said, "Vipsania, we know you love mysteries and suspense, but isn't it time to introduce us to your friend?"

Vipsania put her hands together and looked benevolently at the women gathered in the atrium. "Comrades (a word that drew a few odd looks), this is my friend Conventina, the most wanted woman in Tarraco."

Coventina felt the blood drain from her face, although she thought it unlikely any of the women had noticed given her layers of white makeup. She shot a desperate look at Vipsania. She would have gotten up and left, but where would she go? Indeed, only the good will of these women stood between her and death. She felt caught, trapped, terrified, and angry all at once.

"How wonderful!" said Paccia clapping her hands.

"This is the most exciting thing ever," said Poppaea.

Valeria narrowed her eye, and Annia had no visible reaction.

Cornelia came forward and put her hands on Coventina's shoulders. "Yes, yes, I can see that she is. I saw her several times in the market over the past year. But I would never have recognized her. You did an excellent job, Vipsania. And you must know, Coventina, that you are among friends. You need have no fear of us. We are shamed that the city of the great Scipio has fallen to our enemies without a fight. Our honor is tarnished. You helped restore some of that honor. We welcome you." She kissed Conventina on both cheeks and stepped back.

Conventina was speechless. She had no idea what she should say. She felt a wave of affection for these women, especially for the reserved Cornelia, but the wash of emotions paralyzed her tongue.

Vipsania came and sat next to her. "Now comrades, we have to let Coventina catch her breath, but we also need to be thinking about what we can do to help restore our city's honor. That was very well put, Cornelia." Turning to Coventina, she said, "Cornelia's husband was a centurion. He was killed by these same barbarians."

Cornelia smiled. "Not these barbarians, Vipsania, the Goths. They are different."

"Oh, they are all the same, big and hairy and smelly with no manners. The thing is, what are we going to do about them?" asked Vipsania.

This touched off an avalanche of talking. Poppaea talked mainly to herself, while Paccia spouted ideas, then clapped her hands and dismissed them. Valeria and Cornelia huddled quietly in a corner, and Vipsania tried to pull the ideas together. The problem was that most were hopeless fantasies: poison the aqueduct ("But wouldn't that kill everyone and what would we poison it with?"), assassinate the Frankish leader (all eyes turned to Coventina who pointed out that the man was surrounded by guards and wasn't he a big, hairy guy himself?), burn down the town (which would also kill lots of people, including maybe the "comrades").

"We should protest the market," said Annia quietly.

The comment might have been lost in the noise had not Cornelia heard.

"Wait," she said. "What market, Annia?" The room fell quiet immediately.

"Some of the rich merchants have set up a market near the circus. I was there this morning. The prices are outrageous, but with food so scarce, people have no choice. I saw a woman exchanging a gold bracelet for a sack of onions. It isn't right. And people were angry." Annia stopped, smoothed her dress and seemed to fold back into the couch.

There was silence.

"Is there honor in protesting the price of onions?" asked Vipsania.

"There is honor in fanning anger," said Cornelia.

All eyes turned to Coventina who said nothing for a long moment. "How many people were at this market, Annia?" she asked.

"Around a thousand. They filled the whole plaza in front of the circus," she answered.

"Were there Franks there?" Conventina asked.

Annia frowned. "There were some, but not many. A woman told me the merchants had made a deal with the Franks to give them a cut of the profits. She was indignant. She said it wasn't bad enough that Franks took our city and got all our gold and silver, we also have to pay them taxes?"

The women joined in a chorus of disapproval at this outrage, although Conventina was quiet. What the woman was protesting is exactly what the Romans did all over the empire, to her own people included, but she thought it wise not to point that out.

Coventina began to think out loud. "The Franks have sent their soldiers off somewhere to fight the VII Legion. The rest of their soldiers are guarding the port and the Praetorian Tower. They don't have a lot of other men in the city. If we get people angry enough, they will riot. And the Franks will have to deal with it, which means they may have to bring more troops back into the city, which means fewer soldiers for the VII Legion to fight. I think Annia has a good idea."

Paccia clapped her hands, and Poppaea told herself that this was exciting and that they were all going to be heroines. Coventina said nothing. Annia's scheme might work. It might also get them killed.

XXI

Marcus watched the horsemen crest a hill a mile off. With the VII Legion in sight, the cavalry broke into a trot, staying off the stone road to preserve their horses' hooves. Marcus signaled his officers for the column to halt and, along with Flavius, walked his horse out to meet them.

"Looks like our boy Cassius, sir," Flavius said.

Marcus nodded but said nothing. The two pulled their horses to a stop when they were out of earshot of the column and waited. The cavalry closed swiftly. It was, indeed, Cassius.

The group of horsemen halted, while Cassius rode ahead to meet Marcus and Flavius. Pulling his horse to a halt, he saluted. He looked tired, his horse coated with mud. A dirty bandage was wrapped around his left forearm.

"Looks like you found our Franks, commander," said Flavius.

Cassius gave him a grin. "We did, sir.

Marcus dismounted and led the way to a small copse of trees just off the road. He waited until Flavius and Cassius caught up, then nodded to Cassius to continue. The cavalry commander took a deep breath. "The Franks have built a defense line just east of a river on the road to Tarraco. They have pulled down the bridge and constructed a ditch and a staked wall. Judging from the size of the camp, I would say they have almost three times our numbers, maybe more."

"How wide and deep is the river?" asked Marcus.

"The river is anywhere from 60 to 80 feet wide. In depth, about four feet, though there may be deeper spots. The earth wall is about 30 feet beyond the riverbank. There is an opening with a gate in the wall on its southern end," answered Cassius.

"How far does the wall extend to the south?" asked Flavius.

"It curves in about 400 feet below the dismantled bridge, but then it just ends. The southern flank is vulnerable, not only because the wall is incomplete, but also because the hills to the south are not steep. There can be no attack from the north."

"How vulnerable is the south flank?" asked Marcus.

"That depends on whether there are good fords south of the road and whether they are well defended, sir," replied Cassius.

"Is this good news?" asked Flavius.

"We gave them a thrashing, sir, and the auxiliaries did an excellent job in reserve. Their attack sent the Franks flying back to their camp. Morale is pretty high right now," said Cassius.

"How did you defeat them so easily?" asked Flavius.

"They only had a few pickets out, sir, and no guards at the camp. We caught them in their beds."

"How tough is that ditch and wall?" asked Marcus.

Cassius paused, removed his helmet and ran his hand through his hair. "I don't think I am qualified to judge that, sir. I am not sure what infantry can and can't do. But I don't imagine it will be easy for them to wade across a river and attack a defended position, particularly if the defenders outnumber us. It will also be difficult to ford the river on horseback. I don't see how I am going to get our cavalry into the fight. "

Marcus nodded, put his head down and walked off to stand in a field.

Cassius looked questioningly at Flavius. The optio shrugged. The two stood there for a good 15 minutes while Marcus, his hands behind his back, looked up at the sky, then back to the ground, then at the sky again. He paced. Finally, he turned to them.

"Commander, won't the Frankish cavalry try to do the same thing you did?" he asked.

"Yes, sir, but we will be waiting for them. They won't get close to the legion," replied Cassius.

"On the contrary, I want them to see the VII Legion, commander. When the Franks arrive, I want your men to run for the protection of the infantry," said Marcus.

"Sir! They will know our numbers, and it will demoralize the men," protested Cassius.

"I want them to know our numbers. I want them to think that they are up against a single legion with some auxiliary support. I also want them to think that our cavalry doesn't have a taste for blood," said Marcus.

Both Cassius and Flavius were silent for a moment. "Why would we let them know our numbers, sir?" asked Flavius.

"Because our numbers today and tomorrow will not be what we take into battle. The auxiliary legion at Caesar Augusta is a day's march behind us, and I will send a message for them to split the legion in half. I want half the auxiliary legion to hold back and the other half to speed up and join us. We will slow down and let them catch up. The auxiliary legion from the south is still at least two days off. I want the Franks to see a single legion with some local support troops. I want to hide our true numbers."

"And my cavalry?" asked a stricken looking Cassius.

"I want the Franks to be in the same frame of mind they were before your attack. It was pure arrogance on their part that they didn't put out enough pickets and guards. They beat up our auxiliaries two weeks ago and figured that our cavalry wasn't worth the horses it rides into battle. I want them to think that again. Once they get a good look at us, then you can give us an aggressive cavalry screen. We'll hope they will not see a contradiction in a cavalry that takes to flight in one encounter, to turn aggressive in another. I understand this might create morale problems, commander, but I am confident that you can deal with them. Tell them it's a trick. Everyone likes a trick," said Marcus.

"Flavius," said Marcus turning to his optio. "See that a message gets to Septimius Granius to slow down his auxiliary legion, and send the same message to the legion coming up from Valentia." Turning back to Cassius he said, "Commander, bring me some shepherds."

"Shepherds, sir? Do you want sheep?" answered Cassius.

"No, I want shepherds. Please see to it," answered Marcus. "Oh, and excellent work on your reconnaissance, Cassius." Marcus turned and began walking up the road, his head down, his hands behind his back. "Bring my horse, optio, and get the column up and moving."

"Yes, sir," answered Flavius.

Cassius gave him a puzzled look. Flavius put his hand on the cavalry commander's arm and waited until Marcus walked away from them. Then he whispered, "He is thinking, Cassius. I don't think he has it all worked out yet, but he has something in mind. I wouldn't want to be the Franks."

"If you say so, sir," said Cassius.

"Take my word for it, lad. When he gets quiet and dreamy is when he is at his best. It is how he does things. Now give me two messengers and go get him those shepherds," said Flavius, turning to the group of officers at the head of the column and signaling them to get the Legion back on its feet.

XXII

"You are certain?" asked Grimbald.

"I saw them myself," said Leufrid. "The VII Legion looks like it is at full strength, but it is alone. There are only a handful of support troops."

"Where was the cavalry?" asked the Frankish infantry commander.

"Most of it was in the south. I sent a column south to find out if anything was coming up from that direction, and they bumped into it. Our men were outnumbered and had to back off. There was only a light screen in front of the VII Legion, and we brushed right through it."

"And what do you suppose the Roman cavalry was doing in the south?" asked Leufrid.

"Scouting fords," said the cavalry commander. "Grimbald, don't worry. There are only two places close to the battlefield where they can cross. and I have both of them covered. I am not going to make the same mistake twice."

Grimbald sat back. "All right. How close is the VII Legion?"

"They are a day out of Ilerda, which is at least two days from us," answered Leufrid. "I suspect they will lay over in Ilerda for a day, maybe more."

The infantry commander nodded. "They got a look at our position. That means they will have their engineers working on how to get around or through us. That may delay them for a while."

Leufrid tensed up at the mention of the Roman's successful reconnaissance.

"No rebuke, brother. I am thinking out loud. I think they won't be here for at least five or six days. That means we need to get more rations from Tarraco. I will write out a report and you can send someone with the request."

"Food is getting short in the city," said Leufrid.

"So let the Romans starve. Men can't fight when they are hungry. Get us the food," said Grimbald.

"Yes, sir," said Leufrid, and left.

Grimbald watched him leave, then stood and paced. He stopped, rocked back and forth on his heels, then sat and began writing.

"What do you think?" asked Alberic.

"I think Roman cavalry went from being lions to pussy cats pretty quickly," answered Hildebold.

"My thought also, but if the Roman cavalry screen was light, it had no choice but to retreat, and their cavalry in the south fought hard," said Alberic.

"Maybe they were looking for fords the cavalry could use. Maybe they were doing something else," said Hildebold.

The Frankish commander arched an eyebrow.

"Suppose they are preparing to cover a flank move by the

VII Legion. We focus on the road to the west and suddenly the Legion shows up on our southern flank," said Hildebold.

"Leufrid says he has the passable fords covered. Even if the VII Legion forces a crossing, Grimbold's troops will get the word in enough time to shift our line of defense. They may not have a full wall and ditch, but they can reset their stakes. And remember, we outnumber them."

"The south is our weak spot, Alberic. I hope Grimbald recognizes that," said Hildebold.

"I will tell him to get ready to shift his forces if the VII Legion decides not to attack us at the bridge," said Alberic. "Now, what about the food?"

"I will gather it, sir, but it is getting to be a problem. We executed three hoarders this morning. We are running low, but the market has gotten some food into people's hands. Of course, only those with a considerable amount of money or jewelry to exchange can afford the prices," answered Hildebold.

Alberic nodded. "Within a week the pressure will be off. We can demand food before we open negotiations. Since we hold the city hostage, the Romans can hardly refuse."

"The pressure will be off only if we defeat the VII Legion," said Hildebold.

"We will defeat them, my friend. The killing ground is well prepared," said Alberic.

"Yes, sir. Is there anything else? I need to work on the food problem," asked Hildebold.

"Any news on that madwoman?" asked Alberic.

"No, sir. She has vanished. She may have been able to get out of the city. We will keep looking," answered Hildebold.

"Good. And I think we should ride up and see Grimbald tomorrow," said Alberic.

XXIII

Demaratus, wrapped in a cloak, a hood and scarf covering the lower half of his face, discreetly watched a group of Franks pulling a small coastal vessel along the docks. Several tugged on ropes, while others slipped logs in front of the boat. Others retrieved the rollers once the vessel had passed over them. It was heavy going, and the Franks were cursing and sweating.

"It is the only one that was close to being finished in the ship-yard," said Androdamus. "Many of the shipwrights fled on the boats that left ahead of the city's fall, so the Franks have been using carpenters, but carpenters are not shipwrights. I am not sure I would want to take that boat out of the harbor."

The Franks finally managed to maneuver the ship down a launch ramp and float it. Float it did, but with a list to portside.

"Didn't put the ballast in correctly," said Demaratus. "Unless they know what they are doing, that ship will roll right over once it gets into serious waves. No, I don't think I would like to go to sea in that."

The harbor was jammed with ships, some lashed five deep. It was also heavily guarded. Vallerius shook his head. "Unless we get some of those guards away from the docks, I don't see how we can take the ships. I count at least 200 Franks, and they are well armed.

"We don't have to defeat them," said Demaratus, "just push them aside long enough to take that group of ships over there."

The signifer nodded toward a fleet of about 25 ships moored near the harbor's entrance. The 25 constituted only a small part of the total fleet, but they were large cargo ships, spacious and stoutly built. "If we can take those ships, we will hold almost half their cargo capacity."

"The problem is that those particular ships are all the way out at the end of quay. We will have to fight through most of the Franks to get to them. And even if we do take them, how do we hold them?" asked Vallerius.

"We are not going to try to defend them. We're going to bring flammable material with us," replied Demaratus.

"A suicide mission? We're not going to get a lot of my people to go along with that. It is one thing to fight the Franks, another to burn yourself to death," said the old centurion.

"I have no intention of committing suicide, comrade. All we have to do is take the ships and cut them loose. If they try to take them back, we threaten to burn the ships. I am certain that they will back off and talk. If they lose those ships, Tarraco will become a death trap for them."

"Suppose they don't do what you want them to do, Demaratus?" asked Androdamus.

"Then we fight and die. That is the nature of war. Battle is always a calculated risk. I think this is a pretty good one," Demaratus replied.

Neither of the other men said anything for a while, watching the Franks trying to row the newly launched ship out into the harbor. "Well, it's as good a plan as any, I guess," said Vallerius. "We may lose some of the men, but I suspect not a lot. The veterans are shamed by the way the city fell."

A Frank pushed himself off the wall he had been leaning against and strode over to the three men. "Who are you and what do you think you're doing here?"

Androdamus made a small bow. "I am a clothing merchant, sir. I am checking on my goods. These are my friends."

The Frank waved over three other guards. "Search these men," he said.

The guards ran their hands over Demaratus, Vallerius, and Androdamus, but all three men had been careful not to carry even a knife.

"Show me your goods," said the Frank commander, his voice thick with suspicion.

Androdamus gave another little bow and led the way to a warehouse with a wooden gate. He slipped the hasp out of the lock and swung the door open. The warehouse was piled with goods, not all of them the tailor's. Androdamus led the way toward one of the back corners where scores of bales were stacked in a corner. He loosened a rope binding one of them and pulled out a toga.

The Frankish guard captain grunted. "Okay, but now get out. I don't want to see you around here again." The Franks prodded the three men with their spears and marched them out of the warehouse and off the docks.

"Touchy, aren't they?" said Vallerius, as the three headed back toward the centurion's domus.

"Alert," said Demaratus.

"They are indeed," said Androdamus. "It is clear that they are taking no chances with their fleet."

"That will make our job harder," said Vallerius.

"It will, but it also means they attach great importance to their ships. That is our wedge," said Demaratus.

"Fire-eater for a Greek, aren't you?" said Vallerius.

"We Greeks were fighting the barbarians when you Romans were barbarians, Vallerius," said Demaratus.

"Touchy as well," the ex-centurion teased.

Androdamus and Demaratus looked at each other. "The Romans stopped being barbarians? How did I miss that?" asked the tailor.

Vallerius raised his hands. "All right, I'm surrounded. I yield."

"Wait!," said Demaratus, putting a restraining arm on his companions as they reached Vallerius's house. "I want to see this market."

"That would be dangerous," said Androdamus. "The Dasumi might be there. You cannot afford to be recognized."

"I still need to see it. I will cover my face and be very careful. If food gets scarcer and prices continue to climb, the market could end up being a rock in the Franks' sandals," said Demaratus. "I will hang back a bit so that we are not all together."

"I don't know," said Vallerius. "Androdamas is right. If you are recognized our whole plan collapses."

"I'll be careful," said Demaratus. "Contrary to what Vallerius thinks of me, I am not a fire breather. But if the plan with the boats falls through, we will need a backup. A food riot might be just the thing. Roman riots are impressive. They have, on occasion, brought down emperors."

All right, but don't get us all killed," grumbled Vallerius.

The three men turned and headed toward the southern part of Tarraco and the circus, joining a gathering stream of citizens headed in the same direction.

The market was spread out at the plaza fronting the circus. Several hundred people crowded around makeshift stalls selling vegetables, fruits, grains, bread, olive oil, cheese, and meat, although there was only a single butcher's stand, and it carried nothing but chicken.

Demaratus, keeping a wary eye open for Julius Dasumi, wandered among the crowd, more interested in its mood than anything that was for sale in the stalls. And the mood ran from sour to barely concealed rage. Twice, Demaratus saw shoppers threaten merchants. One kicked over a stall of eggplants that might have been food for the Gods if price were any measure of their value.

There were some armed Franks at the edge of the market, but they got involved only reluctantly in the eggplant incident, separating the protagonists rather than arresting anyone. "Here, here, move along. Fight like this again and we'll shut this all down," one Frank commander told the two men the crowd was egging on to fight.

"Interesting," thought the signifer.

Demaratus made a circuit of the market and counted a dozen Franks. They were keeping a distance from the endeavor. He was returning to where he had entered the plaza—he could see

Androdamus and Vallerius waiting for him—when Julius Dasumi strode by headed for where the fight was breaking up.

Demaratus avoided looking at him, dipping his face further into his cloak. He saw Julius frown and slow his pace, but, at that very moment, a man with a sack bumped into Julius, who shoved him away. "Watch where you walk, clumsy dog."

"Who do you think you are pushing?" replied the man, but the two intimidating-looking bodyguards accompanying Julius grabbed the man by his arms and pitched him off to the side. The man went sprawling, scattering vegetables over the ground.

Demaratus, taking advantage of the diversion, ducked down and melted quickly into the crowd. He walked past his two companions without acknowledging them and strode back the way they had come. He realized that he had been holding his breath the entire time.

When they were out of sight of the market, Androdamus and Vallerius caught up with him. "That was Dasumi," he told them.

"Who? The merchant in the fight?" asked Androdamus.

"No, the man with the bodyguards," he answered.

"Well, that was close, too close," said Vallerius. "Did he see you?"

"He slowed down like he recognized me, but then that man bumped into him and I disappeared," said Demaratus. "If I come back here, I am going to have to have a better disguise."

"I won't say 'I told you so,'" said Androdamus.

"You just did," said Demaratus.

"No, by saying that I won't say 'I told you so,' I didn't," said Androdamus. "Someday, when you are a parent, you will understand."

"I understand why children are crazy," said Demaratus.

The three arrived at Vallerius's domus and gratefully slipped into the dark coolness of his atrium. The old centurion brought out a pitcher of wine and three cups.

"Well, what did you think, signifer?" asked Vallerius.

"There is a lot of anger out there and it is close to the surface. A spark could ignite a riot. And there is little the Franks could initially do about it. I counted a dozen guards, but they seemed reluctant to get involved. I think their policy is to keep hands off this market. They get a cut of the profits, and yet none of the anger at the prices is focused on them. People were angry with the merchant, not the guards.

"Is a riot a better idea than the ships?" asked Androdamus, sipping the vinegary concoction of sour wine so beloved by the Roman army, but hard for anyone else to swallow.

"Not the same thing," answered Vallerius. "The boats might force them to negotiate with us. A riot they would just put down. The first is a threat, the second an annoyance."

"I agree in general," said Demaratus, "but if enough people get involved, there are barely enough Franks to handle it, and if the Third Century breaks out of the tower, the Franks might find themselves in considerable trouble."

"So, we shift plans?" asked Vallerius.

"Let's wait and see what develops. All of this depends on what happens when the VII Legion and the Franks fight it out somewhere in the mountains to the west of us," said Demaratus.

The signifer shifted the subject. "Any problems with the fishermen?"

"None. The captain said my man was there to meet him, and

the guards took no notice of the switch. The young man who came back with them is ready to go back when you need him to," said Vallerius.

"We need to let Marcus know that we have a plan to strike at the Franks' fleet if—and we need to be sure he understands 'if'—the Franks are defeated," said Demaratus, grimacing at the taste of the sour acetum.

"Why?" asked Vallerius.

"The Franks still hold the city hostage, Vallerius. If they lose a battle, they can still threaten to kill everyone in the city. We must be sure to have a counter for that," answered Demaratus. "In the end this might come down to a bargain. I want Marcus to have all the advantages."

"Bargain? Is that what the Roman Army has come to? Bargains?" protested Vallerius.

"It is hardly a victory if you relieve a city and everyone in it is dead," said Demaratus. "And it is not the first time the Roman Army has bargained. Let's work on our plans to seize the boats, but keep in mind that we might have to organize an old-fashioned riot."

"To our plans," said Androdamus, and the three clinked wine cups.

XXIV

"Sir? Ala commander Cassius Cornelius to see you," said a harried clerk putting his head into Marcus's command tent.

"Good, send him in," said Marcus.

Marcus, Flavius, and Septimius were sitting at a table piled high with wax tablets, maps, and old food. Flavius lifted a pile of tablets from the table and dumped them at the back of the tent just as Cassius came through the flap, saluting.

"Commander," said Marcus. "What do you have for us?"

"Four shepherds, as you asked, and a man we picked up who says he needs to speak with you," replied the young cavalryman.

"Everyone in Hispania needs to speak with our legate, Cassius," said Flavius.

"Yes, sir, but he told me to give you a word," said Cassius.

"Which is?" asked Flavius.

"Aura."

Flavius chuckled. "Well, it seems our man in Tarraco is alive and well."

"Shall I bring him in?" asked Cassius.

"Yes, let's hear what he has to say," said Marcus, rubbing his eyes and sitting back in his chair.

Cassius stepped through the tent entrance and motioned their visitor to come, then held the flap while a young man, exhausted and wary, entered. His wariness was not decreased by the silent stare of three Roman officers.

"Who sent you?" asked Flavius.

"Are you Marcus Favonis, the praefectus castrorum?" replied the man.

"Answer me," snapped the optio.

"I was told to talk to Marcus Favonis, no one else," said the man, a stubborn set to his jaw.

"I am the praefectus castrorum," said Marcus. "Tell us who sent you."

"I don't know his name, sir. No one used names, although I knew one of the people who talked with me. He used to be a centurion in the VII Legion. The man who gave me the word for you said it would be safer if no one used names," replied the man, relaxing a little.

Marcus went over to a side table, poured out a goblet of wine and handed it to the man. "Go on."

The man took a deep breath. "He said the Franks' army is not in the city, but elsewhere laying a trap for you, sir. He said the Franks have only a small garrison in Tarraco, and they are not making preparations for a siege. He said they don't look like they intend to stay. They have been gathering ships from up and down the coast and massing them in the harbor. I can vouch for that, sir. There are something like 150 ships, although most of them are just coastal vessels. He also said you should send a message to Valentia and Carthago Nova to send warships north to blockade the port."

The man stopped and took a long pull on the goblet. Marcus nodded to Flavius to get him more.

"Anything else?" asked Marcus.

"No, sir, except that he will be sending more messengers and try to keep you posted on everything that is going on in the city," the man replied.

"What happened to the Third Century?" asked Septimius.

"It has blockaded itself in the Praetorian Tower, sir. The Franks have it surrounded but they don't have any siege equipment, sir," said the man, draining the second goblet.

"Did my man tell you if he was in contact with the Tower?" asked Marcus.

"No, sir. He just told me the things I told you."

"Well, you did a fine job, son," said Marcus taking the man's right hand in both of his. "Flavius, see that this man is fed and has a decent bed. I will have one of my staff talk to you later."

"Thank you, sir," the man said and did a little bow. Flavius took him by the arm and led him out.

Turning to Cassius, he said, "Commander, send a message south as quickly as you can. Be sure the messenger is protected. I don't want him intercepted by Frankish cavalry."

"Good man, your man in Tarraco," said Septimius.

Marcus nodded. "Very good." He was silent for a moment, then added, "Where are they trying to go?"

Septimius shook his head. "Further south? One of the islands? I can't imagine, but then I am not a sailor." At the thought of sailing, Marcus's stomach turned.

Cassius broke into the conversation. "Shall I bring you the shepherds?"

"Yes, yes, let's bring them in, and tell a clerk out there to bring more wine and food," answered Marcus. A long time ago Marcus discovered that waging war was only occasionally about maneuvering troops and leading them into battle. It was mostly about meetings, listening to complaints, and making sure everyone had enough to eat.

Cassius ushered in four men who could only have been shepherds. They wore sheep's wool vests, leather pants, and broad-beamed hats, and they were cooked brown by the sun and cracked by the wind. They pulled off their hats and glanced around with interest, not in the slightest bit intimidated.

Three clerks came in bearing trays of bread, olive oil, cheese, and sausages, and two large pitchers of wine with goblets. The men's eyes lit up.

"Bring some chairs as well," Marcus told the clerks, who quickly did as they were bid. Just as the shepherds were seating themselves and starting to dig into the wine and food, Flavius slipped back into the tent.

Marcus introduced himself, Flavius, and Septimius, and waited as the men gulped down some food and drained their goblets, refilling them on their own.

Marcus put his elbows on the table and clasped his hands. "Gentlemen," he said (all looked at each other with amusement at the title), "you know the valley with the road that runs to Tarraco? The valley with the bridge?"

The men, who had been shoveling down food and gulping wine, paused, and the older of the three answered.

"Yes, sir. We take our sheep to market on that road," he said.

"Is there another route to Tarraco?" Marcus asked.

"You can take the road north to Barcino, and then turn south on the Via Domita," said the man. "You can also cross the river by the southern fords, but you have to go back to the road. The mountains grow steep and treacherous close to Tarraco."

Septimius shook his head. "It is like I said, sir. All the valleys north of the eastern road to Tarraco are dead ends. They go east but the mountains eventually block them."

One of the other men leaned forward and looked at the older shepherd. "There is the bridge of Bormanu, Cotta."

"They can't go that way, Caldus. Sheep can get over the bridge, but not horses. And they couldn't take any of their machines," the older shepherd answered.

"Wait," said Marcus. "What is this bridge of Bormanu?"

"There is a valley north of the road, but it ends in a mountain. There is a way over to the next valley, but it is steep. Horses and carts cannot make it," said Cotta.

"Could mules?" asked Flavius.

"Not ones with loads," answered the old shepard.

"What about men on foot?" asked Marcus.

Cotta shrugged. "I suppose. Are you thinking of going that way?"

"Maybe," answered Marcus. "Where does it come out?"

"Another valley," answered Cotta taking a pull on his wine.

Trying not to sound impatient, Marcus asked, "And where does that valley come out?"

"It comes out at the edge of the forest that the road to Tarraco runs through," said Caldus.

"Have you ever gone over that bridge and to the road?" asked Marcus.

"Sure, many times. You see, they sometimes collect taxes on the other side of that big bridge, so we go over the bridge of Bormanu and they never know," said Caldus.

" Can you guide us?" asked Marcus.

The four men looked at one another. "We can show you the way but, as I said, no horse can get across the bridge, and it will be hard for soldiers," said Cotta.

"Let us worry about that," said Marcus. "Flavius, see them out. See that they get more food and a bed. And we will provide you with a guard."

"What do we need a guard for?" said Cotta, looking puzzled.

"These are dangerous times," answered Marcus. "Optio, see to it."

Flavius saluted and ushered the four out.

"They need to be guarded?" asked Septimius.

"They drank almost all our wine and wine loosens a man's tongue," said Marcus. "None of the plan can get out."

"I am not sure what the 'plan' is," said the auxiliary commander.

"Let's talk to the engineers first, and then I will explain everything," said Marcus. "Cassius, tell my clerk to send in the engineers."

Cassius vanished only to reappear shortly with two stocky men dressed in linen pants and shirts and leather vests. One was carrying a scroll, the other several wax tablets.

"Salvius and Tertius, you know Septimius Granius, I believe?" said Marcus. The men greeted one another, and then Salvius spread the scroll out on the table, weighting its corners with tablets.

"This is the river crossing, sir, and the distances involved." The scroll was a neat drawing that incorporated the dismantled bridge, with notations and numbers at various points of the river. "As you can see, the river is between 40 and 45 feet wide. We could not probe all of it, but it seems to be no deeper than four feet and in places a little shallower. The earthen wall at the other side is approximately 30 feet from the river's edge. We could only see the ditch at an angle, but it looked to be about four feet deep. The wall above the ditch is six feet. It is staked at three-foot intervals. "

"The wall is too low," said Flavius quietly, "and they left too much room between the river and the ditch."

"We concur, sir," said Salvius. "Whoever engineered the wall and the ditch was an amateur. We have a suggestion about how to breach it."

Marcus loved engineers. To them the world was simply a series of obstacles that you overcame.

"Go on," prodded Marcus.

"Now understand, sir, we are not saying this is going to be easy. The camp looked quite large to us, and we think the wall will be heavily manned. The men will have to cross the river and fight their way through it," said Tertius.

Flavius frowned. "Wading the river will break up the units and the men will straggle onto the other side without any formation."

"We can reduce that with portable bridges, sir," said Salvius.

"Explain," said Marcus.

"We make a bridge with wheels, sir. It will be 10 feet wide and 40 feet long. The men push it to the edge of the river and drive stakes in where the bridge is close to the river. We have a block and tackle system that will pull the bridge erect and then we will drop it across the river. We think you will need three of these, sir," continued Salvius.

"Won't they be short?" asked Flavius.

"Yes, sir, but it won't be a problem. The banks of the river are not muddy and the slope down to the river is gentle. Even if the bridge doesn't make it all the way, the men will only have to wade through water less than a foot deep and with a gravelly base," answered Salvius.

"We will also build siege ladders that will allow the men to bridge the ditch and assault the walls," added Tertius.

"Excellent, men. Get to work on this immediately," said Marcus.

"Excuse me," said Cassius. "Can you build something like that for horses?"

"Sure, but it doesn't need to be so elaborate, sir. We can build you a bridge that you can drop on the bottom of the river to give your horses good footing. It takes a while to cross, but you can carry the bridge in pieces yourself. Of course, it can't be a really deep river," said Macro.

"Won't the bridge float away?" asked Flavius.

The engineers gave him a look that they reserved for the in-fantry and children. "We attach weights to it, sir, and the horses weigh it down further once they start crossing," said Salvius.

"Can you make me three?" asked Cassius.

"Yes, sir. We can have those for you in two days. The other bridges need to be built closer to the crossing," said Tertius.

After the engineers left, Septimius turned to Marcus. "Sir, I don't understand. We are attacking the Franks across the river and also taking some mountain god's bridge to bypass the Franks?"

"Both," said Marcus. "Let me show you." He spread out a variety of objects—ink pots, cups, and tablets—to make a crude map. "This is the valley," he said, "with the river here (a quill pen stood in for the river) and the Franks' wall (two ink pots became the ditch and timbered stockade). To the north are the steep mountains." By this time all of the officers were crowding around the table.

"The VII Legion takes the valley just north of the mountains and crosses over this 'bridge of Bormanu' and into the valley on the other side. That valley parallels the one the Franks hold." Marcus pushed a coin alongside a scroll that had come to stand for the steep northern escarpment.

"I will take VII Legion into the Franks' rear. Cassius will find a way to cross the river in the south (a coin stood in for the ala). The auxiliaries will march down to the river and make a lot of noise, but do nothing until the VII Legion attacks the Franks from their rear. They will know this because we are putting a signal unit in the northern mountains that will have a view of the whole battlefield. The Franks will have to drain forces from defending the river to confront the VII Legion. This will give the auxiliaries the opportunity to cross the river and assault the Franks from the west. Cassius will fight his way up from the south and attack the southern flank. The Frankish army will be caught in a three-way vise with no place to retreat."

By this time all the coins had converged in the center of the table.

There was dead silence. Finally, Septimius spoke up. "Sir, isn't dividing our forces in the face of the enemy a recipe for disaster? Scipio the Elder did that in Hispania and lost his life and two legions. The Franks outnumber us, sir. And as for Cassius, his cavalry did a fine job on the reconnaissance, but, with all respect, he caught them unawares. They outnumber our cavalry two to one, and Cassius says they have blocked the two main fords," said the auxiliary commander. "Plus, the Frankish army will see that they are facing auxiliaries in their front and will immediately prepare themselves to defend against the VII Legion from another quarter, although I doubt they will look to their rear. Lastly, you may never make it across this 'bridge of Bormanu,' or will arrive so late that the Franks may just decide to cross the river and destroy us."

"Anything else?" asked Marcus.

"I am sorry, sir. I feel it is my duty to point out the problems with your plan," said Septimius.

"Cassius?" asked Marcus.

The cavalryman frowned. "I will have more men when the auxiliaries arrive from the south, sir. The southern legion is three days off and they brought about 500 cavalry. I think our numbers will come as a surprise to the Franks. I am not as pessimistic about being able to push the Frankish cavalry out of the way and assault the southern flank. But it will be hard-fought."

"Anything else?" asked Marcus.

The two commanders were silent.

" I know this is risky, but we have a responsibility to our citizens in Tarraco. If we do not deal forcibly with this invasion, it will be the first of many. And the Franks will think they are being attacked across the river by the VII Legion."

"Sir, these Franks are not fools, or at least we cannot assume they are. They know the difference between an auxiliary legion and a main-line legion," said Septimius.

"Not if your front rank is wearing legion armor, instead of auxiliary chain, and is carrying the eagle of the VII Legion. We will turn your auxiliary legion into the VII Legion, commander, and the auxiliary legion that arrives from Valentia will become you. The Franks will see two legions, the VII Legion and an auxiliary legion, exactly what they expect to see, and while it won't be as large as the Frankish force, it will be too powerful for them to come out of their defensive wall and attack across the river," explained Marcus. "Cassius will take all our archers and slingers, which he has used effectively in the past to disrupt superior forces. All he has to do is keep the Frankish cavalry busy until the VII Legion strikes the Franks from the rear. Then the Franks will be caught between a hammer and an anvil."

"Sir," put in Flavius, "our men are not going to like giving up their armor, especially to auxiliaries."

"We will use the 10th Cohort's armor and they will be compensated. I will talk with them," said Marcus.

"And the eagle, sir?" said Flavius with a slightly horrified look on his face.

"The VII Legion is not going to give up its eagle. We will make a fake eagle and cover it with gold foil. I also want a false signum for each century. Flavius, I want you to take charge of this transformation. Think of it as a play," said Marcus.

"Except a lot of our people are going to get killed if the Franks don't buy it," mumbled Flavius.

"All the more reason for you and Septimius to get to work," said Marcus. "Cassius, I want a plan from you by tonight." They rushed off to carry out their orders, and Marcus stood over the table and looked at the map.

With his commanders gone, doubts began to crowd into his mind. The Franks might sniff the plan out. The timing left little room for error, such as the VII Legion getting lost in the northern valleys, or Cassius being driven back across the river. If one part failed, the entire operation would collapse. He started to pour himself a cup of wine, but thought better of it. He pulled himself to his feet. He would first have to talk with the 10th Cohort.

XXV

The Women's Legion of Tarraco— the title Vipsania had come up with—was gathered in their host's bedroom. Vipsania had turned it into a meeting place, with couches, pillows, and a large central table. All the windows were covered with different kinds of material that she had dug out of chests. The varicolored cloths gave the room a vaguely festive feeling.

"There was very nearly a riot yesterday," Vipsania said, "and over the price of eggplants and onions. People are very angry."

Leaning in to hear her conspiratorial whisper were Coventina, Valeria, Paccia, Annia, Poppaea, and Cornela. Poppaea was having a difficult time staying still. She darted about, circling the group of women and then sitting down again. Paccia was visibly excited. Anna and Valeria were quiet, and Cornela sat back, almost as if she was an observer rather than a plotter.

"What happened?" asked Coventina.

"Just what I told you," said Vipsania. "A man kicked over a stall because the prices were so high."

"We need the details, Vipsania. What happened when he did that?" pressed Coventina.

"Don't you believe me?" asked Vipsania, looked both injured and insulted at the same time.

"Of course she believes you, dear," said Cornela quietly, "but we need to know what happened after. Did the men fight? Who broke it up? Were there soldiers?"

Coventina shot her a grateful look. Cornela seemed almost an outsider—Coventina suspected she was born to a higher status than the other women in the room, certainly than herself—but the older woman listened carefully and homed in on the heart of things.

"Oh, well, the crowd supported the man who knocked over the stall and told him to give the merchant a beating," said Vipsania. "But the Franks showed up and broke it up."

"How many Franks?" asked Annia softly. Coventina gave her a surprised look. Annia was so quiet and unobtrusive that the rest of the women seemed to forget she was there. But it was Annia's idea to attack the market, the only sensible plan any of them were able to come up with. Coventina had been about to ask the same question, but Annia beat her to it.

Vipsania sat back and thought, "Only three. And they didn't do much, just broke up the fight and told people they would close the market if it happened again," she said finally.

"All told, how many Franks were at the market, Vipsania?" said Annia in the same quiet voice.

"Eleven," answered Vipsania brightly, proud of herself that she had remembered to circle the market and count them.

"So, they are keeping a distance," said Cornela thoughtfully.

"And there are only 11. If a real riot gets going, they wouldn't be able to stop it," said Vipsania. "And if they did try, it would just demonstrate to everyone how stupid these barbarians are."

All the women were silent.

"We should do what that man did," said Valeria, her first contribution of the afternoon. "If each of us had an argument over the prices, I am sure people would join in. We might have to do hardly anything."

"I agree," said Coventina. "We should just go shopping as we always do. But we should argue and say we can't feed our families."

"Oh, yes, children," piped up Paccia. "If you say you can't feed the children, that will make people all the angrier."

Slowly a plan emerged. The women would go tomorrow, but separately. Vipsania, Paccia, and Valeria had been to the market several times and had a good idea about its layout. Paccia set little cakes out representing the stalls, and Vipsania scattered dates around to show where the Franks usually were—near the fringes of the market, which meant that they could not immediately intervene. All three women agreed that the city was simmering with anger, an anger that could explode quickly.

"Then what happens?" asked Cornela.

"I am not sure there is anything we have to do, or can do, for that matter," said Coventina. "If a full riot breaks out, it will destroy the market and put a strain on the Franks. We want them to have to send soldiers into Tarraco to keep order so they won't have as many when the VII Legion finally arrives."

"What if people get killed?" said Annia.

The remark silenced the group for a moment.

"They may get killed, Annia," said Cornela calmly. "We may

be among them. But if we do not do something to divert the attention of these Franks, it will be our soldiers who die, and they are our only hope for deliverance." She adjusted her gray shawl. "My husband died to keep the barbarians out of the Empire. Every day soldiers die in Gaul, in Mauretania, in Pannonia, in Cappadocia. Their deaths allow us to live the lives we do, to eat Vipsania's honey cakes and drink her wine. Is it not time for citizens to do their duty?"

"I also have a debt to repay," said Coventina softly.

"Yes, and you Celts take your debts as seriously as we Romans do," said Cornela, giving her a bleak smile.

Vipsania leaned into the group. "Are we in this together?"

All put out their hands and grasped the others' over the table scattered with cakes and dates.

"May the Gods guide the Women's Legion of Tarraco to victory," said Vipsania.

Coventina had powerful and conflicting emotions. On one hand, a surge of joy and blood lust. She would strike at those who had tormented her uncle. But then a wave of fear, for the women sitting around the table and for herself. Coventina had no illusions about what would happen to them if they were taken.

XXVI

All day the I Ausetanorum auxiliary legion from Valentia had straggled into the camp at Ilerda. First came the I Augusta Nerviana Alae, which pleased Cassius. The most he had expected were 500 cavalry, but almost 1500 showed up, herding extra horses and mules. There were slingers, the rest of the Cretan archers, engineers, carpenters, blacksmiths, and even some boatwrights. The mules were laden with supplies, with ox carts a day behind.

The auxiliary legion was actually larger than the VII Legion, and its praefectus, Publius Marius, had served in Pannonia, although he had never actually been in a battle.

Marcus, Flavius, Cassius, and Septimius watched this avalanche of men and materials pouring in from the south. "Did you expect this?" asked Marcus of Septimius.

"I am not surprised, sir. The cities and towns know that if the Franks defeat the VII Legion, the entire peninsula is open to them. It will be weeks, if not months, before Rome is able to mount an effective relief campaign," answered the auxiliary commander.

"Nothing like fear to get people to cough up men and materials," commented Flavius. "But I wonder how good they are?"

"They will be defending their homes, optio," said Septimius. "What they lack in training they may make up for with enthusiasm."

"Enthusiasm is important, but it is also fleeting," said Cassius. "If there is a reversal, they will not have the experience to understand that battles consist of ebbs and flows. That is their major weakness."

Marcus shrugged. "They are what we have. Thank the Gods it is more than we expected. It will also make our ruse easier. The Franks will see two full legions marching down to the river crossing. As long as Cassius can keep their cavalry from doing a full reconnaissance and learn we have three legions, not two, we might pull this off. Let's meet with the Legion's commanders. We need to finalize plans and get the VII Legion on the road."

The camp was a patchwork of chaos and order. The marching camp that the two legions had built was laid out with streets in neat, geometrical order. The tents were aligned—less sharply in the auxiliary camp than the VII Legion's camp—and a steady stream of traffic went in and out the camp's four gates. Besides the noise of men shouting and mules braying, there was a constant pounding and sawing as the carpenters cut pieces for the bridges, siege ladders, and ballista machines.

Publius turned out to be a competent commander with a good understanding of his legion's shortcomings, but a distant and slightly chilly personality. "The men are out of shape, sir," the tall, lanky praefectus told Marcus. "It was hot in the south and most of them haven't marched that far in full gear for years.

We came as fast as we could, but I didn't want to the men to arrive exhausted."

"Quite right, Publius. They will have a full day of rest, and we will see they are well fed," said Marcus. "The VII Legion will leave tomorrow to go north. Cassius and the cavalry will retrace your route for several miles and then turn east. Septimius will be in overall command of the auxiliary force. His legion will lead the attack on the river line, your legion will be in reserve."

The five men, plus Publius, his chief of staff, his three tribunes, and various other officers, had spent more than two hours going over the plan. The praefectus castrorum of the Valentia Legion was a retired centurion, Appius Thorius from the XII Fulminata, a veteran who had seen many battles in Galatia, and while a little old for his job, was focused and competent. He asked most of the questions.

"Risky, dividing our forces like this," Appius said, leaning over a map with the positions of the two auxiliary legions, the VII Legions and the cavalry marked by small stones.

"Riskier to assault a fortified river line against superior forces," said Marcus.

"If we get beat, at least we are all together, and we can go on the defensive. If the Franks discover what we are up to they can destroy us in detail," put in Publius. "This is a very complex plan, sir, and complex plans have a way of going wrong once a battle starts."

"Nevertheless," said Marcus quietly, "that is what we are going to do. I need Septimius' legion to look and act like the VII Legion. I need Publius' legion to back them up and appear as threatening as it can. You are right, praefectus castrorum, that when battle is joined, the best of plans can go awry. But they go astray, too, for the enemy. He is looking to fight us on the ground of his choosing. We are going to change that. If we can force a change in the Franks' plans, it will be their plans that go badly, not ours."

"Sir, we have to coordinate three different military units. How are we going to do that if we aren't in contact with one another?" Publius countered.

"Good question," said Marcus. "The coordination here is important. Septimius' command has to rivet the attention of the Franks, which does not mean your auxiliary legions will play a secondary role. You will move up to the river, but you will not attempt to cross it until you receive our signal. The signaling unit will come with the VII Legion as far as the Bridge of Bormanu. When you see their signal, you will know that the VII Legion has launched its attack on the Franks' rear. If you do not see it, it is because we have been unsuccessful, in which case you will establish a defensive line on your side of the river. If the Franks attempt to cross, it is they who will be wading into a defensive position. They outnumber you, but not by enough to take the river line from you."

Flavius discreetly examined Publius. His comments and questions were proper, but there was an underlying edge of hostility to them. What's his problem, wondered the optio? Could it have anything to do with that matter at Capria with the Lusitanians? That could complicate things. If Publius dragged his feet getting his auxiliary legion into battle, the VII Legion would be without sufficient support. He would bear watching, thought Flavius.

Marcus pointed at the small stones in the southern part of

the map. "Cassius has found an undefended ford, and one that is only lightly defended. His portable bridges will allow him to cross the river in force. I do not think the Franks are expecting us to show up with 1500 more cavalry. The Franks will expect us to try a crossing and, if successful, to drive up the east side of the river to flank the Frankish defenders at the river. But Cassius will move east, and then swing back north. He may be able to arrive on the southern flank of the enemy undetected, but even if he doesn't, the Franks will have to send cavalry to confront him."

The VII Legion commander stood. "The VII Legion will try to get as close to the Franks as possible before they notice us. Our guides say there is a forest that spans the road to Tarraco. We will assemble in this forest, then march out as quietly as possible. When the signal unit on the north mountain sees us deploy, it will signal your legions on the west bank of the river. The minute you receive their signal, you should lay your bridges and cross the river. The Franks will have to strip soldiers from the riverfront to confront the VII Legion. As for Cassius, if he eludes the Frankish cavalry, he will arrive on the southern flank just as the Franks become aware they are in a trap. If he is discovered and cannot fight his way north to the main battle, he will still keep the Frankish cavalry occupied."

"There are a lot of 'ifs' in this," said Publius.

"There are, but I doubt the Franks will be thinking along these lines, and outthinking the enemy is the key to victory," said Marcus.

"Maybe the Franks don't think along these lines because they think anyone who would try it is crazy," said Publius.

It was a bold comment, and Flavius flushed, clinching his teeth. But he kept his mouth shut. Marcus had given him explicit orders.

"I am depending on that. We need to do something the Franks least expect.We want to panic them. I am less interested in dead Franks than disarmed ones," said Marcus, looking around the tent at the men assembled.

"Sir?" asked Publius.

"We need hostages, comrades. Remember, the Franks have the citizens of Tarraco. We need something to bargain with,"

The auxiliary officers glanced at each other. "How can we bargain with barbarians?" asked Publius.

"Rome bargains with the Goths and Parthians," said Cassius. "Bargaining doesn't mean you don't get what you want. It is just a different way of achieving victory."

"Once a battle gets going, sir, it is not easy to stop it," said Publius.

"Our legate has been in a few of those," said Flavius acidly, unable to remain silent any longer, "more than anyone else in this room."

"It is a legitimate point, optio," said Marcus. "Yes, Publius, that will be a problem, but there is no sense in trying to figure it out here. First, we have to defeat the Franks. Let me worry about bringing the battle to a conclusion."

Publius said nothing but his sour look lingered.

Another hour was taken hashing out timetables, order of march, and the different scenarios that might emerge from the battle. In the end, all was settled. The auxiliary commanders went off to their legions, and Cassius, Flavius, and Marcus poured wine and sat in silence for a while.

"If we pull this off, sir, it is going to be grand," Cassius said finally.

"Having doubts, commander?" said Marcus, with a smile that took any sting out of the comment.

"I always have doubts, sir. They make me careful. But as complex as this plan is, I think it is going to work. We will hold up our side of it, sir," answered Cassius.

"I have no doubt about that, Cassius. I would not have envisioned this plan had I any concerns about your end of the battle," said Marcus.

"What about the auxiliary legions?" asked Flavius.

Marcus ran his hands through his hair and sat back in his chair. He was drained and exhausted, not the best way to begin a campaign. The life of a legate was not all it was made out to be. "Septimius will be fine, and it will be his legion that leads. He is intelligent and innovative. If something opens up on the battlefield, he will take advantage of it. As for his troops, that is hard to say. We will just have to see."

"And Publius?" asked Cassius.

Marcus was silent for a long moment. "He is not enthusiastic."

"An understatement," commented Cassius dryly.

"Or maybe something else," added Flavius.

Both the men looked a question at him.

"There are some people in Hispania who bear you no love, sir. I have always wondered when that Capria stuff would rear its head. We annoyed some powerful people that day," said the optio, "people who would rather see you take a fall than defeat the Franks."

Marcus frowned. "That seems a little far-fetched, Flavius. If the VII Legion is defeated, everyone in Hispania is at risk."

"Maybe, maybe not, sir," replied Flavius. "From what we learned from Demaratus, this doesn't look like an invasion. If it were, the Franks wouldn't be gathering all those ships. Maybe some of those powerful people know that, sir."

Marcus chuckled. "So, all of this is just to get back at us?"

The option reddened. "I didn't say that, sir, I just said there may be more than one agenda at play here and we should pay attention. My worry is that Publius won't back Septimius if it comes to a battle."

"I hadn't thought of all this," said Cassius with a worried frown.

"Well, I hadn't either," said Marcus. "You may be right, Flavius, but there is not a lot we can do about it at this point. And I think if Publius holds back, he will find a formidable foe in Septimius."

"He's a good man," conceded Flavius, "and I agree, the die is cast. But we should go into this battle with open eyes, and I don't trust Publius."

The three were silent a moment, and then Cassius rose and saluted. "If you don't mind, we need to get going sir. We have a long ride south, and I want to rest the horses before we cross the river."

"Fortuna be with you, commander," said Marcus, rising and embracing the young cavalry commander.

"Now be careful yourself, Cassius," said Flavius. "If anything happens to you, I would have to explain it to our temperamental Greek, and that would not be to my liking."

Cassius grinned at the optio. "Demaratus just might take the city before we get there."

"He might," laughed Flavius.

"Now be off with you, commander. We shall see you next in battle," said Marcus, returning the salute.

Cassius slipped on his helmet and vanished through the tent's door.

"I worry about our young Cassius," said Flavius. "He leads from the front."

Marcus nodded. "I worry too. But we are not likely to talk him into sitting back while his men fight. And leading from the van does inspire the troops."

"As long as you don't get killed," said Flavius.

"My, we are gloomy this day, optio," said Marcus.

"Not gloomy, just realistic. No, I think we can pull this off. My one worry is Publius and the Valencia legion," said Flavius.

Marcus changed the subject. "Did you get an eagle and the proper armor?"

"The carpenters and blacksmiths are working on the eagle, and we have the armor at the expense of a very unhappy 10th Cohort," replied Flavius.

"And you did what about this unhappiness? Does it require my revisiting them?" said Marcus.

"No, sir. You explained the ruse and the 10th Cohort will be compensated with light guard duties and extra pay," answered Flavius.

"Extra pay?" asked Marcus. "I don't remember mentioning that."

"Yes, sir. We can expect a generous contribution from the merchants of Tarraco when we liberate them, and I pledged them 100 denarii in extra pay."

Marcus blanched. "Flavius, that is 48,000 denarii. The legion's treasury would be deeply strained by that kind of outlay."

"Demaratus will figure it out, sir, don't worry yourself about it. A plea to the merchants will cover it, and I am sure your lady" (at this Flavius stumbled, since he wasn't quite sure how to characterize Aelia or exactly what her relationship to his commander—and friend—was), "ah, could, help us with the Corduba merchants."

Marcus gave him an oblique look. "Suppose we lose?"

"Well, sir, we will all be dead so we won't have a problem," replied Flavius.

Marcus laughed. "Every contingency covered, is it?"

"Yes, sir. That's my job," answered Flavius.

"All right, optio. Let's get our legion on the road. I want to be at this Bridge of Bormanu by tomorrow evening. Be sure we carry torches and rope, and I want extra javelins," said Marcus.

"Yes, sir," replied Flavius, keeping the impatience out of his voice. They had gone over this twice already. But Flavius realized that immersing himself in such details was his commander's way of dealing with his own nervousness. Flavius saluted and left.

Marcus looked down at the table. He was worn out and also nervous. The plan that had looked fine spread out on a table could turn into a nightmare in the execution. If he lost this battle, he would never get another command (if he survived, that is). There were those who would demand he commit suicide to preserve his honor. But for all the uncertainties and headaches, he liked being legate. His word was law, not just for his century, but for the entire legion. It was not that Marcus liked power per se, but he did like being able to put his ideas into practice. And a legate had that power. It was seductive, and it would be hard to give up.

He caught himself. This was dangerous thinking. He was not a legate, he was a praefectus castrorum who found himself in command by accident. Titus might yet recover, and, if he did not, it would be more likely for Rome to appoint one of the tribunes in his place or send out a new commander than keep Marcus as the legion's commander.

Marcus made himself stop thinking about command and concentrate on writing a letter to Aelia. He smiled at Flavius stumbling as he spoke of Aelia. He knew his optio was uncertain as to his relationship to the beautiful and wealthy merchant. That was hardly surprising, because so was Marcus. Aelia certainly didn't seem interested in the subject of marriage, and Marcus was too shy to raise it.

He unrolled a blank scroll of papyrus and considered what he was going to say, which brought him back to how he really felt. Aelia was brilliant, courageous, and fun. She was also regal, demanding and stubborn. But he was in love with her, a thought that allowed him to start the letter. Aelia hated formality in letters, so he tried to make it as chatty and personal as he could. He never quite succeeded, but Aelia was patient.

Marcus sighed. As if leading a legion and coordinating a battle against a superior enemy wasn't complicated enough, he also had to write a letter to a woman who made him feel awkward.

Doggedly setting himself to the task, he eventually found a certain tenderness and longing creeping onto the page. He also explained the battle plan in detail. Aelia was not bored by things male and, while she was no fan of war— "bad for business" she once said—the organization and tactics fascinated her. When he questioned her interest, she replied that war was a little like business, only not as ruthless.

He spent the morning writing the letter, then filled out orders until mid-afternoon, when Flavius returned to the tent in full uniform.

"Ready, sir," he said.

Marcus rose from the chair, and Flavius helped him into his armor, then handed him his helmet while he buckled on his sword and pugio. They stood looking at one another. "We've gone through much, comrade," said Marcus quietly.

"Yes, sir, that we have. And there will be more after this," answered Flavius.

Marcus nodded and pushed himself out of the tent. Beyond, in the road, was the VII Legion, its eagle sparkling in the bright sun, the men drawn up in rigid ranks, his staff mounted at the head. A mule began braying in the Legion's rear, answered by several more. Marcus saluted and strode toward his horse, followed by Flavius. Having mounted, Marcus turned to look back at the long lines of men organized under the cohort and century banners. Turning to Flavius, he nodded and gently urged his horse forward. Like a huge metal beast, the VII Legion followed.

XXVII

One by one, the comrades of the Tarraco Legion slipped into Vipsania's domus. All dressed conservatively, like good Roman matrons, as indeed they were. Poppaea and Paccia were so excited they couldn't sit still. Valeria nervously rubbed her forearm, while Annia and Cornela appeared calm and detached. Vipsania bustled about like a mother hen, although her eyes and mouth were lined with tension.

For the last time, they went over their plan: the women were to return home, then make their way separately to the market. Cornela and Vipsania would initiate arguments at both ends of the market, and the rest of the women would join in. There was to be no violence unless the arguments led to a riot, in which case, what happened, happened. If the Franks showed up in force, they were to disperse and meet back at the house ("for wine and honey cakes," said Vipsania).

Just as they were ready to leave, Coventina stopped them in front of the door. Her dress was plain, with red trim, belted just below her breasts, and her wig simple and brown. Vipsania had wanted her to wear either a long blond wig or the Egyptian one she had worn that first time the Legion had gotten together, but Coventina explained that both wigs would make her stand out for different reasons: the Egyptian too exotic, the blond unmistakably Frankish. "I want to be so inconspicuous that the crowd will stand out," she said firmly.

Reaching under her dress, Coventina drew forth a thin-bladed boning knife from Vipsania's kitchen. A pugio was too large to hide under her dress. "Comrades," she said softly, pointing the knife's tip at the half circle of women in the atrium. "What we are planning to do is dangerous. If we are taken, our deaths will be beyond our worst nightmares. I do not say this to discourage you, but we must all be clear about what is at stake. If anyone wants to drop out, there is no shame in that. I have a blood debt to repay, you do not. I do this because I swore by the goddess who watches over me and my people that I would repay these Franks for what they did to my uncle. The Franks have done you no harm."

"Why do you speak so?" asked Cornela. "I hope you will not take offense at what I am going to say, my dear Coventina. You say the Franks have done us no harm. But, my dear, you can only say that because you are not a true Roman. Please, this is not meant as an insult. But we Romans do not surrender. We do not tolerate others over us. We rule the world. We are humiliated by these barbarians who dare to come among us uninvited. The empire endures because we Romans endure, and the moment we falter, then all the tribes and people and nations who lurk in the dark forests of the north and the deserts of the east will fall upon us. All our cities, our roads and bridges, aqueducts and theaters, our literature and poetry, our temples and great forums, will be swept away."

Cornela stopped and adjusted her cape. "No, my dear, we know what we do, and we know the risks. We Romans have borne those risks for time almost beyond reckoning. I gave up my husband on the altar of Empire. Paccia may smile a great deal, but she also weeps for her two sons who serve with the XVI Flavia Firma in Syria. Annia's grandfather died fighting Goths in Thrace with the I Italicia. Valeria's cousin was killed fighting for the V Macedonica in Dacia. If we die, our fight to the death will strike fear in these unwashed pigs who dare think they can rule over Romans."

The women all fell silent, even Poppaea. Coventina realized just how much an outsider she was, one of those of "unwashed pig" stock. She masked the anger within. She had made a pledge on the bier of her uncle, a pledge she would keep, and she needed these women to do so. But she would not worry about them anymore. They were Romans, and they would bear what they would bear. Yet she could not help but feel pained by their reassurance: she had grown to like and admire these women, but she would never be one of them.

Demaratus played dice with Vallerius as he discreetly watching the port. One Frank—Demaratus had learned his name was Wallgard—seemed to be in charge. The Franks had swept the coast from Tarraco to Emporiae for any ships. There was no way to calculate if they were sufficient to carry all the Franks because Demaratus had no idea how many soldiers the Franks had outside the city.

"They haven't let down their guard, have they?" asked Vallerius, rolling a set of knuckles out on the cask they sat around.

"No," answered Demaratus. "We will have to arrange for a diversion. Can we be sure the men in the Praetorian Tower got our message?"

"My man hits what he aims at, and he saw the two guards take the message below. What they make of it, who knows?" replied Vallerius.

"Is there no way we can get a message from them?" asked Demaratus.

Vallerius rolled the dice again. "I can't see how. The Tower is well guarded. The Franks won't let anyone get close. And any attempt by the men in the Tower to make contact would expose us to the Franks."

"Why not try another arrow and ask them to shoot it someplace we can find it and the Franks can't?" asked Demaratus, taking his turn at rolling the dice.

"Maybe, but if the Franks find it, then the whole plan will be revealed," answered the old centurion.

"We can devise a code. The Franks will know that the men in the tower are in contact with someone in the city, but they won't know who or why," said Demaratus.

Vallerius considered this. "What do you suggest?"

"That we tell them what we are going to do, that we are arranging for a diversion to draw Franks away from the Tower. If they can break out of the Tower and fight their way to the port, it would greatly aid us."

"How will they know it is not a trick to get them out of the Tower?" asked Vallerius.

"Suppose we have a limited attack of the Franks in the plaza, maybe just with arrows and slings. If we can kill a few Franks, that should convince them it isn't a ruse," answered Demaratus.

The centurion shook his head. "Pretty complex, comrade."

"Do you have a better plan?" asked the signifer.

Vallerius shook his head. "None I can think of."

"Then let's proceed," said Demaratus, gathering up the dice, pulling his hood forward, and starting back toward the city's center.

Coventina mingled with the crowd at the market, placing herself in almost the exact center, so she could watch both ends. Each of the comrades had made her way to the market and were hovering near Vipsania and Cornelia.

Vipsania had picked out a grain merchant, while Cornelia had chosen a vegetable seller. Vipsania started the action.

"How much for a bag of these oats?" she asked the merchant. The man answered ten denarii "What! That is an outrage! Who can afford these prices? I have a family to feed, and you want me to spend my entire household budget on some oats?" At the end of each sentence she raised her voice, so by the time she had described the dire straits of her household budget she was almost shouting.

"Lady, oats and everything else are scarce. There is nothing I can do about it. I paid a high price to bring them to the market, and my markup is small. I have a family, too," said the merchant, a rail thin man with bad teeth.

"Show me what you paid for these oats," shouted Vipsania, her hands on her hips, the very image of an outraged matron.

"Look, I don't keep my receipts with me," replied the man hotly. "If you don't like my prices go buy someone else's oats."

"There are no other oats," shouted Valeria from the back of a small but growing crowd drawn by the argument. "You know that, you thief!"

Paccia pushed herself next to Vipsania. "I couldn't even buy a handful of these oats at his prices," she said. "Here we are imprisoned in a city, and these merchants are making a profit off it. Is this what citizens do to one another in time of need?"

People from the growing crowd began calling out as well, and some shook their fists. The merchant realized that this was trouble. "I understand about families," he said with an ingratiating smile, "so for you I will lower the price." It was exactly the wrong thing to say.

Vipsania threw her arms out. "Everyone here has family. I will not feed mine if others go hungry. The Franks take our food and don't pay for it, why should we have to pay some fat merchant?"

At the other end of the market, Cornela was examining a onion. "You are not serious," she told the short, heavy man behind the stall laden with onions, cabbages, cucumbers, beets, and apples.

The man shrugged. "That's the price. Onions are hard to come by. You look like you can afford it."

"How dare you," said Cornela drawing herself up. "I am a widow whose husband fell in the defense of Rome, died to keep the barbarians away from our cities. And now I find the barbarians are Romans who would gouge and cheat their own people, just because they can get away with it." She dropped the onion on the ground and crushed it with her foot.

"You can do anything you like with your onion, because you just bought that one," said the man, his face reddening with anger.

"Try to collect it, pig," said Cornela, keeping her voice calm and even.

"Here, here, what is going on?" said Julius Dasumi pushing himself through the crowd.

"This old crone just smashed an onion because she didn't want to pay for it," said the merchant coming out from behind his stall and pointing at Cornela.

Julius grabbed Cornela by the arm. "You owe this man for the onion," he growled.

"Take your hands off her!" shouted Poppaea, who emerged from the crowd and shoved Julius so hard that he lost his grip on Cornela.

"How dare you touch me," shouted Julius.

"How dare you attack a war widow. How dare you defend this theft from our people. And just you put your hands on me, sir, and I will give you a thrashing you won't forget," said Poppaea.

"We will see about that," said Julius reaching for Poppaea, only to have a large man step between the two. "You'll be keeping your hands to yourself, mister. We respect war widows around here, and this young woman was just defending her."

By this time, the crowd had grown to 40 or 50 people, and comments were flying at Julius and the merchant. The latter, seeing which way things were going, retreated behind his stall.

Julius was angry, but growing wary about what to do. The

crowd was getting ugly, and they had shifted their enmity to him rather than the vegetable seller.

Suddenly, the crowd parted and three armed Franks pushed their way into the middle of the crowd. "All right, break it up, or we are closing you down," one growled.

"Shut it down, Frank, we don't give a shit," someone shouted.

"Who said that?" glowered the Frank. A chorus of voices claimed credit.

"Arrest these two women and that man," said Julius pointing to Cornela, Poppaea, and the man who had intervened between Julius and the women.

The Franks looked uncomfortable. The crowd had grown larger, and there was some kind of disturbance going on at the other end of the market. The Franks were suddenly aware of the fact that they were in the middle of a crowd of visibly angry people, outnumbered 10 to one. Arresting someone seemed like a bad idea.

"Shut your mouth, Roman," the Frankish officer said. "No one tells us who to arrest."

"I was authorized to set up this market," said Julius. "I was given permission by Alberic himself. If I report your conduct to him, you will be severely punished."

An arm came from out of the crowd and pushed Julius. "This is your idea? Your idea to rob us blind? And you're working with the Franks? That's treason!"

The crowd took up the chant: "Treason, treason, treason!"

Julius Dasumi suddenly realized he was in trouble. He heard a crash next to the vegetable merchant, and a melon came sailing through the air. It missed Julius, but hit one of the Franks on the shoulder. The man staggered back, then lunged forward with his spear. A man at the edge of the crowd screamed as the spear point pierced his upper arm. But rather than scattering in panic, someone behind the Frank struck him with a cobblestone, sending the man sprawling on the ground.

The two other Franks called out in their language and drew their swords, standing back-to-back with shields up. The crowd kept away from the swords, but stones and vegetables began raining down on the men. The Frank who had been knocked down staggered to his feet and joined his comrades.

With the crowd focused on the Franks, Julius slipped away.

Coventina watched with delight as the riot spread. Vipsania had started first, but the crowd around Cornela had grown violent faster. Now both crowds began to merge, and a number of stalls were knocked over. Food was flying everywhere. Suddenly, the edge of the crowd recoiled, and Coventina could see a line of shields and helmets pushing the horde back toward the circus. But the anger was so great that people began hurling stones and pieces of the stalls at the Franks, and for a time the soldiers had to retreat. Beyond them she could see more soldiers running up the street that fed into the plaza in front of the Praetorian Tower.

Coventina saw Annia in the crowd near Cornela and caught her attention. She held her palms up, signaling it was time to withdraw. Annia vanished into the crowd. Coventina began to work her way toward Vipsania. Suddenly a group of Franks appeared, attacking the crowd from another direction. Coventina had no idea where they had come from, but she was caught up in the crowd trying to escape. She was jostled and then knocked to the ground. The crowd stampeded, preventing her from getting up. Just as she was getting to her knees, she was jerked erect. Turning to see who had ahold of her arms, she looked right into the face of a young Frank. He was wearing a pointed helmet with a sword guard that ran down below his nose, His beard was blond and scruffy, and he had a sword in his right hand.

She tried to pull away, but, pushed from behind, she slammed into the Frank's chest. He said something in Frankish, cursing most likely, then suddenly looked closely at her. She realized with horror that her wig had come loose. Reaching up with his sword hand he pulled it off her head.

Coventina's hair was still very short, but it was red, very red. The man narrowed his eyes and yelled something. She felt her other arm seized, jerking her in the opposite direction. The other Frank holding her was older and wore a Roman soldier's helmet.

"Well, well, look what we have here, Arnuf. I would bet you a chest of gold that this is our witch." He squeezed her arm so hard she thought she would faint and pressed his face up to hers. "Witch, you are going to die."

A bolt of fear and despair ran through her. They held her arms so tightly that she couldn't get at the knife under her dress. She twisted to one side and drove her knee into the man's groin. He gasped and bent over. The second man jerked her arm painfully and grabbed her by the neck. She turned her head and bit deeply into his arm. The man shouted and pulled back to strike, but suddenly pitched forward into her chest. Behind him, Coventina saw Valeria raise a piece of planking from a stall over her head, then bring it down on the Frank, who staggered and stumbled to his knees.

Coventina, her arm freed, reached under her dress and whipped out her knife, as another Frank slammed the hilt of his sword pummel against her jaw. Her head spun, and she staggered back. The Frank drew his sword back for a thrust, but the man suddenly stopped, a confused look on his face. Then he slowly pitched forward onto the ground.

Standing behind him was a man in a hooded cape with a knife in his hand. Coventina was still spinning, the rush of fear and battle overwhelming her.

"Coventina, quick, we must be gone. The Franks are sending reinforcements," the man said. How could he know her name?

She stood staring at him, trying to make sense of what was happening. He reached out and grabbed her arm, but she twisted free and leveled her knife at him.

"Mad Celt," said the man, pulling back his hood.

"Demaratus?" she said.

XXVIII

The light had turned gray in the east by the time the VII Legion reached the dead end of the valley and looked up at what the shepherds called the Bridge of Boromanu. It looked as if the Titans themselves had designed it. Shaped like a three-sided box, the canyon had high, steep, and inaccessible walls on all sides. In the distant past, some cataclysmic event had collapsed part of one wall, so that a steep slope led to the crest of a ridge between two of the peaks. It was narrow—no more than 20 feet wide, at one point even narrower—covered with thorn bushes and rocks, a thin path etching its way up the center of the fell.

The 10 cohort commanders, along with Marcus and Flavius, stood at the bottom of the slope looking up.

"Can be done," remarked centurion.

"How are we going to get the equipment up that thing?" asked another.

"We strip down to the basics. Nothing but water," said Marcus.

"The extra pila and the javelins?" asked Certicius from the First Cohort.

"I think we need to keep two centuries back, sir," said Flavius squinting at the slope. "After we get the rest of the cohorts over, then one century deploys in a chain on the bridge. The rearguard can pass the javelins, pila and equipment up the chain and over the top."

"Good plan," agreed Marcus. "I suggest that the men tie their scutums to their backs and use their pila to help them climb. What about a rope?"

Flavius shook his head. "I think a rope will just get in the way. I don't think it is necessary, sir. The biggest problem we have is making sure the men get some rest once they are over. Do we know how far it is to the forest, sir?"

"The shepherds say three hours," Marcus replied.

"The shepherds aren't in full armor carrying a scutum, pilum, and sword," said a centurion from the fourth Cohort, "and sheep are like goats. They can go anywhere."

"If shepherds and sheep can get up that slope, so can the VII Legion, gentlemen. We will do as Flavius suggests. The Second and Third cohorts will lead. The Fourth Cohort will assign a century to form the chain. Arrange to securely bundle the extra pila and javelins. Flavius and I will ascend first and take a look," said Marcus. "Let's get moving."

The cohort commanders returned to their units and gathered their centurions around them. The centurions in turn convened their optios and tesserariuses to hand down the orders.

"Optio," said Marcus. "Get the shepherds and some men. We

want to know what the other side looks like before we have everyone crowding over the top."

A few moments later the two shepherds, Cotta and Caldus, along with some tough-looking legionnaires from Marcus's old First Century, appeared, and Marcus set himself to climb the Bridge of Bormanu. The slope started steep, then moderated. The footing was uneven—some places were packed soil that made climbing easy, but others consisted of gravel and stones that were easy to slip on, especially when burdened with armor. At one point, Marcus grabbed a bush, only to be painfully reminded that Hispania's vegetation armed itself against intruders.

It was hard going, and Marcus was gasping for breath, but the ridge grew steadily closer. Near the top the slope steepened again, so that Marcus had to scramble up the last bit. Finally, he stood on the ridgeline. He could see the VII Legion forming up below, their faces turned toward him, watching his progress and waiting for a signal.

Using a pilum as a walking stick, Flavius pulled himself over the edge and joined Marcus. The rest of the men followed until all stood on the crest.

The slope to the east was gentler, slanting down a broad valley, only to vanish in the growing evening. "We will need the torches at some point, Flavius. I think the first two centuries can get up without them, but by then it will be close to dark. The moon will not appear for several hours," said Marcus slowly mastering his wind.

"It is as we said," remarked Cotta, pointing down the valley. "Once you are over it is not difficult."

"You have been an invaluable help, Cotta and Caldus. The VII Legion will not forget this," said Marcus formally.

Caldus shrugged. "It is our Hispania as well, sir. These barbarians would steal all our sheep if they could."

"Nevertheless, we are in your debt," said Marcus. "I have one more favor to ask of you. Can you guide a signal team to the mountain that overlooks the valley where the Franks are?" asked Marcus.

"It is just over that ridge and beyond a bit," said Cotta, pointing to the huge mountain that loomed up from the south. "I have never done it before, but we can, I know. We should start, however, because the ground is rough and parts will be steep.

Marcus turned to Flavius, "See that the signal team comes up as quickly as possible."

Flavius turned to a legionnaire and told him to go back down and bring up the signal team before the main body began to climb. Turning to Marcus, Flavius said, "I had the team near the front, sir. I thought you might want them up early."

"Well done, optio, get them started," said Marcus, who then turned and beckoned to the legionnaires from the First Century. "You men come with me. Cotta, I will need one of you to help us find the path ahead."

The eight men formed up behind him as Marcus and the shepherds led the way. When the sheep came up the Bridge, they did so in twos and threes, wearing a groove into the slope. Once they got to the top, they spread out and moved down the valley, grazing as they did. There was no path, just the low spot in the valley. The route was largely obstacle free, but, while it was uneven ground, it wasn't easy to make one's way down. Marcus, the shepherds, and the soldiers followed the valley to a large copse of trees at the bottom.

"What comes next?" asked Marcus.

"A little ahead a stream comes into the valley, and you follow it until it turns off to the north. Where the stream turns, a forest that straddles the road begins," answered Caldus.

"Is the forest dense?" asked Marcus.

"No," answered Caldus.

"Is there an open space near the road, one far enough from the bridge so they won't see us?" asked Marcus.

Caldus thought for a moment. "There is an open field about a mile from where the forest ends. You could put your men there until it gets light. But the forest is not thick. The Franks might see your torches."

"We will only use the torches until the moon comes out. Can you guide us to the meadow you are talking about?" asked Marcus.

"Yes. I will go ahead now and make sure of the way. Maybe you can let me have a few of your soldiers?" asked Caldus. "My cousin will stay here with you," he said, indicating a young shepherd whose name Marcus had not heard before.

Marcus searched his memory for the legionnaires' names. "Lucius, choose four men and go with the shepherd here. Watch for places that might cause us problems, and see if the field is big enough for us. Keep us informed by sending messengers back."

"Yes, sir," said the big legionnaire, saluting, and calling out four names. The five soldiers and the shepherd disappeared into the copse of trees.

By the time Marcus got back to the ridge, the first members

of a century from the Second Cohort, the men huffing and puffing, were breasting the top. Marcus told the centurion to form the century up at the north side of the valley. "Let the men get some rest," said Marcus.

Slowly the cohorts, century by century, worked their way up the slope and into the valley. By the time the last of the cohorts were approaching, the light began to fail. The torches were brought out, and the pila and javelins made their way up the slope, handed from man to man. Flavius had scattered torch holders all the way up the slope so that the men could not only find their footing, but also see the bundles as they were passed up.

Marcus was struck by the beauty of it. As night fell, the line of torches stood out on the slope like some enormous snake of fire. He couldn't decide if that was a good or a bad omen, but then he didn't believe in omens.

Finally, the deed was done, and the last century came scrambling up the slope and into the valley. It was smoothly done, but it took longer than he had anticipated and time was running out. Marcus called a quick staff conference of the cohort's pilus priors and the centurions of the First Century, and got the legion underway. He could see the blocks of men, the torches illuminating their way, heading off down the valley. The torches made him nervous. If any Franks were around, they would figure out what was afoot, but there was nothing he could do about it. The final part of the march would be under a moon that was almost full, and the shepherds had assured him that the ground was clear and open all the way to the forest.

Flavius suddenly loomed up out of the darkness. "Sir?"

"Yes, optio, I am coming. Have we heard anything from the men we sent ahead?" asked Marcus.

"Not yet, sir. Shall I send out a runner?"

"Yes," said Marcus, and started off in the wake of the Legion, a path marked by flame and the occasional fiery reflection off a helmet or shield. a march of light into darkness.

The VII Legion was struggling—and straggling—down the long valley that led from the top of the Bridge of Boromanu. The shepherds said the way was easy once the Legion was over the top, but what was easy for shepherds and sheep was slow and difficult for men encumbered with armor, shields, and pila. The plan had been to use torches until the moon came out, but the moon was not quite full and the light was marginal. Men stumbled and tripped and knocked other men down. Men stopped and the men behind them ran into them, sometimes knocking a whole line of legionnaires down. It was also difficult to keep unit cohesion, and Marcus feared that the Legion would arrive and have to spend valuable time reorganizing itself into cohorts and centuries.

Marcus glanced anxiously toward the east for the first hint of gray.

Flavius loomed up beside him. "Slow going, sir," he said, quite unnecessarily. Marcus was about to make a cutting remark that he was quite capable of seeing that for himself, but then realized that Flavius's comment was more a reflection of his optio's nervousness than information he thought his commander needed.

Marcus ran through the potential disasters that could occur if the VII Legion were not in place at first light. The most obvious was that the Franks would figure out that they were facing only a couple of auxiliary legions and attack. It would be a hard-fought battle, because the Franks would have to attack from across the river, but they would outnumber the auxiliaries almost three to one. Marcus was not confident that the two legions would hold up, and, if they broke, it would be a slaughter.

Then, too, the VII Legion would face odds of almost five to one, and enemy soldiers drunk on victory. He made himself stop this line of thought.

A runner from the troops he had sent forward suddenly appeared. "Sir, we have reached the forest."

"And?" asked Flavius.

"Lucius told me to tell you that it is thicker than we were led to believe, and it is really dark, sir. He suggests we should continue to use the torches," replied the man, still panting from his run.

Flavius looked at Marcus. "Shall I go have a look, sir?"

"Yes, optio. Hold up anyone going into the forest with torches.

Flavius and the runner disappeared into the night.

So, something else has gone wrong, thought Marcus. What were the chances that the Franks would see the torches and conclude they had a hostile force in their rear? They could hold the river line with a scratch force and concentrate on the VII Legion, defeating his plan by destroying each part in detail. And if the Franks destroyed the VII Legion, they could simply ignore the auxiliaries.

He would have to swing the VII Legion further east to avoid the possibility of being spotted, but that would lengthen the time it would take to get the Legion in place for the attack on the Franks' rear.

The Gods were not with him this night.

Flavius finally returned. "It is thick, sir, too thick to go through without torches. I sent Lucius to scout out a route that will take us further east to avoid our torches being seen."

Marcus smiled. It was not the first time that Flavius had read his mind. "Proceed, optio," he said.

Flavius vanished and Marcus went back to his litany of disaster scenarios.

Cassius lay on his stomach watching the ford in the first light of dawn. A large group of Frankish horsemen sat around small fires or lay wrapped in cloaks, sleeping.

"How many?" the man next to him whispered.

"I can see maybe 100. There are more on the other side of that ridge. You can see the smoke from their fires," answered Cassius. "The main force is back at the first ford."

Cassius had divided his cavalry into two wings. The local auxiliaries and half the men who had come from the south were at the ford where the Franks had anticipated the Roman cavalry would try to cross, a part of the river that was deeper and swifter, but also narrow. The portable bridge could span it easily. The trick was to get across in enough numbers as to overwhelm the Franks. And that would depend on how well the diversion went.

Cassius had infiltrated 200 cavalry across the river at a place downstream. The Franks had not bothered to guard the river at that point because it was deep and swift, so the men had dismounted and swum the horses across. Unfortunately, few of his men could swim, and every one of them was with the diversionary unit.

But the downstream crossing was also a long way from the ford he now saw. If the diversionary force got across safely, if they could turn north and find the Franks, and if they could attack the Frankish camp and draw off some of the defenders at the ford, then Cassius could drop the bridge across the river and get his men across.

A lot of things could go wrong.

He said a brief prayer to Nabia, the river goddess, and to his patron goddess of horses, Epona.

He wiggled back from the edge of the bank leading to the river and scrambled down a slope to the men waiting on horseback.

"Sir?" one of them asked.

"There are too many to force a crossing at this ford. We need the diversion attack. But move the bridge up. Where are the bowmen?" asked Cassius.

"Here, sir" said Cleomanes, the commander of the Cretan archers, slipping between the horses to come to his side. "Do you mind if I take a look?"

"Go ahead, just be careful," said Cassius.

Cleomanes and his second-in-command climbed the bank and lay on their stomachs, pushing themselves forward until they could see the ford. They whispered back and forth for a while, then slid back down the slope.

"What do you think?" asked Cassius.

"The distance is easy bowshot, sir. I think we can clear out a lot of horsemen for you. I just wish I had all my men," said Cleomanes.

"So do I," said Cassius, "but the auxiliaries are going to need them at the bridge. I seem to recall you causing the Mauri a lot of trouble with no more men than this."

"Oh, we can cause them trouble, sir. But trouble doesn't mean we can force a crossing for you," said bowman commander.

"I know that, Cleomanes. But all we need is an edge. I don't think those horsemen over there are expecting an attack. Move your men up."

Cleomanes's second-in-command disappeared, returning shortly with 25 bowmen. They gathered in a circle and began stringing their bows. All carried two quivers of arrows.

Cassius began to pace. He went back over the plan. The bulk of his force lay on the other side of a small hill, well away from the river crossing. Around him were two hundred selected cavalry, men who had fought with him in Mauretania. Another group of men surrounded a bridge made of planks, nailed and then tied for extra strength, to four stout logs. The engineers guaranteed him he could gallop horses across it two abreast. Two of them were directing the operation.

The sky began to lighten, and the east turned a shade of rose. as the sun fought to climb over the mountains.

Maybe his horsemen from the south had not made it across the unguarded ford. Maybe they had gotten lost, despite only having to follow the river. Maybe the Franks had ambushed them, destroyed them all, and were sitting over there having a good laugh at his expense.

He crept back up the bank and was just looking toward the

valley across the river when the Franks began looking back at their camp. The rise on the other side of the river blocked his view of the camp, but there were shouts and a horse screamed. The men nearest the ford mounted and galloped back toward the main camp.

Cassius decided that it had to be his diversionary force attacking the main Frankish camp. He took a deep breath, stood and pointed to the archers and the group of men with the bridge, and then waved his arm. The archers strode over the bank and slid down to the riverside, fitting arrows to their bows. The men with the bridge lifted and lumbered forward with it. The remaining Franks on the far side of the river looked back toward their main camp. Finally, one Frank turned his horse. Seeing the archers and the men with the bridge, he shouted to his men before an arrow unhorsed him. The Franks whirled around but seemed confused by what they were seeing. The bowmen unhorsed several of them, and the Frankish horsemen scattered to avoid being targeted.

With the engineers directing its course, the bridge was approaching the river. Several men ran in front of the bridge, and hacked away at the bank with dolabras, the ubiquitous trenching tool of the Roman army. They quickly cut a trench about three feet wide and four feet deep. Just as they finished, the bridge arrived. The engineers had explained to Cassius how they were going to get the bridge across, but engineers talked in language that no one but other engineers understood. Now he could see what they were doing.

The bridge was dropped on the edge of the trench. The four logs furthest from the river had a pulley apparatus attached to them, and a crowd of men grabbed hold of the ropes that extended from the pulleys.

The engineers checked the trench and the rope attachment, and had the men lift the back end of the bridge, while they slipped wooden supports under it. Men swarmed around the bridge, some pulling on the rope, others holding down the edge of the bridge near the trench. Slowly the end of the bridge slid into the trench, anchoring it. In the meantime, the pulley apparatus that attached the rope to the bridge began to lift it. As it got higher, longer support timbers were slipped below so that the bridge gradually rose at one end, while the other was anchored in the trench. The weight of the bridge could break down the trench and slide the bridge toward the river, but the engineers had enough muscle power to overcome this problem.

Cassius looked back across the river. The Frankish horsemen had gathered at extreme bow range further upstream. Several raced off toward the camp, most likely to sound the alarm about the new attack. The archers had stopped shooting, hoarding their arrows for better targets.

By now, the bridge was close to vertical, its plank side facing toward Cassius. The engineers signaled another group of men to grasp a pulley mechanism that mirrored the pulley apparatus on the other side of the bridge. The bridge would have to be lowered slowly to prevent any of the logs breaking or the planks shattering. The engineers told him they could drop it the last 10 feet when the physics of block and tackle could no longer hold the bridge, but any drop higher than that risked the entire enterprise.

The bridge reached 90 degrees and began slowly tipping

toward the river. The men who had hauled the bridge now dropped their ropes and, under the direction of the engineers, ran to grasp the ropes on the other side. Wedges had been driven into the log ends resting in the trench so that they would not slip back away from the river, and the bridge slowly descended.

Cassius waved forward a group of horsemen who gathered behind the men pulling on the rope. Once the bridge reached a 45-degree angle, the pulley mechanism was at a disadvantage, and the bridge's descent accelerated. When it reached about eight feet from the other side, it fell with a rush, pulling several of the rope holders onto the bridge. While the bridge made an enormous crash and actually bounded up and down once, it emerged unscathed, one end on each bank of the river.

Cassius spurred his horse toward the bridge, drawing his sword and scattering the men who had lifted the bridge. His horse hesitated a moment in the face of the unfamiliar object, but Cassius drove him onto the planking and galloped across it. He could hear horsemen following him.

The Franks on the other side crowded together and attacked, but the bowmen disrupted the Frankish charge by downing their horses. Cassius whirled his horse to make sure his men were behind him, then led the counterattack, slamming into the milling Franks. He parried a javelin thrust and slashed down at his attacker's leg, opening a gaping wound. The Frank spun away. There was little structure to the fighting. The Franks held their own for a brief time, but the Roman cavalry poured over the bridge, pushing them back. With the Franks driven back from the bank, more of the Roman cavalry pushed across.

Cassius worried about his flank. He had no idea what was

happening in the main Frankish camp, and he did not want to be surprised by a sudden assault from that direction. A large group of horsemen loomed up to the east, but they were Roman, not Frankish. One officer in the group worked his horse in Cassius's direction, finally pulling himself alongside the commander.

"What is going on at the main camp, Macro?" Cassius shouted over the shouts and screams and clash of weaponry.

"This is all the Franks there are, sir. We hardly had a fight. It looks like they really didn't expect us," the man shouted back.

"Swing your men around behind them. Try to stop any from escaping to spread a warning," shouted Cassius.

The man spun his horse and dashed back up the bank, waving to his men. The group vanished over the hill, hoping to cut off any retreat by the Frankish cavalry.

The Roman cavalry gradually overlapped the Franks' flanks, pushing them in a circle, where most could not fight in the press of horses. Several Franks made an effort to break out of the encirclement, but they were cut down. One group, however, exploited a gap in the Roman attack, drove through it, and raced off. Cassius hoped Macro and his men would cut them off, but he had to concentrate on finishing the Franks in front of him.

By now, the bowmen had crossed the river, were deployed on a high bank overlooking the battle, and methodically picking off Frankish horsemen. Slowly, the Frankish line contracted. Many no longer had javelins and were fighting with their swords. The Roman encirclement was so tight that the Franks at the center could hardly move. Some of them panicked, spurring their horses to try a breakout. But the horses and men were so packed that they merely knocked one another over, increasing the chaos.

The Frankish commander had fought badly, thought Cassius. He should have run for it once he could see that the battle was not going in his direction. Instead, he had stubbornly tried to push the Romans back to the bridgehead. Maybe he thought the Roman cavalry wasn't worth much. If so, it had been a fatal mistake.

XXIX

Great battles begin with small events. In the telling afterwards, men remember blaring sounds, the tramp of thousands of feet, the blast of war horns, the shouts and cries of combat, the fear, pain, blood, and exhaustion. But memories are composed and edited into a coherent narrative, stories with less to do with what happened and how it happened than with what men want to remember.

The battle at the bridge began with a tiny flash of gold that disappeared almost as soon as it appeared. Coming up out of the east, the rising sun had found a reflective surface, too far off to identify.

Dagobert saw the flash, blinked his eyes, rubbed them, and squinted into the west. For a while, nothing. Then, another spark, and still more. The Frank summoned a man. "Tell the commander the Romans are coming."

The man looked to the west, then made his way down the defensive embankment, and disappeared into the tents filled with men beginning to stir in the morning light.

Dagobert was young for his command, but he had seen hard fighting over the past four years. He had worked himself up to command a unit of 100 men, the men who were currently manning the embankment and thicket of wooden stakes that faced the river and the dismantled bridge. He was an easygoing commander and the men liked him. They also respected him. In battle, Dagobert was always in the front. He favored a battle-axe and swung it with power. Now, he loosened the haft slipped into his belt and watched the procession of reflections coming toward him.

Slowly the reflections transformed, a wall of silver and red. Dagobert could make out a flash of gold behind the silver: the Agelia, a Roman Legion's most precious symbol. Other objects on tall poles gradually came into view—cohort and century signifers—but the eagle rose highest, marking the legion's commander.

Dagobert had fought Romans before, but always in small units. This was the first time he had seen a full legion. There were no cornus blasts, no drums. Instead, a great body of men marched in perfect sync and absolute quiet. It sent a chill down his back. It was as though an army of statues was approaching.

Grimbald and Leufrid scrambled up the embankment and looked out. The latter turned to Dagobert. "How long since you noticed them?"

"The time it took for me to send a messenger and for you to appear, sir. Not long at all."

Grimbald squinted at the army marching on the Frankish position. "That's the VII Legion. I can see its eagle."

"Where are the auxiliaries?" asked Dagobert.

"We aren't certain, commander. But I would guess behind the VII Legion," answered Grimbald.

The infantry commander's uncertainty explained why Leufrid had not answered the question: his cavalry had not been successful in scouting out the Romans. Well, Dagobert was not surprised. As far as he was concerned, cavalry were useless.

The three men watched while the Romans spread out in formation a quarter mile long. It was hard to see beyond the front line, but men were pouring into the valley. There were now scores of cohort and century poles, far more than a single legion would carry. The auxiliaries must be behind the VII Legion, in reserve.

"The VII Legion will lead the attack. I am not surprised. Not very imaginative but what do you expect from the Romans. They see something, they take it," said Leufrid.

Grimbald looked at him but said nothing. Finally, he turned to Dagobert. "Commander, I am moving men up to the embankment here. You and the other commanders should be prepared to cross the ditch and fight the Romans as they wade across the river. If for some reason they establish a foothold on this bank, you can always fall back on our defenses."

Leufrid snorted. "The Romans have no chance of getting a foothold on this bank, Grimbald. The river will break up their formations, and they will have to fight with water up to their waists."

"We do not know what the Roman plans are," replied Grimbald, putting a slight emphasis on the word "know." Leufrid flushed. "Sometimes Romans do stupid things. Sometimes they fool you. We need to be prepared for the unexpected. Is your cavalry set?"

Leufrid nodded, "They will cover your southern flank in case the Romans get across and try to flank our defenses."

Grimbald nodded in the direction of the southern flank. "That some of them there?"

Leufrid turned to look for a long time. He frowned. "No, those are my men from the downstream fords."

"They're in an awful hurry," said Grimbald quietly.

Without a word, Leufrid strode down the camp side of the embankment and grabbed the reins of a horse held by an orderly. Mounting swiftly, he turned the horse in a circle and galloped off to meet the group of horsemen, scattering infantry in all directions.

"Cavalry," muttered Dagobert.

"We need them, commander," said Grimbald.

"Let's hope they fight better than they do reconnaissance," said Dagobert.

By now, the armor-clad Romans, still in absolute silence, had deployed 100 yards from the river.

"I wonder what they are waiting for," said Dagobert. A number of other officers had joined them, and a steady stream of men was piling up behind them. "Shall we get the men over the ditch to the river?"

Grimbald nodded. "The Romans look sluggish with all their banners and formations, but they aren't. A cohort can move very quickly when it wants to. We need to stop them before they can emerge from the river."

Several of the officers began moving men over the embankment and across the ditch toward the river. Many carried bundles of spears and javelins. Similar bundles were piled behind the defense wall. There was no movement on the Roman side.

Grimbald studied the silent, still legion lined up on the other side of the river. "There is something odd about that legion," he said.

"Sir?" asked Dagobert.

"Don't you think that first line looks a little ragged?" asked the infantry commander.

Dagobert squinted in the direction of the Romans. "I have never seen a legion drawn up, sir, so I couldn't say. They can't be auxiliaries, sir. That's legion armor on those men over there. It might be that the VII Legion isn't much of a legion, sir."

"That's what Leufrid said about their cavalry, and they whipped us five days ago," said Grimbald. The infantry commander shook his head. "Well, keep a close eye on them. I want to find out what news those riders were bringing, Leufrid." Grimbald slid back down the defense wall and took the reins of a horse from an aide. He mounted and trotted off, following Leufrid. He reached the group to find them in the middle of a heated conversation.

"What do you mean you don't know where they are?" Leufrid asked an exhausted man with a bloody cut on one leg. Grimbald did not like the implications of that wound or Leufrid's question.

"We were ordered to break out and alert the main body at the other ford, sir, and we did. But when we rode back, the Roman cavalry was gone," said the man.

"A thousand horses can't vanish. You couldn't track them?" said Leufrid, his voice steadily rising.

"The commander didn't know what to do. The Romans were on our side of the river, lots of them. And they were riding east. The commander was not certain if they were trying to ride to Tarraco or to get into our rear. He thought it was safer to bring the cavalry back here sir, rather than trying to chase after them," replied the man.

Almost as if on cue, a large body of Frankish horsemen came over a low hill and trotted down toward the camp.

"What is going on, Leufrid?" asked Grimbald.

"The Romans forced a crossing at one of the fords, sir, and we don't know where they are," answered Leufrid.

"How could that happen?" asked Grimbald.

"They used a ford we didn't think they could get across. It was deep and swift. They would have had to swim their horses. But they somehow got cavalry on our side and attacked our camp. It was a diversion. While the men were defending the camp, the Romans laid a portable bridge across the river and came over in force," said the man.

"What happened to our cavalry?" asked Grimbald.

The man shook his head. "The commander attacked the Romans and they surrounded our men. These were the only ones that got out," put in Leufrid. "But we still outnumber them."

"That doesn't seem to be doing us a whole lot of good," roared Grimbald, finally losing his temper. "This is the second time the Roman cavalry has defeated us. And we outnumbered them each time. You want to explain that, Leufrid? You keep saying the Romans are girls. Well, it's a good thing we haven't met the boys in battle."

"Sir," protested Leufrid. "They fooled us the first time, and who knew they had a portable bridge."

"The way you win battles, Leufrid, is you fool the people you are fighting. We have been fooled twice. What's next?" shouted Grimbald.

Leufrid turned red but said nothing.

Grimbald pointed at the southern flank. "Somewhere out there are a thousand or so Roman cavalry. You better make sure they don't attack us on our one vulnerable spot."

Leufrid saluted and galloped off, followed by his staff and the handful of riders, all that were left of the guard at the southernmost ford.

Turning to his own staff, Grimbald said, "We have to assume the VII Legion has portable bridges as well. That was probably one of the reasons for the raid last week. Give Roman engineers a week and they will dream up some mischief to plague you with. Spread the word." The aides raced off toward the river defenses.

Grimbald dismounted and squatted on the ground to think. Portable bridges were a problem he hadn't considered, but he still had more soldiers than the Romans, and they would have to establish beachheads and fight their way through the defenses. They might even carry the ditch and the embankment, but at great cost, and they would be too exhausted to pursue. If disaster hit, he could always fall back on Tarraco, using his cavalry to keep the Roman horsemen from cutting off his retreat or harassing his rear guard. "Relax, Grimbald," he told himself. "Battle is always a surprise, but we can handle this one." He stood to lead his horse back toward the river. He would have to detail some troops to cover this southern flank in case there was more trouble with the Roman cavalry than Leufrid anticipated. He would also have to make it up to the cavalry commander. Commanding officers can't be fighting one another, particularly deep in enemy territory.

A man came running from the back of the camp. "Romans, sir, Romans."

"Yes, lots of them. We are going to stop them from crossing that river," replied Grimbald, distractedly. He was thinking about those bridges. How many would they have? How did they set them up?

The man cut in front of him. "Romans, sir, Romans."

"I heard you" bellowed Grimbald. "Do they so terrify you?"

The man shook his head, his face alight with alarm. "No, sir, look," and he pointed back toward the camp.

"Well, I guess we know where the Roman cavalry went," said Grimbald glancing at road leading toward Tarraco. What he saw froze him to the spot.

"What?" he asked, rubbing his eyes and looking again.

"Romans," said the man dumbly.

A solid wall of legionnaires was moving out of a line of trees. They were followed by another wall, and yet another. Grimbald watched in growing horror. The lines were perfectly dressed, the eagle glowing in the morning light. Silent and lethal.

"How?" he said, and then it hit him; the ragged line of the legion across the river. That was the auxiliary legion, maybe more than one, and marching on his rear was the real VII Legion.

There were men who would have fallen to pieces at such a time, men who would have given into despair and fallen on their swords, or succumbed to fear and dashed for the hills. Grimbald was none of these. And he still outnumbered his enemies. He took a deep breath and willed himself calm. He would play it out. If the Romans wanted to divide their forces, he would try to take advantage of that.

Grimbald turned to his staff, who had begun gathering around him. They were 12 men, and, while they looked anxious, no one was panicking. "Listen carefully. Stop the flow of men to the riverbank, but leave those that are already in place there. Have a line of men stand on the embankment, so it looks like we have a lot of soldiers there. Pay attention. We have to convince the Romans on the other side of the river that we are prepared for them. We will take everyone else and attack that legion in our rear. We will hold the auxiliaries at the river and crush the VII Legion in our rear. Do you understand?"

Most of the men nodded. "Go, now. But don't run. We have time. Running means panic, and we can't panic the men," he said. "You," he said, pointing at an aide holding a horse. "Go to Leufrid and tell him to throw every horseman he has at that legion." The man leapt on his horse and galloped off. Almost involuntarily, Grimbald looked at the hills on his southern flank. If the Roman cavalry suddenly showed up his plan would collapse. He put the thought out of his mind. First, deal with the VII Legion.

By the time he got to the rear of the camp, commanders were forming up their men, and soldiers were streaming in from the riverfront and falling into units. "We fight pretty much like the Romans over there," he thought to himself. He fervently wished the Franks at the river were good actors. They had to hold off the auxiliaries. But as long as he could keep the VII Legion from communicating with its auxiliaries across the river, that was not a bad bet.

A reflection caught his eye. He narrowed his eyes looking for where he had seen the flash earlier on the steep mountain to their north. There. A flash, and then another. Could the Romans have soldiers on that mountain? Impossible, and even if they did, they couldn't be in large enough numbers to threaten his northern flank. Then it dawned on him. They didn't need soldiers, just a few men with mirrors.

The auxiliaries and the VII Legion were in contact.

Grimbald fought down a wave of fear, not for himself, but for their entire enterprise. To come this far, to get this close. He fought the surge of despair. The Romans had tricked him, but plans rarely survive the first clash of battle. The Romans might stumble. The auxiliaries might make a mess of the river crossing. The Roman cavalry might never show up. Roll the knuckles until the game is lost.

The VII Legion was closing, and suddenly the morning was rent with blasts of the Roman war horns. A great block of Frankish cavalry thundered down on the Roman's line. That should slow them down, thought Grimbald. But a shimmering wave arched out of the Roman ranks and scores of horses went down screaming and kicking. Javelins. The cursed Romans were using javelins to break up the cavalry attack and keep the horsemen at bay.

The horses whirled like a huge band of starlings and dashed off, only to spin again and attack. Once again, a cloud of javelins broke up the attack. If Leufrid would only think to hit the Roman's left flank, they would have to move troops there to ward it off, giving Grimbald a chance to hit the Roman center and split the legion in half.

But Leufrid kept attacking the center, where the Romans were strongest. Glancing at the left flank, he saw a horsemen mount a hill to the south. Then a line of horsemen. So, the Roman cavalry wasn't lost after all, nor was it bound for Tarraco.

Grimbald watched the Frankish cavalry back off and regather to face south. The lines of horsemen from the hill began to descend, while the Franks trotted forward to meet them. Well, there was nothing he could do about the cavalry. He turned back to the VII Legion.

It was close now. The centuries, their shields locked, their great infantry pila jutting upwards, moved relentlessly toward the Frankish infantry.

An aide appeared at his side. "The Romans are trying to cross the river, sir."

Grimbald nodded. There was nothing more he could do. The men would fight well and win, or fight poorly and lose. No plans, no maneuvers would mean much now. He would watch his flanks, keep a reserve to throw into a gap in his line or maybe exploit a mistake by the Romans, but in the end, it would come down to men against men.

Septimius stood behind the first line of auxiliaries watching the mountainside.

"There it is," he said. "The VII Legion is attacking."

Publius spat. "This is a fool's game. This Marcus is going to get us all killed, and then there will be no protection for the rest of Hispania."

Septimius frowned. "So far, the plan is going well, Publius."

"This Marcus just wants to be a tribune. He is not from Hispania. We should hold here and see what happens."

"If we don't attack, the Franks will throw everything against the VII Legion and destroy it," said Septimius. "In any case, we have our orders, sir."

"Why should I take orders from an outsider, and why should we gamble the last fighting force on the peninsula just to gain Marcus glory?" Publius shot back.

Septimius was silent for a moment. "I am in command here, Publius, and I am going to attack that river line. If you do not attack in support, we will fail. But if we fail, I will let everyone know exactly why we failed. I doubt you would survive that revelation." The legate slipped his helmet on, and turned back to Publius. "Return to your command and follow your orders, sir. We have a battle to fight."

Publius looked like he was going to say something more, but swallowed it. He turned on his heel and walked back through the deployed legion.

Septimius watched him go. Turning to his stunned staff, he told them, "Remember this conversation, gentlemen, now it's time to build some bridges." He raised a hand and pointed at the river. Centurions signaled optios and tesserari and the auxiliary legion began to move.

But rather than marching down and wading across the river, the soldiers formed a wall of shields. Rolling on logs placed in front of them, three great bridges lumbered forward. Several dozen men were already hacking away near the riverbank to provide the bridges an anchor and a pivot point from which to lift them. At the other side of the river, the Franks began shouting, as some threw javelins. Missiles from slings and bows came sailing across the divide, but the wall of shields the legionnaires had thrown up absorbed most. The Romans returned fire. When the Frankish archers stretched their arrows over the shields to strike at the men laying the bridges, soldiers formed a loose testudo of shields to protect them.

The bridges were bigger than the cavalry bridge, but the increase in manpower more than made up for the awkwardness of the three structures. The bridge ends were dropped into the trenches, and wedges were driven in to keep them from slipping. Then, foot-by-foot, the bridges rose until they stood almost straight up.

Septimius signaled to his staff, and three blocks of picked auxiliaries congregated near each bridge. Behind them were archers and slingers. The engineers looked back at the legate, and the men gathered around him. Septimius dropped his arm and the bridges began to slowly, and then more rapidly, descend. Finally, with a rush, they fell the last 10 feet, bounced slightly when they hit and settled in. Before they stopped rocking, Roman auxiliaries poured across the bridges to meet a solid wall of shields and Franks on the other side.

For a time, the Romans were restricted to the bridges, but then they began to carve a half-circle around the end of each bridge, which allowed yet more soldiers and replacements to filter in. In the meantime, soldiers on the west bank hurled pila and javelins, taking a steady toll on the Franks, as did the arrows and sling missiles. Small groups of Romans began wading across the river. Most were prevented from climbing the other bank, but they served to drain men from the Franks fighting to hold the bridgeheads.

None of these attacks would have been a problem had not the Franks stripped the river of defenders in order to attack the VII Legion.

Slowly, the bridgeheads expanded, and the soldiers managed to wade the river and scramble ashore in two places. The engineers had one more trick up their sleeves. The stone bridge had been dismantled, but both ends were still in place. A group of soldiers carrying several long planks climbed one side of the bridge. The planks were not tied together, so they were much lighter than the portable bridges. Few men could cross over the makeshift bridge, but it was one more thing to defend, which required some of the Franks shifting to defend yet another front.

To the south, the Frankish and Roman cavalry whirled around one another, attacking, retreating, and counterattacking. As with most cavalry battles, it was harder on horses than men, and neither side could get the upper hand. The minute one side tried to encircle the other, there was a breakout, a retreat, and a swift counterattack.

The VII Legion had plowed into the Franks, initially driving them back. But the Franks were fighting hard, and Grimbald tried to use his superior numbers to surround the Romans' flanks. A Roman legion, with its flexible structure of cohorts and centuries, is almost impossible to flank. Each time, it looked as if the Franks might slip around an edge, the Romans sent a reserve century to seal the flank. The Romans were also rotating men to keep them from being exhausted. Allowing the men to rest was harder for the Franks, because they were fighting a two-front battle, three if one counted the cavalry clash in the south.

A messenger appeared at Grimbald's side. "The Romans are across the river, sir, but we are holding the defense line."

"Tell them to hold it at all costs," said Grimbald, watching a Frank counterattack drive back a Roman century that had done a fearful amount of damage to his right flank. The Romans retreated in good order, and Grimbald watched as a fresh line of legionaries moved into place and advanced once again. Grimbald cursed the Romans. It was like fighting a machine.

Most battles are not lost by big missteps, but by the accumulation of small ones. It is rare that a great charge wins the day, or even that some brilliant maneuver turns the tide. A man breaks and runs, and his comrades suddenly lose heart. There is a slow drift of men to the rear, not a stampede, but a trickle. The Franks were fighting well, but the men knew they had enemies both before and behind them. Their enemies were men, but they were men who did not shout or scream or bellow when they fought. They fought like war was a business, with profits and losses totted up in the midst of madness. When they were stabbed or bludgeoned or trampled, the Romans died like all men die. They bled like men everywhere. But to the Romans it was still a business, cold, efficient, relentless. There are times, of course, when efficiency is not enough, when spirit or numbers overwhelm even the best-trained legion in the empire.

Not today.

Today, a man from north of Noviomagus, near where the

great Rhenus River divides Rome from the world north of it, lost heart. He was not a coward, but something snapped in him as the Second Cohort of the VII Legion advanced for the third time in less than an hour. The man saw the wall of shields marching toward him, the lethal Roman short sword sticking out from between them, the identical markings on the scutums, identical helmets and uniforms, the almost expressionless faces beneath those helmets. He turned and ran.

The two men on either side of him tried to grab him—they were his friends, had fought side by side with him in many battles—but he dragged them away from the front line. They followed him. A gap was opened in the Frankish line, which filled in, this time by men who were now glancing over their shoulders and then looking forward into what the man from north of Noviomagus had seen. And some of them also slipped away.

A dam break begins with the shifting of a few stones.

The center of the Frankish line began to crack. One by one, men slipped to the rear, drawing others with them, until the trickle became a stream, the stream a river, the river a deluge. Grimbald saw it, and it surprised him. He was always ready for disaster, but he thought it would come from his rear, or maybe his southern flank. His infantry was good, very good. They had fought together for years, and they fought for a reason, not pay or loot or enmity.

And yet they broke.

Not all of them. Some fell back in good order, swords and shields forward, slowly backing up toward the camp. Grimbald looked behind him. He could see the defense line at the river was still holding, although he could also see that the fighting surged around the wall of stakes. The line was holding, but it was under assault. Grimbald grabbed an aide. "Go to Leufrid. Tell him to save the cavalry. Get it back to Tarraco."

"Sir!" the young man stated to protest.

"Go! Or I will cut your throat. Go! Tell Alberic to load the ships and fly. Go! Go! Go!" Grimbald shouted, pushing the man toward a horse. The aide hesitated a moment, then mounted and dashed off.

Grimbald slipped in behind the rallying Frankish troops, but the line would not hold for long. The Roman commander had ordered one of his reserve cohorts to shift toward the south, and they would soon flank the Franks from that direction. "You already figured that our cavalry was not a threat any longer, didn't you, you bastard," muttered Grimbald.

Well, he could still bloody these cursed Romans. "Fall back! Fall back!" he called out. "Rally at the river defense line." Frankish soldiers looked over their shoulders at him, their faces betraying exhaustion, tense with fear.

The Frankish line began to steady as it shortened, and some of the men who ran toward the rear were returning to the front. We will lose, thought Grimbald, but there is more blood to shed, and it will not just be ours.

The VII Legion cohort sealed the southern flank, and Roman cavalry filled in behind them. He hoped this meant the aide had gotten to Leufrid. He would have to see that his men did not get too packed together, so packed that they couldn't fight. He was measuring the possibility of a counterattack on the cohort on his southern flank to buy time and fighting space when the Romans stopped advancing.

Grimbald blinked. Why had the cohort stopped? He turned to look at the main body of the VII Legion, and it too had stopped. Exhaustion? What was going on? The fighting still continued at his rear, but that too began to slack off. Finally, it stopped.

Grimbald stood in the middle of the camp. To the east, the VII Legion was marching another cohort out to flank him from the north. He was in a box with no way out. He still had troops, but they had no heart for this. Were the Romans playing with him, like a cat with a mouse, torturing it before the final kill? He brought down all the curses he could imagine on the Romans, but his northern curses did not seem to work well in this hot, dry land.

Several of his officers gathered around.

"What are the sons of bitches up to?" grumbled a man, his face cut and his shirt soaked with blood under his breastplate.

"Playing with us is what," said another. "We should gather everyone and attack those bastards from the VII Legion. Maybe we can hurt them enough to keep them out of Tarraco."

"We haven't hurt them much so far," said an older officer in a weary voice.

Grimbald said nothing as he watched the Eagle of the VII Legion. It was moving forward. Several horsemen emerged from the front line, riding forward until they were about a hundred yards from the Frank rear guard. A man in a red cape dismounted and walked forward. A stocky man followed him. They stopped and waited.

"What do you make of that?" an officer asked.

"Looks like the legate, and it looks like he wants to talk," said another.

"About what? Whether we get fed to the lions or crucified?" said an officer with a face wound, spitting on the ground.

Grimbald took a moment to look at his soldiers, now formed in a phalanx of shields and swords. The lines were still solid, but the men played out. And worse, afraid, though they did their best to hide it. He could not hold their eyes, The men looked at the ground and the Romans rather than at one another. Grimbald had been in many battles, battles won and battles lost. He could smell defeat, and the odor now was powerful.

Grimbald looked at his officers. They were brave men, and they would die if he asked them to. But they were beaten men. They cursed the Romans, but there was no fire in the curses, just resignation and weariness.

"Let's find out what they want," said Grimbald. "Arnuf, come with me. If we don't come back, Thankmar is in charge. Make our deaths expensive."

"Yes, sir," said the tall Frank with the blood-soaked shirt. "We'll do that."

Grimbald and Arnuf walked out to meet the two Romans. The Frankish commander studied the two as he and Arnuf approached them. The legate was stout with brown eyes and a broken nose. His aide was broad and looked tough. The Franks stopped several feet away, and the legate nodded a greeting.

"Legate Marcus Favonius, commander of the VII Legion Hispania Gemina Pia," the man with cape said. "This is my aide-de-camp, Flavius Priscus, former optio of the First Century, First Cohort.

"Grimbald, commander of the infantry," said Grimbald. "This is my comrade, Arnuf. What can we do for you, Roman?"

Grimbald watched Flavius stiffen at the insolence in the remark, but if it bothered the legate, he didn't show it.

Marcus looked out over the field, at his troops surrounding the Franks, at the Frankish rear guard drawn up in a block. "You fought well, Grimbald."

The remark startled the Frankish commander. "We are not done yet," he said.

Marcus was silent for a long moment. "We both have a problem, Grimbald. I thought we might discuss it," he said at last.

Grimbald and Arnuf both looked at one another. "And what would that problem be?" asked the Frankish commander.

"You have an army that is about to be exterminated. That is your problem," answered the legate.

"We still have a lot of fight in us, Roman," said Arnuf.

"No you don't. Gentleman, we are professional soldiers. Yes, we will lose some men, but not enough to do us damage. In fact, I might just let the auxiliaries finish you off while we go into defensive mode. How successful do you think your attacks would be against us if we are on the defensive?" asked the legate.

"Not very," said Grimbald, drawing a startled look from Arnuf.

"Good, our first agreement. Let's build on it," said the legate.

"Wait," said Grimbald, "what is your problem?"

"You hold Tarraco, which means you hold our citizens hostage," answered the legate.

Grimbald nodded.

"I propose an exchange," said the legate. "You will have to surrender your army, but in return we will not harm any member of it."

"All that means is that you sell us into slavery without any bloodshed on your part," said Arnuf.

The legate shrugged. "That may happen, but are you ready to say the game is over? You do not have much bargaining power, Grimbald. You hold the city hostage, but the city is a trap. The fleet from Valentia, Gedes, and Carthago Nova should arrive any day now to blockade your planned escape by sea. You do not have enough troops to defend the city from three legions, and, in any case, we Romans never lose a siege."

Grimbald tried to keep his face expressionless but the remark about the ships staggered him.

"Yes, we know about the ships, Frank," said the legate's aide.

Grimbald was silent for a moment. "Are you suggesting that there may be another alternative than death and slavery?" he finally asked.

"Maybe," the legate replied. "A commander of a legion has a good deal of power, but he is not all powerful. I am suggesting that there is a possible alternative to the certain death of your army."

"How do we know we can trust you?" asked Arnuf.

"Listen, Frank, who do you...," started the aide, but the legate put his hand on his shoulder and silenced him.

"You don't know. Even if I give my word, I do not guarantee I can keep it. The alternative is your deaths. Choose," said the legate.

XXX

Demaratus held Coventina to him in a dark bedroom in Vallerius's domus. She was trembling, but silently, her hands bunched up into tight fists. He stroked her softly, and gradually the trembling subsided. They remained still for a long time. Then Coventina pushed him back and put her hands to his face. "My Greek," she said.

"My Celt, who just tried to stab me," he said with a grin.

Coventina touched his cheek with the back of her hand. "Oh, Demaratus, I dreamed you would come." Then, puzzled, she asked, "But how? Where is the VII Legion? What are you doing here?"

"I was sent into Tarraco to spy on the Franks," answered the signifer. Coventina just stared at him. "And I came for you, my love. My friend Flavius dreamed up the spying mission, and Marcus let me go."

"You did this for me?" she said softly, again touching his cheek.

He pulled her toward him. "Yes, but I have also been spying."

"Well, Greeks like to do more than one thing," she said stroking his chest.

"I take it you no longer wish to stab me?" he said, trying to lighten the conversation.

"I am sorry, but I did not know who you were," she said, laying her head on his chest.

"I could not afford to be recognized. Julius Dasumi is in Tarraco, and he bears me no love," said Demaratus.

Coventina frowned. "The brother of your friend Marcus' mistress?"

The signifer laughed. "I am not sure he would appreciate that title, and I am certain Aelia would not."

"Why does her brother dislike you?" she asked, leading him to a sleeping couch. She suddenly felt exhausted, drained.

"I did not give you all the details of our final encounter with Aelia and her brother, but Julius then accused me of being a thieving Greek. I explained to him that he was in error," said Demaratus, as the two sat down on the couch, still facing one another.

"Explained?" she said, arching an eyebrow.

"He wears the explanation across his chest. It was deep enough to leave a scar," he answered.

She smiled and ran her hands up his cheeks and into his hair. "How is such a pretty man so dangerous?"

"All Greeks are pretty and dangerous," he said.

"And full of themselves," she said. She put her finger to his lips as he began to reply. Then she pulled him forward and kissed him.

Demaratus kissed her back. "I found out about you from Androdamus. We have been searching everywhere, but it was as if you had vanished."

"I was lucky," said Conventina, "but you are a spy?"

"We are planning to strike back at the Franks," he answered.

"Tell me," said Coventina.

Demaratus laid out the scheme to attack the ships in the harbor and his communication with the Roman soldiers in the Praetorian Tower. "Vallerius has raised up a secret army of retired soldiers. Of course, all depends on what happens when the Franks meet the VII Legion in battle. If the Legion is defeated, then we escape. If the Franks are defeated, then we attack."

"I want to be with you," said Coventina fiercely.

"You have done enough, my love. You will be safe here. The chances that we will be successful are not great," he answered.

She grabbed him by his cloak. "I made a blood pledge on my uncle's funeral bier, a pledge I will keep. And I will not be separated from you again."

"Coventina, this will be a battle. If we fail, we die. I will not permit it," said Demaratus.

"Permit it? You will not permit it? You have an inflated view of your powers if you think I require your permission," she said, a steely note in her voice.

"Now, listen to me," started Demaratus, but Coventina cut him off. "I have lived in fear for more days than I can remember. Do you expect me to cower here in this house while you go off to fight the Franks, these Franks who murdered my uncle? To sit here and hope they do not find me, and drag me into the plaza to be raped and tortured?" She stood and strode over to the chest where she and Demaratus had lain their weapons on entering the room. She drew Demaratus' dagger and handed it to him. "Kill me now, my love. Make it a clean death and hold me while I die."

"You are a mad woman," said an exasperated Demaratus, reaching for the knife.

"If I am mad, it is because I can no longer bear what they would do to me. I cannot bear it!" she almost shouted. "I will not live in fear, Demaratus. I will not! We live together or we die together, or kill me now. If you do not, I will do it myself." She placed the blade near the great artery on her neck.

There was silence in the room.

"I could not bear your death, Coventina. That is why I want you to stay here and be safe," he said softly.

"And I cannot live that way, my love. I cannot, I will not. I do not wish my own death, but I will embrace it if it releases me from this fear. I do not fear battle, I fear a lonely death. It is not even the pain and humiliation I tremble at, but to die alone. That I cannot bear. This is who I am, Demaratus." She reached into her dress and withdrew the pendant she wore around her neck. "Look at this, Demaratus. This is my life. This is mighty Coventina, the great bear of the mountains. She flows through my veins, she is in my bones. She has watched over and protected our people since we came into this land. There is none fiercer than Coventina. I will fight because we are as one. Try to understand that, my love."

Demaratus shook his head. "I do not entirely understand, but sometimes that is not important."

He took her into his arms and held her in a long embrace. After a silence, she said, "Not understand? That's a very un-Greek thing to say."

The signifer put both his hands to his head. "You really are impossible. One moment you are going to cut your throat, the next you joke with me."

"Well, we Celts are an ancient people, older than the Greeks. When you mature, you too will be able to feel many things at the same time," she said with a smile, knowing that she had won.

"So be it," said Demaratus. "I will have to convince the others, however."

"No one defeats a Greek in an argument," said Coventina, tossing the knife back on the chest and reaching out to him once again.

"I just lost one," muttered Demaratus.

She looked at him solemnly. "My love, if we fail, and it looks as if we will be taken, you will release me, yes?"

He sighed. "Yes."

She kissed him.

XXXI

Alberic sat on a low stool, his elbows on the table. Hildebold, tense, almost rigid, paced. Leufrid stood before them looking tired and defeated. There was none of a cavalryman's bluster about him.

"How? How did this happen?" asked Hildebold, whirling on Leufrid. "You outnumbered them. You had a defensive position. And they were, what did you call them, 'girls and old men'? Our army defeated by girls? What have you done!"

Leufrid said nothing, his face contorted with anguish.

"Tell us how this came to pass," said Alberic quietly, putting a restraining hand on Hildebold, who shook it off.

"It happened because we sent fools into battle, so puffed up with vanity that they allowed themselves to be defeated by a smaller army," shouted Hildebold. "Do you know what you have done to our people, Leufrid? Will you go and tell them they are sentenced to a life of slavery, those who are lucky enough to survive?"

"Hildebold, be silent. We need to hear what happened. The

game might not be over," said Alberic. Again Hildebold paced, but said nothing.

"Now, Leufrid," said the Frank leader.

The cavalry commander shook his head. "Hildebold is right, sir. We thought their cavalry was no match for ours. It was. We thought the VII Legion was a shell. It was not. We thought the auxiliaries would not fight. They did. Most of all, they fooled us, and they fooled us because my cavalry—no, I—did not do the job. We were blind, and they saw everything."

"I want details. How did they fool you? How did they get across the river?" asked Alberic.

Leufrid sighed. "Their cavalry used a portable bridge to cross a part of the river we never thought they could cross. Our commander should have made a run for it, but instead he stood and fought, and only a few of our men got away."

"Go on," prodded Alberic.

"By the time the main body of our cavalry got to the battle, it was over and the Romans had left. Our commander pulled the cavalry back to defend our infantry."

"What happened with the infantry?" asked Alberic.

Leufrid took off his helmet and ran a hand through his hair. "They tricked us. They dressed their auxiliaries as the VII Legion. They had all the shields and armor right, even an eagle. But the real VII Legion somehow got behind us, and we found ourselves caught between the VII and two auxiliary legions."

Alberic rolled a bronze seal back and forth across the table. "I take it their cavalry wasn't the only part of their army with portable bridges?"

"No, sir. The auxiliaries had three. We did a good job of

holding them off, but Grimbald had to use most of the men to fight the VII Legion in our rear.

"And where was your cavalry in all this?" put in Hildebold.

"We attacked the VII Legion, but they used javelins to break up our charges. Then the Roman cavalry arrived, and we had to keep them off our southern flank," said Leufrid wearily.

"Javelins?" asked Alberic.

The cavalry commander nodded. "Yes, sir. These Romans know how to fight cavalry."

"But our infantry outnumbered them?" said Hildebold, still pacing.

"The VII Legion fought well, as well as any Romans we have encountered. And we could never throw everyone into an attack, because the auxiliaries were pounding at our river line," said Leufrid.

"Grimbald?" asked Alberic quietly.

"I don't know, sir. I got an order from him to break off and retreat to Tarraco. The messenger said for me to tell you to take the boats and flee," said Leufrid.

"With what!" shouted Hildebold, his temper boiling over. "What will we take to Mauretania? Women and children and cavalry that cannot fight? Why delay being taken into slavery? Let it happen here."

"Silence!" roared Alberic. "We are not slaves. We have our garrison and, yes, our cavalry. It was not their fault. They were ill-led, and the Romans were better than we thought they would be."

Hildebold put both his hands on the table. "I warned you about the Romans, Alberic. I warned you that Grimbald and this fool were overconfident. Now it is our women and children who will pay for this."

Alberic flushed red but mastered his anger. "You are right, my crow. I also bear responsibility for this disaster. Now, shall Leufrid and I fall upon our swords for you?"

"I never said you should fall upon your sword, sir," grumbled Hildebold. "I was just pointing out our situation."

"And you think I was not aware of our situation, Hildebold?" said Alberic.

Hildebold said nothing, but started pacing again.

"Listen to me, both of you. Grimbald was right. We need to leave as quickly as possible. Sooner or later they are going to find out about our ships and set up a blockade. How many cavalry do you have, Leufrid?"

"I haven't counted, but I would estimate a little over 2,000, " he answered.

"We have 1,000 in the garrison," said Alberic, rising and beginning to pace himself. "That is a good fighting core, maybe enough to get us a piece of land. How long will it take us to load the ships and be gone, Hildebold?"

"I would have to ask Brocard and Wallgard, sir. The riot at the market has strained things a bit," answered Hildebold, ceasing his pacing.

"How did that happen?" asked Alberic.

"That madwoman, the red-haired witch was behind it," said Hildebold, "and she got clean away in the chaos. We arrested a lot of people and are holding them in a warehouse near the docks."

"She is a witch, isn't she?" said Alberic. "Well, that is not our concern now. Get Bocard and Wallgard. Keep the people you arrested penned up, and I want every important merchant in the city arrested and put in there with them. The only things we hold over these Romans are hostages. Leufrid, I want an exact count of your men. Go."

Momentarily confused, Leufrid saluted and left.

"Fool," hissed Hildebold when he was out of sight.

Alberic seized his second-in-command by the shoulders. "We can't afford that now, Hildebold. We must pull everything together and be gone by the time the Romans arrive. I need you now, comrade. Put aside your anger. Our people need us."

"Of course, sir, it is just that this might have come out differently if we had been there at the river," said Hildebold.

"This Roman commander is bold and innovative. We might both be dead on some field now. But we have no time for regrets, Hildebold. Let us play this out to the end."

Hildebold nodded. "I will fetch Bocard and Wallgard. I will also see that the gates are defended in case the Romans show up."

"How long do we have?" asked Alberic.

"A day, maybe less. Victory lends wings to an army's feet," replied Hildebold.

"Let us fix wings to our own, brother," said Alberic.

The small fishing skiff slid close to the shore, where two men, their faces muffled with cloaks, waited. The tiny beach was just wide enough for the boat to run up on shore, and the two fishermen jumped over the sides, holding it from sliding back into the sea.

"If you will climb in, sirs, we can get going," one of the

fishermen said. "The Franks are seizing everything afloat, and I have no intention of losing my boat."

The two men waded into the surf and clumsily pulled themselves over the gunwales. The fishermen pushed the boat back into the sea, then nimbly jumped aboard. Both seized oars and backed the ship free of the beach. Once she was clear, one of them scrambled aft and turned the rudder to head her out to sea, while the other pulled with both oars.

"This boat stinks," said one of the cloaked men disgustedly.

"Yes, sir. That smell would be fish, which is what we do. Now, before we go any further, I would like to see your gold," the man at the oar said.

The larger of the two men elbowed his companion. "Show him," he said.

The other man reached into his cloak and extracted a purse. Opening it, he poured out a handful of gold coins. "Satisfied?" he said.

"When they are in my hands I will be satisfied," said the man at the tiller.

"When we get to where we are going, you get your gold," the larger man said angrily.

"That's not the way of it, sir. The gold now or you can swim ashore," said the man at the oars.

The two men glanced at each other. Both reached into their cloaks and drew out short swords. The man with the gold put his sword to the throat of the fisherman with the oars, while the larger of the men put a sword point to the tiller man's breast.

Slipping off his hood, Julius Dasumi pressed the point of the sword until the fisherman flinched. A tiny stain of red appeared on his shirt. "Take us south, dog, or you're dead."

XXXII

Under the watchful eyes of the Franks, a stream of Tarraco residents carried sacks and jars down through the streets and onto the docks. Ox carts piled with goods, sometimes pulled by teams of men, creaked slowly down from the town. At the long wharves, men were unloading carts and packing them aboard ships. Since the ships were tied up three to four deep, teams moved the supplies from the inner ships to the outer vessels. Still, the goods were piling up dockside faster than they could be loaded on the ships.

"Move it, Roman," a Frankish soldier yelled at one man who was slowly dragging a sack toward one of the ships. The soldier followed this order with a sharp rap of his spear on the man's back. Despite all the threats, the loading was going slowly and porters were standing in small groups waiting their opportunity to load the ships. As the morning progressed, the groups grew larger.

"These Romans are dragging their feet," fumed Wallgard, who was trying to coordinate the loading of the ships.

"What did you expect? If you were in their place how enthu-siastic would you be?" said Brocard examining a wax tablet.

"Maybe we should make an example of a few of them," said Wallgard. "That might get them off their asses."

"It is not all their fault, Wallgard. It isn't easy loading ships four deep. And given what happened yesterday at the market, it might not be wise to provoke them. It took a hundred men to bring order, and most of the rioters were women. I suggest we be patient," said Brocard.

Wallgard stomped off to bellow at a group of men seated on sacks of wheat. "Pick them up, you lazy bastards, and get them over to those ships," he said, pointing at a cluster of mid-sized coasting vessels. The men took their time getting to their feet, but instead of each picking up a sack, four of them seized the corners of one and carried it over to the ships Wallgard had indicated.

"It takes four of you to carry one sack?" Wallgard yelled.

"We have been on short of food since your lot showed up," one man said sullenly. "We don't have the strength to each carry a bag. Maybe if you feed us something we could carry more."

"Guard!" called out Wallgard. "Take that man over there and kill him," he said pointing at the sullen worker.

Immediately the other men surrounded him and began shak-ing their fists at Wallgard. Others dropped what they were car-rying or got up from their seats and began to form a half-circle around the men.

Two Frankish soldiers approached but neither looked en-thusiastic about seizing the man. "What's going on here?" one of them growled.

"We're tired and hungry." A shout from the back of the crowd that was followed by a number of jeers and growing hostility by the dragooned workers.

Wallgard pointed at the man who had answered him back. "Take that man," he told the soldier.

By now the crowd had grown to about 30 and the Franks glanced around nervously. "You there," one of them said, "get back to work."

The man shrugged. "Sure, just keep that guy away from us," he said pointing at Wallgard. A group of men walked over to the sacks, and once again four of them picked up a sack and carried it to a ship.

Wallgard was livid, but before he could speak, Brocard intervened, taking him to one side. "Wallgard, we don't have enough soldiers in this town to handle a riot. Most of the men are on the walls looking out for the Romans. We don't need this. We still have time. Let it go."

The Frankish ship commander made an effort to calm down. "All right, but this is more than laziness, and none of those men look like they have missed a meal. They are trying to keep us from leaving, Brocard."

"Of course, but we will leave. So push them, but don't threaten to kill anyone. If they think they are going to die, they've got nothing to lose by turning on us" answered Brocard. "When can I send our women and children?"

The change of subject diverted Wallgard. "Not until we are loaded. The loss of our army means we don't have to take the smaller ships, and we can use some of midsize as supply ships.

But it will be a while, and the women and children would just clog the docks or the ships. I need half a day."

"That may not be in our hands, brother," said Brocard.

"I know, I know. But I doubt the Romans can be here until tomorrow. If this cursed lot doesn't sabotage us, we should be able to do it. Don't send the gold and silver until we have the ships loaded and can get rid of these Romans."

"All right. I should get back. I will alert our people that they should be prepared to move by late afternoon," said Brocard. "Good luck, Wallgard."

"And to you, Brocard. We are going to need it."

Wallgard looked around. There looked to be more Romans than a few minutes before. He started to puzzle over this, but a commotion down at the end of the wharf grabbed his attention, and he strode down to sort it out.

A hooded man wandered over to the group slowly loading the wheat sacks. "Don't do anything to convince them they need more guards down here," he said quietly, picking up a corner of a sack. "And be ready. If things go right, some of these guards are going to head up toward the Praetorian Tower."

"Okay. I just don't take kindly to that ratty little barbarian talking to me that way," said Wallgard's intended victim.

"Save your anger for the fight," said the hooded man. He slipped away and fell in with a group that had set up a chain carrying jars of oil toward one of the boats. A tall youth looked out from beneath his hood and winked at him. "Shameless," he whispered with mock severity.

"If we come out of this alive, I will show you shameless," Coventina whispered back.

A group of six men emerged from a taverna near the plaza that fronted the Praetorian Tower singing bawdy songs and playfully pushing one another. As the group neared the plaza, the horseplay turned rougher. A squad of Franks moved toward the group.

"All right, move it along," said one. "No one allowed in the plaza."

Two men squared off, swaying in a way that suggested a fight wouldn't inflict much damage on either one.

"You should be happy about that ugly face of yours, Fabius, happy that you never had a father who could look on it," one of men said to the other.

"That beats having hundreds of fathers, Arrius," the other said, shifting his weight from foot to foot. "Your mother was so great a whore you had your pick of them."

"I'll show you a whore," said the first man and began flailing away at the second, who grabbed him by the waist and wrestled him around in a circle. The other men cheered on the fight and started taking bets as to the winner. "Two denarii on Arrius," yelled one. "Three on Fabius," yelled another.

"Here, here, break it up," a Frank squad commander ordered, grabbing one by his neck. The man, suddenly quite sober, spun around and drove a pugio into the Frank's neck. The other drunken fighter leapt on another Frank, pinning his arms, while one of the bettors stabbed him in the chest. The remaining Franks were so stunned they froze, a fatal reaction. Within moments, the six Franks were dead or dying.

There were at least a hundred other Franks in the plaza, and after a moment of shock, they picked up shields and spears and charged the group of men backing out of the plaza toward the taverna. When the Franks got close, they turned and ran, followed by the Frankish soldiers.

Half way down the block, doors on either side spewed forth men, many in the full legionnaire's armor. Others appeared on the roofs of houses and sent arrows and sling missiles into the ranks of the Franks. The ambush killed half a dozen men and sent the others retreating back toward the plaza.

"Come on, barbarians. You want to conquer Tarraco? Well, come and conquer us if you have the courage," an older man dressed as a centurion shouted. A line of Romans with swords and infantry scutums formed a wall, blocking off the street. The shields were from a variety of legions, some slashed with lightning bolts, some sporting lions, others numbers and symbols.

Three Franks dashed out of the plaza and headed for the docks, while the others, recovering from their surprise at the initial ambush, advanced on the wall of shields. The two groups came together in a crash, the Franks stabbing with spears and swords, several slashing away with battle-axes. Lifting a leaf from the Romans, the back ranks of the Franks formed a roof of shields that largely neutralized the archers and slingers barraging them from the roofs.

Slowly, the line of Roman shields fell back. Most of the men wielding them had long retired from the ranks, and while they wore the uniform, they were no match for an army of young men. Aged arms and legs tired easily. The Franks, sensing the weakness of their foes, renewed their attacks and more Romans fell. The wall retreated further.

There were shouts in the plaza as more Franks crowded into the street.

The old centurion cried out. "Comrades! They have brought reinforcements from the port. Strike!"

The Roman wall surged forward. For the first time, heavy infantry pila fell on the Franks, but the roof of shields blocked most. The Roman attack smashed into the Franks, driving it back, but it soon exhausted itself. The Franks pushed it back, faster and further this time. There was a feel of desperation to the Roman attacks as more and more of them fell.

Suddenly, the Frank attack slackened.

"Ready, comrades," panted an exhausted Vallerius. The men surrounding him were wheezing, many of them wounded. As the Frank attack slackened, they gratefully rested their huge shields on the ground as they tried to catch their breath, waiting for the next attack.

The attack did not come.

"What's happening?" a man asked Vallerius.

The centurion shook his head. "I don't know. Maybe they are pulling out to defend the port. We should attack now!"

"Vallerius, old friend. We are not going to do anything of the kind. We are going to sit here and catch our breath and thank the Gods for this respite," said a grizzled man with a paunch, sucking in air with huge gulps.

Vallerius looked up toward the few men who were still on the roofs. "What can you see?" he shouted.

"The Third Century is marching out of the Tower! The Franks are pulling back to fight them!" the man yelled back.

"Well, comrades," said Vallerius, straightening his helmet and lifting his shield. "Have we got a little more fight in us?"

"Oh, I suppose," sighed the man with the paunch. "Let's get some fresh men up here and go at them again. I knew I should never have come out of retirement."

"Now, Petronius. Doesn't this make you feel young again?" grinned Vallerius.

"No, it makes my back hurt and reminds me I have a bad knee, that I drink and eat too much, and that my shield has gotten heavier," the man replied, but he lifted the scutum, squared his shoulders and moved forward. Slowly, the wall of shields moved down the street, this time faced with a single line of Franks.

"We're under attack in the plaza," a Frank panted to Wallgard, who had come back up the dock as soon as he had seen the soldier running down from the city's center. Wallgard glanced around. The loading was going slowly, but it was moving along. "Clovis," he called out, and a broad Frank soldier left the group of men and strode over.

"Clovis, the men in the plaza are being attacked. They need support. I was thinking you could send half your men. Leave 50 here to keep the loading going."

"What kind of attack? Who is attacking us?" asked Clovis.

"Roman infantry. They tricked us into an ambush," the man answered.

"The Romans in the tower?" Wallgard asked.

"No, they didn't come from the tower, sir. They came out of houses near the plaza, and they had men on the roofs shooting arrows at us. I was ordered to alert the port and ask for help, so I didn't see exactly who the attackers were," the man answered.

"Orderic," called out Clovis. A tall Frank, older than Clovis, detached himself from a group of Franks overseeing the loading of amphorae of olive oil. "Sir?" he said.

"You're in charge. I am going to take half the men into the city. There is an attack going on near that tower where the Romans are holed up. Keep the loading going. We need to have these ships ready by mid-afternoon," said Clovis, already striding up the dock and calling out names. Frankish soldiers broke off what they were doing and followed him, several picking up shields stacked against a warehouse wall.

"You, Romans! Get to work," yelled Orderic. A group of residents had dropped their labors to watch what was going on. Slowly and reluctantly, they returned to hoisting jars and lifting them onto the ships.

"Keep a sharp eye, Orderic," said Wallgard. "The timing of this is suspicious. This could be an attack aimed at the ships."

"I'll put a heavy guard on the entrances to the docks, sir," said Orderic, who began calling out names and pointing out where they should go. A number of Franks stopped prodding the Romans loaders and ran up the dock toward the streets leading toward the city's center.

As the Franks thinned out on the docks, Wallgard noticed that many of the Romans were gathering in groups.

"Orderic, break those men up and get them to work," said Wallgard.

The broad Frank motioned at several soldiers, who joined him and moved toward the men. "Break it up and get to work," Orderic ordered, and the soldiers began striking the Romans with the butt ends of their spears.

One Roman youth was dragging a sack toward a gangway. A Frank shoved him, knocking the youth sprawling. "Come on, move it along," said the guard. The youth struggled to his feet, stumbled, and fell into the Frank's chest. "Clumsy fool," said the Frank and shoved the youth back. But the Roman held onto his assailant's arms, dragging him toward the gangway, then suddenly dropped to his knees. As the Frank was catching his balance, someone shoved him from behind. He tripped over the youth in front of him and pitched over the edge of the dock with a loud splash.

"Kill those men," shouted Orderic, but another Roman had slipped behind him, and Orderic gave a gasp, staggered and fell to the pavement. A surge of men dropped what they were carrying and overwhelmed the Franks around the downed Orderic, stabbing at them with knives and short swords or grabbing them while others disarmed them. Wallgard reached for his sword only to find a blade across his neck.

"Make a sound or a move, Frank, and you're dead," said a voice behind him. He felt his arms being pinioned and a rope tying his hands together. He was shoved toward the ships, pushed up a gangplank and thrown onto the deck.

The attack happened so quickly that many of the Franks were confused. Some were still looking up toward the city. Groups of Romans retreated toward the ships, some facing the Franks, others pitching bundles on board the vessels. Others slipped the cables tying the ships to the dock or hacked at them with swords. By the time the Franks saw what was going on and ran toward the ships, most of the Romans had boarded and were untying the boats from the docks.

With Orderic dead or badly wounded, and no one giving orders, the soldiers were paralyzed. The Romans, however, had a plan. While some of them held the Franks at bay by kicking the gangways back onto the docks, others smashed beakers of oil on the ships' decks. Wallgard watched with growing horror as other Romans unbundled torches and set them alight with flint lighters.

Some Franks had finally figured out what was up and were trying to pull the boats back to the docks. Others leaped over the gunwales of those still tied to their moorings to attack the Romans. Because they had no armor, shields, or spears, the Romans were at a disadvantage. While surprise had allowed them to overwhelm the Franks, the advantage was shifting to the soldiers.

One of the boarders—a Greek— took a torch and lit several oil-soaked bundles. Flames licked the bundles and began to spread. Turning to Wallgard, the he said, "Call them off, Frank, or we burn these ships to the waterline."

"You would burn with them," said Wallgard, as calmly as he could manage while tied up with a knife at his neck.

The Roman youth who had started the fight grabbed him by the shirt with one hand, and with the other swept back the hood. Staring at Wallgard was a woman with short, bristly red hair. "Yes, the madwoman, Frank. Do you think we care if we burn? And if we burn, so will your women and children. Call them off, now."

Wallgard watched the fire grow, and saw, too, other fires spring up. Some of the Frankish soldiers had left off fighting the Romans and were trying to smother the flames. The Romans had concentrated on the big ships and some of the midsize coast vessels. The ship Wallgard was on had drifted too far from the dock for the soldiers to board it, but several were rounding up gangways preparing to breach the gap. Some of the Romans had retreated to the outer ships, starting fires as well, while their comrades slowly retreated from the Franks on the inner ships.

Wallgard considered. It might be possible to put out the fires before they spread. Once the Franks came to grips with the lightly armed Romans, they might subdue them, although the insurgents were fighting desperately and inflicting casualties. If he had not sent the guards to the plaza he would tell this mad woman to fuck herself. But while the Franks were making progress, so were the fires.

"Decide, Frank, now," the woman said, pressing her face right up to his. Her face was bright red, her nostrils flared, her teeth set in a death grimace. He decided that she was mad and probably quite prepared to burn alive.

"All right. Stop the fires," he said.

"Call off your men, then we stop the fires," said the Greek, who was eyeing a group of Franks getting ready to cast grappling hooks from the dock and pull the boat back to shore.

Wallgard pushed himself to his feet. Taking a deep breath, he called out. "Cease fighting. We need to put out the fires."

Many of the Franks looked at him and hesitated. Some were locked in combat and kept fighting.

"Cease fighting," Wallgard called again, louder this time.

"Comrades, fall back," called the Greek.

Slowly the two forces fell apart, still armed and wary, as the fires kept burning.

"You said you would put out the fires," Wallgard said to the Greek.

"And we shall, after your men get off the ships and let us float them into the middle of the harbor," the man answered.

"That wasn't part of the agreement," said Wallgard.

"We make the terms of the agreement, Frank. What are you worried about? We can't get these ships out of the harbor anyhow because of the chain," said the Greek.

"How do I know you won't burn them anyhow?" asked Wallgard.

"Don't be stupid, Frank," said the woman. "The VII Legion will be here today or tomorrow. Why would we kill ourselves now? You have hundreds of hostages. We have your ships. These ships guarantee the safety of the hostages. If we burn them, we have nothing to bargain with."

Wallgard was silent a moment. "Agreed, if you let me go."

"Why would we let you go?" asked the woman.

"Because he is the only Frank who knows how dangerous we are to his precious boats," said the Greek. "We need a sailor over there to talk some sense into those thick Frankish heads." Turning to Wallgard, he said, "Agreed, but call them off."

Wallgard turned toward the Franks on the dock and those who had made it onto the ships. "Onshore, men. Don't interfere with the ships." The men on the shore backed up from the docks, while those onboard the ships reluctantly began climbing over gunwales to inner ships and, finally, onto the docks.

"Now put out the fires!" said Wallgard to the Greek.

Instead, the Greek called out to his men, "Cut those smaller ships loose, free the ships you are on from the others. Once you are clear, put out the fires." Romans hacked at the ropes that bound the ships together and shoved their oars to launch their ships. As soon as there were gaps between their vessels and the inner ships and the dock, they began dousing the fires with buckets of water or smothering the flames with sails.

The woman cut Wallgard's hands free, then put a knife to his chest. Pressing it painfully into his breast, she backed him up to the side of the ship. "Frank, you murdered my uncle and earned a blood debt to my people. It is not yet repaid, but the Cantabri keep their word. I hope you can swim." With that, she shoved him over the side of the ship and into the cold harbor waters. He surfaced sputtering and began threading his way through the thicket of ships toward the dock.

"We did it!" said Coventina, turning to Demaratus and throwing her arms around him.

He grinned at her. "Yes, but we have only bought some time. And we need to get these boats together." Releasing her, he called out orders, and slowly the larger boats began to come together, while others were set adrift. Some were already drifting back toward the docks or the long stone mole. Demaratus noticed that Franks were running along the mole headed for the harbor entrance. He wondered how the fighting in the plaza was going.

After a quick show of force, and gathering together the survivors of the retired legionnaires, the century retreated to the Pretorian Tower. The great iron portcullis came down with a crash, and the huge, studded gates slowly closed. The Franks were keeping their distance from the rain of stones from the top of the tower.

"So, you've rejoined, have you?" said Antonius Crispus, the Third Century's centurion.

"Not likely," said Vallerius slumping against a wall, with half a dozen cuts and nicks oozing blood.

"I'm not sure you needed us, old friend," said Antonius.

"We needed you," said the old centurion wearily. "How many did we get in?"

"Most of your men. The men on the roof presumably scattered. We couldn't get to the badly wounded," said Antonius squatting down by him.

Vallerius nodded. "The lot of the army. We knew what we were getting into. Your lads fought well. If it hadn't been for those reinforcements, you might have done the Franks in."

"I wonder what happened at the harbor?" said a young tesserarius, coming over to stand by the two men.

"I imagine we will find out soon enough, Tiberius," replied Antonius.

"Sir," said the soldier, coming into the small gatehouse near the northern wall of the city.

Without a word, the Frank officer got up and ran lightly up the steps to the top of the gate. Several hundred yards from the gate was a group of horsemen. One wore a gold mask, another carried a banner, another some kind of medallion on a tall pole. They sat on their horses facing the gate, not moving.

XXXIII

Alberic and Hildebold looked out at the motionless Roman cavalry.

"How long do we have?" said the Frank commander.

"They will be here tonight," said Hildebold. "Unless they are dragging their own siege equipment, however, they will have to build it after they arrive. That could take a few days."

"It has not been a good day," said Alberic leaning on the parapet over the gate.

Hildebold said nothing.

"No rebuke, my crow?" asked Alberic.

"It is too late for rebukes, sir."

Alberic nodded. "So let us see where we stand."

Hildebold ticked off several points on his fingers. "We have a little over 3,000 men if we arm some of the older boys. Most of them are cavalry, however, so they are lightly armored. We have bowmen and slingers, but not many and not enough to cover all the walls."

"Go on," said Alberic.

"The Romans are back in their tower, but their attack was a

ruse anyhow. Most of the large ships and some of the medium ones are clustered in the middle of the harbor under the control of the Romans and that madwoman. We lost very few men in the fighting but we lost control of a good portion of our fleet," said Hildebold.

"We do not need as many ships, of course," said Alberic, "not nearly as many."

"No," said Hildebold a bitter sound in his voice.

"Hostages?"

"We have more than 300 Roman merchants and their families gathered in two warehouses near the port. Some others must have heard the news and gone into hiding," answered Hildebold.

"Then let us move our people down near the port. Leave the Romans holding our ships alone. I don't want burning ships in the harbor. We could lose them all," said Alberic.

"The walls?" asked Hildebold.

"Make it look like we have more men than we do. Put old men and boys up here. Make the Romans stop to build siege engines. We have the hostages. Maybe we can make a deal for our women and children." Alberic pushed himself erect. "I will go and talk with these hostages. Get Brocard to organize moving our people. And let me talk with Wallgard. I need to know if it is possible to make a run for it. You handle keeping the walls manned and let me know when the legions arrive."

"Yes, sir," said Hildebold, still staring at the Roman cavalry.

Alberic squeezed his second-in-command's shoulder and ran down the stairs to the street level, where a crowd of officers awaited orders. The Frank commander told them to see

Hildebold and then indicated that three Franks should come with him.

The streets were deserted. In the aftermath of the fighting around the Praetorian Tower and the port, many of the Frankish soldiers had beaten and even killed a few random Roman citizens. His men were enraged that the attack had killed some of their comrades, and that the madwoman had reappeared, clearly having been hidden by people in the city. Now Roman families barricaded themselves into their homes and waited for the VII Legion to arrive. He had a perverse desire to burn them all out, but that would accomplish nothing so he let the sentiment go.

The Franks with him were almost running to keep up with Alberic's long strides. He could see the tower in the distance, a group of Romans clustered at the top. There was nothing he could do about them.

The closer he got to the port the more cluttered the streets became. Supplies were still moving down and out onto the docks, although a large bloc of ships was anchored in the middle of the harbor. He could see torches burning and men manning the sides. Not a lot of men, fewer than 100. But they had struck swiftly and cut the boats loose before his soldiers had time to react. Whoever organized the attack was a dangerous man, and also a bit lucky. But luck is an important part of war. The Franks had had very little of it since they had taken Tarraco.

Alberic strode into a cavernous warehouse packed with people ranging from old men to infants. It was noisy and hot and his reception drew looks that ranged from fearful to hateful. Slowly, the noise died down, although some children continued to squabble, and an infant was wailing somewhere in the back.

"Listen to me, Romans," said Alberic. "You are our hostages. Choose three to represent yourselves and be prepared to come with me when I need you."

A heavy-set man pushed through the crowd. "We won't do anything until we get food and water."

Alberic nodded to two Frankish soldiers and strode forward, grabbed the man, and dragged him to where the Frank commander was standing.

"What did you say, Roman?" said Alberic quietly.

"I said we need food and water, especially for the women and children, and until we get them we won't elect anyone to do anything," said the man who seemed not in the slightest bit intimidated.

"I can think of one way to reduce the number of mouths that need to be fed," said Alberic.

The man looked at him evenly. "Do what you wish, Frank. I am a veteran of the XXII Primigenia. My legion fought you barbarians in Germania. We do not scare easily."

There was a rumble from the crowd that had begun to press forward.

Alberic gave him a wintry smile. "Your legion didn't do a good job, did it, Roman? Because here we are in the heart of your empire. The barbarians are hammering at every border. How long do you think it will be before one of us pulls down Rome itself?"

"Long after you are dead, Frank," yelled a man from crowd. "And that won't be long once the VII Legion gets here." Jeers and cheers greeted the remark.

The man folded his arms across his chest. "Food and water, barbarian."

Alberic was reaching for his sword pummel when a calm voice behind him said, "I do not think this is necessary."

Standing just inside the door to the warehouse was the head duoviri, Fabius Porcius. He gave Alberic a small bow and turned to the man with his arms crossed. "Domitius Oppius, your courage is admirable, but I believe we can fulfill your request without any bloodshed. You should choose two others because your participation in this process is essential, and we will make sure that food and water is delivered here and to the hostages next door." Turning back to Alberic he said, "Sir, I believe the request for food and water is reasonable as is your request for the hostages to choose a spokesman. I wonder if I might talk with you in private?"

The little mouse was good, thought Alberic. It was almost as if an adult had appeared and intervened in a squabble between children. He was also right. The last thing the Franks needed was another riot, and keeping the hostages healthy was in the Franks' interest. Alberic told the three men who had accompanied him from the wall to get food and water for the hostages. Taking Fabius by the arm, he led him out into the docks. He noted that the man called Domitius was calling out some names,

Outside he turned to the Duoviri. "Well?"

"I have information you need to be aware of, Alberic," said Fabius.

"What information?"

"First, shortly, several of our warships are going to appear off of the harbor and you are going to be blockaded. I tell you this because your choices are now limited and growing more limited by the moment, and I urge you to open negotiations with the legate of the VII Legion. I also have information that suggests such a negotiation might reach a conclusion that is to all our advantages," said Fabius.

Alberic said nothing for a moment, considering. The remark about the warships might be a bluff, and for some reason Wall-gard did not seem overly concerned with the possibility that the Romans might send such vessels. But if it was true, he had to admire the mouse's ability to get that kind of information. As for the comment on the negotiations: that could be a ploy to keep the hostages alive. "What information might that be?" he finally asked.

"It appears that there has been a change in the command of the VII Legion. Its legate, Titus Valens, was taken ill and its command fell to his praefectus castrorum, Marcus Favonius," replied the Duoviri.

"Why is this of any interest to me? " asked Alberic, wondering how it was the mouse knew these things. Of course, it could be a bluff, but Alberic did not think so. It had a ring of truth to it, which meant that the Duoviri had a source of information outside of the city, and was also probably keeping the VII Legion informed on what was happening inside the city. For the first time a wave of depression engulfed him. He had been outmaneu-vered, outfought, and now it appears that the Romans had a regular way of getting information in and out of the city.

"Because this Marcus Favonius is man who thinks with his head, not just his sword arm. I will not go into details, but because of something he did, Hispania has so far been able to avoid a civil war in our western province of Lusitania," replied Fabius.

"You just want to keep the hostages safe," said Alberic.

"Of course," said Fabius, "that is my job. I also consider it my job to spare Tarraco a siege, although I do not think it would be an extended one."

"And why do you think that?" replied Alberic.

"I can count, Alberic. I know how long the walls are and how many men you have to defend them. It will take the VII Legion and the auxiliaries no more than a few hours to break in," replied Fabius.

"But then the VII Legion will find the city's inhabitants dead as well," said Alberic. "We also have options, Roman."

"You will kill a lot of people, and maybe even all the hostages, but you cannot kill a city and also defend it. You don't have the soldiers. Really, Alberic, I thought you were a sensible person, certainly more so than that gloomy little creature, Hildebold," said Fabius. "What will you gain by killing your hostages? Revenge? That is a pointless and empty emotion, and illogical. Let me go out and talk with the VII Legion. You have nothing to lose."

Alberic suppressed a smile at Fabius's characterization of Hildebold. The man had a point, and in any case, Alberic needed time. If talk could bring it, so much the better. "I agree. I will give you your parole to leave the city and make contact with the VII Legion and this Marcus."

"Excellent," said Fabius. "If you do not object, I will do so directly. You will escort me to the gate so that that Hildebold creature does not cut my throat?"

Alberic grabbed the Duoviri by his toga and pulled him close. "Hildebold is my friend and comrade. You keep a civil tongue in your head, Roman."

Fabius looked directly up at the taller Frank. "He is not my friend or my comrade, and you are wasting time with this posturing. We do not have to like one another to do business together. If you do not escort me, send a message to Hildebold to allow me to pass. If he cuts my throat all of your people will die. That is as civil as I intend to be."

The big Frank held him for several seconds then laughed and let him go. "You must have done more fighting than clerking with the XI Legion."

"Clerking is harder than fighting, Alberic, and in the Roman Army infinitely more dangerous. Information is worth 10 legions," said Fabius, straightening out his toga.

"Harmut," Alberic bellowed. A tough-looking soldier trotted over to the two of them. "Take this man and give him free passage through the gate."

"Yes, sir," the man said, and motioned to Fabius with his spear to walk in front of him. The Duoviri nodded to Alberic and walked briskly up the street toward the town's center.

Alberic watched the two go and then turned back to the docks. Wallgard was waiting for him.

"What's our situation?" Alberic asked.

"We have most of the ships we are going to use loaded. Because there are far fewer of us, we can get by without the ships the Romans are holding in the center of the harbor. We will be crowded, but as long as the weather holds, I think we can make it. What happens when we get there," he shrugged.

"The duoviri says the Romans are going to show up with a fleet to blockade us," said Alberic.

"Do you believe him?" asked Wallgard.

"Suppose one does show up?" asked Alberic, ignoring the question.

"It depends. I don't think the Romans have a fleet in Hispania. They can pull together some liburnas and maybe a few old triremes. I doubt they have anything as large as a quinquereme, but even if they do, it won't be much use against our smaller, faster ships, even overloaded, as they will be. The problem is that we won't have as many soldiers, so the Romans will be less shy about closing with us," answered Wallgard. "It concerns me but I think we could still get most of our people out."

"Prepare for that, Wallgard. We may have to make a break for it. You will be in charge of getting our people to safety," said Alberic.

"Sir?"

"Someone is going to have to command the rear guard. That will be Hildebold and me. You will have to take over, brother," said Alberic, taking the ship commander by the shoulders.

"It was you who brought us all this way, Alberic. We can't do this without you," said Wallgard.

"You may have to, brother. Do your best. If it comes to a dash, we will buy you time. Now, get it ready. I will need to be at the wall from now on. May our gods look over you, Wallgard." Alberic grabbed the thinner man and hugged him for a long moment, then turned and walked back toward the city.

XXXIV

The command tent was crowded with cohort commanders, Cassius, Marcus, and Flavius, the two auxiliary legion praefectus, and four staff clerks taking notes. Fabius took a sip from a wine goblet. For almost an hour he had been laying out the situation in Tarraco, his analysis of the strengths and weakness of the Franks, and his opinions of what should be done. The fact that a civilian, even a duoviri, felt he could recommend courses of action for the military was an indication of how much weight civilians carried in Hispania.

"To sum up, sir, I believe they would be open to negotiations on surrendering the city and freeing the hostages," said Fabius. "Their commander, Alberic, seems to be a sensible person, and I have to say that, all in all, the Franks behaved rather well. There were very few citizens violated, and they kept their word not to loot the city."

"Open to negotiations? That is rather presumptuous of them, duoviri," said Septimius.

Fabius lifted both his hands, palms up. "I was giving you my opinion on the matter, sir. There is no question that you and the

VII Legion can retake the city. I doubt that the Franks would kill a large number of citizens in revenge, although I cannot speak for the hostages they hold. I raise the issue of negotiations because that is one option."

"They are barbarians that have violated the Empire," growled Pubius, the other auxiliary commander. Septimius shot him a frosty look. Marcus caught the glance and wondered about it. Something must have happened at the river, because he has not seen Septimius address a word to Publius. Later, he would ask Flavius to find out what the coldness between the two men was about, but that was of no importance right now.

"Actually, I rather think they are citizens, sir. Certainly many of them have fought as auxiliaries, and most speak Latin," answered Fabius.

"Then they are guilty of treason!" shouted Publius.

"I was not defending them, sir, I was pointing out that this is a more complex matter than it first appears. For instance, if they are guilty of treason, then are not those who helped them equally guilty? Should we not send our legions north to Narbo to inquire how it was that such a large body of people could pass the length of Gaul and no one notice? Or warn us? Is Rome prepared to ask those questions and insist they be answered?" said Fabius adjusting his toga and taking another sip of wine.

His reply was met with dead silence.

"I would add that there are a number of prominent families in Tarraco, families that have a significant presence in Hispania, who were," he paused to consider, then continued, "shall we say 'helpful' to the Franks while they were in Tarraco. Shall we arrest those people for treason?"

If it was possible for the group to grow more silent, it did.

Marcus broke the quiet after a long moment. "We thank you for your thorough report, douviri. We will consider its implications. In the meantime," he said, turning to the rest of the people in the tent, "we need to surround Tarraco. I want the two auxiliary legions in the south, but delegate a cohort from each legion to guard the prisoners. The VII Legion will invest the main wall in the north. I want you to start building siege machines, but wait for my word before there is any attack. The cavalry will seal the city and spread out so that the Franks are forced to cover the whole wall. Gentlemen, we have much to do." Nodding at Fabius, he said, "Duoviri, please stay. You too, Cassius."

After a moment's hesitation, the commanders saluted and filed out, leaving Marcus, Flavius, Cassius and Fabius. "Please sit, duoviri," said Marcus, indicating the others should also. Flavius made himself inconspicuous by sitting at the back wall of the tent. Marcus poured Fabius more wine and handed the jug to Cassius, who put it down without taking any.

"I want to speak for a moment, douviri, and I would appreciate you correcting me if I am wrong," said Marcus.

The man nodded assent.

"It is my impression that this so-called 'invasion' was not a surprise to our friends and comrades in Gaul, and that it was probably known about in Rome, am I correct?"

"Yes, although I cannot speak for Rome. Let me say that there are some in Rome who would not be opposed to a certain 'independence' developing in parts of the Empire. Many in Palmyra and Mesopotamia hold similar sentiments," answered Fabius.

"Would you say that there are similar sentiments in Hispania and Mauretania?" asked Marcus.

The duoviri frowned. "Hispania, yes, and it is long standing, sir. I cannot speak for Mauretania, although I have heard talk of an 'African empire.'"

"These families you speak about? I am new to Hispania so I am only beginning to understand it. Are these leading families in the province?" asked Marcus.

"They are," answered Fabius.

"With influence in Rome?" continued the legate.

"Considerable influence, sir. A move against them would encounter stiff resistance in the Senate, particularly because they were careful about how they cooperated," said Fabius.

Marcus rose, which brought everyone to their feet. "You have done a great service to your city and the Empire, Duoviri. I would like you to arrange a meeting with the commanders of the Franks. You will inform them that we hold over 10,000 prisoners."

"Really?" said Fabius, rising to his feet. "They surrendered?"

"They did. In part, because I promised to negotiate with their leaders in Tarraco," answered Marcus.

"Negotiate about what?" the douviri asked.

"That is yet to be determined. We have much to think about. I would like you to be part of these negotiations," said Marcus.

"Of course, sir. I will transmit your message to Alberic. When and where?"

"Tomorrow morning at the main gate."

Fabius bowed and left.

"I am not sure I followed all of that, sir," said Cassius, looking puzzled.

Marcus smiled at him. "I am not sure I did either, but a few thoughts occurred to me."

"Yes, sir?" said Cassius.

"Well, optio, have you figured out where they were headed?" asked Marcus.

" I had that one worked out a week ago, sir," replied Flavius, rising up and joining them.

"Where?" asked Cassius.

"There is only one of two places they could be going, Cassius. Either Mauretania Tingitata or Caesariensis," replied Flavius. "They didn't come all this way south to return north. Italia, Sicily, and Greece are too crowded and with lots of Roman soldiers. Aegyptus and Cyrenaica are too far. What's the one place in the Empire right now that doesn't have a regular legion, because Rome dismantled the III Legion Augustus?"

"The Franks would know that?" asked Cassius doubtfully.

"No, lad, but there are people in Gaul who would, and a whisper here and there that there is land for the taking with only auxiliaries defending it makes it a tempting target," said Flavius pouring himself a goblet of wine.

The cavalryman shook his head. "I am not sure I will ever be able to sort this all out."

"Yes, well, the problem with you Lusitanians is you believe in being straightforward and honest," said Flavius taking a long drink of wine. "That's why you never stood a chance against us Romans."

Cassius looked sharply at him trying to figure out if Flavius was joking or insulting Lusitianians.

Flavius laughed. "That was a compliment, Cassius. We Romans can get so twisted up that we wring our own necks. Anyhow, that is how I see it. What do you think, sir?"

Marcus smiled and poured himself a goblet. "And what are we going to do about this?" he said.

"I know what I would do, but of course I'm just a lowly optio," said Flavius.

"That never stopped you before from giving advice," said Cassius.

"Go on, Flavius," said Marcus.

"I think we should help them out, sir," replied Flavius.

"What!" exclaimed Cassius. "These people just killed a lot of our men and also seized a city. We're going to help them out?"

"Why not? True, they did give us a bad time, but remember, Marcus and I spent several years beating up on them or their relatives up north. And Cassius, did you hear that clerk's remark about setting up an African empire?" asked Flavius.

"He is a duoviri, Flavius, and a pretty good one at that," said Marcus mildly.

"I stand corrected, and I agree. He looks like a mouse but he doesn't behave like one. But if I may continue...," Marcus waved him on. "Now Cassius, who do you think might be behind this 'African empire' stuff?"

Cassius gave him a blank look.

"Our old friend, the governor, Domitius Antonius himself, lad," said Flavius. "You know that snake has to be in this up to his neck. And as I recall, he tried to get our legate here killed, not to mention me and Demaratus and the rest of our century."

"Do you think he knew about this?" asked Cassius.

"I doubt that," put in Marcus, "but I think it is a good bet that he is involved in this African empire plan."

"And these people who want to break up the Empire just tried to kill us all, Cassius. Where I grew up, that is something that needs to be repaid," said Flavius quietly.

Now it was Marcus's time to frown. "I think you have guessed correctly as to where the Franks were bound, but what are you suggesting?"

"That we send the Franks to Mauretania and make them the governor's problem," replied Flavius.

"But how do we know the Franks weren't recruited to come and help the governor set up this empire?" asked Cassius.

"We don't know that. But we are holding the whip hand here," said Flavius. "I think we could get an oath from these Franks. As I recall, they take them a lot more seriously than many Romans do."

Marcus smiled. "I am not sure the civilian administration would think very highly of this idea, Flavius."

"They might if they thought it was the only way to get those rich hostages out alive," said Cassius, warming to the idea.

"It appears I am besieged," said Marcus, looking back and forth between the two men.

"Sir, all I am suggesting is that we talk with the Franks and see what comes of it. I think the clerk, ah, duoviri, is right about blame here. There are people who ought to be brought to accounts. But I doubt it will happen, which means the Franks will pay for everyone else's treason. If we could get the Franks to swear a sacramentum to the emperor, if we could get our superiors in Carthago Nova to agree, and if the Franks arrived in Mauretania to upset our friend, the governor, then everyone would make out," said Flavius, tapping his palm with each point. "I know it's a lot of ifs, but it isn't the first time the Empire has made a deal with barbarians."

"It is a lot of ifs, Flavius, but I agree there is no harm in trying to find out if we can do it." Marcus stood up. "Cassius, I am going to write out a negotiating position, and I need you to send it with some fast riders to Carthago Nova. After that, I want to see this Grimbald."

Coventina slid her arm around Demaratus, and the two looked out toward the harbor entrance. At mid-day two liburnas and an ancient-looking quinquereme had shown up off the port. The liburnas were sleek and fast, but smaller than the ship on which they stood. The big quinquereme looked as if someone had pulled it out of a museum and sent it off to sea. If the Franks really tried to break out, the Roman ships would not be able to do much about it. But it was a psychological lift for the men on the ships, and Demaratus suspected it would have a demoralizing effect on the Franks.

"Are we saved?" asked Coventina. She had a hard time keeping her hands off him.

"Hardly. First, those are Romans out there. If they can avoid running ashore, they will be lucky. Second, there are not enough ships to blockade the harbor," he said, slipping his arm into hers. He recognized her need for touch. She had been through much.

She laughed. "You don't think a lot of Romans, do you?"

"Not when it comes to sailing. Otherwise, they are all right, although they have an affection for violence," he said.

She shuddered. "All men have such an affection, my love."

He stroked her cheek and said nothing.

"What do you think they will try to do?" she asked.

Demaratus stood and surveyed his little fleet. Two dozen ships were clustered together, three quite large. Demaratus had made one of the larger vessels his command ship, and torches were burning in all the vessels. All had been soaked with oil. If the Franks tried to seize them back, he would fire them all. The larger ships were anchored with stone anchors, and the smaller ships were tied to the larger ones. If the ships were set alight and the anchor cables cut, they would drift toward shore. In almost any direction they went, they would end up firing other ships. If Demaratus and his crew were trapped, so were the Franks.

"There are not as many Franks as there were, are there?" observed Coventina.

"No. More than half have gone, to the walls I suspect. But there are plenty of women and children." Ashore, a group of children chased one another around the docks, and groups of women sat in the warm sun, some around small fires.

Coventina's face stiffened. "It is always the women and children that suffer for the folly of men."

Demaratus rubbed her forearm. "I would not argue that point," he said softly and pulled her closer to him.

Antonius Crispus, centurion of the Third Century, 10th Co-hort, his optio Domitius Celer, his tesserarius Tiberius Cicero, and headquarters Tesserarius Sextilius Germanus all leaned over the parapet of the Praetorian Tower and watched the Franks below.

"How many?" asked the centurion.

"Just short of 200 that I can see, sir," answered Tiberius.

"They're cutting it close," said Domitius.

"I doubt they have much choice, sir," said Sextilius. "Their forces must be thin on the walls, and the VII Legion is sure to arrive any time now."

"Think it's worth it to take a whack at them?" asked Antonius.

The other men said nothing. They had no intention of dis-agreeing with a superior officer, and because of the centurion's tone, it wasn't clear whether he was serious about wanting a response.

"No, I guess not," Antonius answered his own question. "We probably do more good here tying up troops and keeping them off the walls."

The others nodded agreement.

"Well, that's the army: fight, wait, fight, wait, with the wait the longest part," said the centurion.

"Don't they get tired or bored?" asked Alberic.

Hildebold looked over the cavalry that had remained frozen in place all day. "Romans are not quite human." He spit over the wall.

"Look who is coming," said Alberic. Even from a distance the head duoviri was distinguishable, if for no other reason than he was so unprepossessing.

The duoviri nodded at the cavalry, who took no notice of him as he steered his horse toward the main gate. He dismounted and waited until the gate opened just wide enough for him to slip through. Alberic and Hildebold ran down the steps to meet him.

"What do you bring us, Fabius?" asked Alberic.

"The legate of the VII Legion wishes to meet with you to-morrow morning outside the gate here. I would recommend you do so," said Fabius. "He has requested that I be at this meeting."

Alberic nodded assent, but said nothing.

"Then if you do not mind, I would like to visit the hostages," said Fabius. "If you agree to talk with the legate, I will ask you to permit me to choose one of the hostages to ride to the camp of the VII Legion."

Alberic motioned for a Frank soldier to accompany the duoviri. "Let him choose someone and give him a horse," he said.

Fabius and the Frankish soldier walked toward the port. Once they were out of earshot, Hildebold looked at Alberic. "The Romans want to talk?"

"The game is not yet over, comrade," said Alberic.

XXXV

The gates of Tarraco swung open just enough to let a small party of men depart. Alberic and Hildebold led the way, followed by the head duoviri Fabius Porcius and two other men, both wearing expensive togas, but looking a bit the worse for wear.

Two hundred yards from the gate stood Marcus and Flavius, with Grimbald at their side. A small group behind them consisted of the two auxiliary commanders and some staff.

"Hostages in the togas?" asked Flavius.

"I would guess. The small dark one is second in command?" asked Marcus to Grimbald.

"Yes. His name is Hildebold," replied the Frank commander softly, a dirty bandage around one arm.

Marcus looked at the man. Grimbald's shoulders slumped, and he was drawn and pale. Marcus had never had to surrender to anyone, but he thought he might look much like the Frank did now. He felt a certain sympathy for the man. Turning back to the group approaching from the gate, he studied the two Frankish commanders. Alberic wore a breastplate and helmet and was armed with the long sword the Germanic tribes favored.

Hildebold, shorter and darker, had no armor or helmet, but wore a long sword as well. The two strode swiftly across the ground.

Negotiations were always a matter of keeping the other side off balance. Marcus hoped that having Grimbald by his side would disconcert the Franks. He had gone over his proposals with the other commanders and gotten their reluctant approval. He could have simply ordered them to agree, but that was not the way Marcus worked, and his instinct was that Hispanians did things differently. They had to be convinced.

Publius had resisted, saying that the Romans had won a great victory and should reap its benefits. "Yes, a great victory," said Septimius. "I am sure you have much to report on that, sir." Publius froze, then went silent. Again, Marcus wondered what happened at the river, and why it should silence Publius. From that point on, the auxiliary commander said not a word.

Marcus eventually won them over by stressing the safety of the hostages.

The group from the gate finally arrived. After a long and somewhat awkward pause, Fabius stepped forward and made the introductions. With each, the party gave a short, stiff bow. Flavius introduced Marcus and himself.

Alberic looked over at Grimbald. "You are well, Grimbald?"

The man looked down at the ground. "I have failed you, sir," he finally said.

"In this you are not alone, my brother," replied Alberic. Turning to Marcus, he said, "You wished to talk, commander?"

Flavius bristled. "He is giving you a chance to talk, Frank, and his title is legate."

Alberic gave the stocky Roman a wintry smile. "I have talked, optio. And as I believe I am only in a position to refuse, not to offer, I do not have anything else to say at this point."

Marcus had been studying the Frank in the exchange with Flavius. If he was beaten, he was a good actor. His second-in-command had a sullen, dangerous look about him.

"We are wasting time, gentlemen," said the douviri. "May I suggest we get down to business?"

Flavius had been about to reply to Alberic until Marcus put his hand on his shoulder. "Agreed, Fabius. Let us consider the matter as I see it. Commander," he said addressing Alberic, "you are surrounded and blockaded. We hold 10,000 of your men as hostages. You do not have sufficient men or supplies to resist a siege. If it comes to a siege, it is not only you and your men who will die, but your women and children as well. Your only choice is to surrender and to call upon our mercy."

"I did not think you had that word in Latin," said Hildebold, his voice tight with anger.

"We do, and it is all you have, Frank," replied Marcus evenly.

"We hold 300 of your most prominent families," interjected Alberic, touching Hildebold's arm to silence him.

Marcus smiled to himself. It appears we both have hot-tempered aides, he thought. "Ten thousand of your warriors and your families against our 300, commander? That seems a poor exchange," said Marcus.

"Let me tell you how I see it, Roman," said Alberic. "Your blockade will not be difficult to break. You do not have sufficient ships to stop us, and if they are not careful, we will take them away from you. We have enough men to withstand a siege until our boats are away, and more than enough to cut the throat of every hostage. And we are not afraid to die, Roman. When we came south, we knew the risks. I will mourn my soldiers, but soldiers are always prepared to die. We will not be slaves, nor will I sentence any of our women and children to such a fate. If it comes to that, death would be a better alternative."

"Where are you bound?" asked Fabius.

The question caught Alberic by surprise. "None of your business," he snapped.

"Gentlemen," said the duoviri, "we are at an impasse. Alberic, you can kill the hostages and delay our legions long enough to send your women and children off, but to what? Where will they go? Undefended, they will end up slaves, in any case. You can kill the hostages, but so what? It will gain you nothing but revenge, an empty sentiment which profits none."

Turning to Marcus, he said, "Sir, there is no doubt that you can retake the city. I also have no doubt but that the commander here will kill our people. Since it is inevitable that you will win in the end, what does it profit us to lose our most prominent people? In spite of what you both have said, I believe there is common ground here."

Alberic shook his head. "I do not see where it lies, duoviri."

Marcus said nothing. He had decided that Fabius was the key to a peaceful resolution, and knew far more than he did about how to make that work.

"That is why I asked you where you were bound," replied Fabius.

"He already told you it is none of your business, Roman," growled Hildebold.

"I was not addressing you," Fabius said, glancing at Hildebold,

"I was speaking to Alberic." The dismissive tone in his voice prompted Hildebold to grab his sword pommel, but he did not draw it. Flavius put his hand on his sword handle just in case.

Fabius ignored Hildebold, keeping his eyes on Alberic. "I was not asking because I wished you to reveal something that would be to our advantage and your disadvantage. You know what I said about boatloads of women and children unprotected by soldiers is true. If this is not to end in a bloodbath, we need to know where you were bound. If it is to attack another place in Hispania, then let us get about the business of bloodletting. If it is elsewhere you are bound, we need to know where. Surely you can see the logic in that, Alberic."

Hildebold started to reply, but Alberic silenced him with a look. "We were not bound for any place in Hispania," he said.

"Italia?" asked the Duoviri.

"No," answered Alberic.

"You are bound to Africa, are you not?" said Fabius.

Alberic mastered his surprise, but Hildebold looked startled, then tried to mask it, a sure sign that Flavius had been right about the destination.

"If I am correct," said Fabius, "and Hildebold's face seems to suggest I am, then I believe we can have a discussion about something more than how many of us we can each kill."

"How did you know?" asked Alberic.

"You have betrayed us," exploded Hildebold, turning on Alberic.

"The optio here figured it out," said Fabius, nodding toward Flavius, "although it was hardly a difficult puzzle to solve." The last sentence drew a frown from Flavius. "Tingitana or Caeseria?" asked Fabius.

"He has not betrayed anything," said Marcus. "We knew you would go to the one place in the Empire that did not have a regular legion. The only place you can go is Mauretania. We just did not know which province you would choose."

Alberic shook his head. "We traveled the length of Gaul without raising a ripple, but since we have arrived in Hispania everyone knows our secrets."

"You raised no ripples because it was in the interests of the Gauls to keep your secrets," said Fabius.

"We knew this," said Alberic. "But we told none our destination. If I answer your question, how do I gain?"

"There are two ways to consider gain," replied Fabius. "It can be at another's expense, or it can be mutually beneficial. You do not 'gain' anything if it is not in our interests. But it is possible that a peaceful resolution of this matter is in all our interests."

Alberic turned to Marcus. "You have said very little, legate. Does this man speak for you?"

"I am no admirer of war and slaughter," replied Marcus. "But I am also sworn to uphold the interests of the Empire. The VII Legion will fight anything that threatens it. Do you challenge the Empire, Alberic?"

"We do not, although we bear it no affection. We are a single tribe, pressed by Rome from the south and others who crowd in from the east. We were bound for Tingitana, because we were told that there is land and water aplenty and not many Romans," answered Alberic. "I do not say this as an insult, legate. We are people who do not like the shadow of others blocking our sunlight."

"You are right about there not being many Romans," put in Flavius, "but the locals may have a say about land and water."

"We were told they were horsemen who did not cultivate," said Alberic.

"Oh, they're horsemen, all right, but they will still have a say," said Flavius.

"The optio and the legate here have just returned from Tingitana and know a great deal about the locals," said the douviri, with a trace of impatience in his voice. "But we must return to the main point here. If you do not challenge the Empire, Alberic, then are you a subject?"

The Frank commander looked puzzled. "I do not understand. We have been fighting you for weeks and you ask us if we are subjects?"

"Are you citizens of the Empire?" asked Fabius.

"No!" spat Hildebold.

Fabius looked over at Marcus and raised an eyebrow.

"Then you are not in rebellion against the Emperor," said Marcus.

Still looking puzzled, Alberic shook his head. "No, I guess not. But I don't see what that has to do with anything." .

The duoviri sighed. "That is because you are barbarians and not subject to the laws of Rome. If you are citizens and rebel against the Emperor, then you are guilty of treason, and the only punishment is death. If you are not citizens, but misguided barbarians with no understanding of law or rules or order, then you are in need of enlightenment, after being duly punished and swearing allegiance to our august Emperor, of course."

"We have laws and rules, Roman, and...," started Hildebold, but Alberic silenced him.

"And if we swear allegiance to the Emperor?" asked Alberic.

"Then you will have seen the light of civilization and will rest within the bosom of the Empire," answered Fabius. "Of course, there will have to be compensation for the damage you have caused."

"Compensation?" asked Alberic suspiciously.

"Horses, gold, silver, and goods," said Fabius. "I am sure we can work something out."

Alberic turned to Marcus. "What about Tingitana?"

"That decision will be made in Nova Carthago, but there is a shortage of citizens in that province, particularly in the south. I cannot guarantee anything, but the request does not seem unreasonable," replied Marcus.

Alberic glanced at Hildebold who managed to look suspicious, angry, and confused all at the same time. "Legate, may I have a moment with my second-in-command?"

Marcus nodded, and the two Franks went off to huddle.

"Suppose Nova Carthago says no?" whispered Flavius.

"I doubt they will," answered the duoviri. "The whole peninsula is in an uproar about this, and there is nothing more that Nova Carthago would like than to make this go away. Particularly if it becomes Tingitana's problem. There is no love lost between the leaders of our two provinces. Plus, those 300 hostages have cousins and nephews and relations all over Hispania. No governor or military officer wants their deaths on his head."

"I do not know Hispania as intimately as you, duoviri, but I agree. The question will be what we let them take when they leave," said Marcus.

"Weapons," said Flavius.

"Weapons?" asked Fabius slightly horrified.

"First, the governor is not going to like this, but it is mainly the Mauri who are not going to like this. The Franks are going to need weapons," answered Flavius.

"And what would keep them from setting up their own little empire?" asked the douviri.

"The Mauri," answered Marcus. "There are not enough Franks to conquer Tingitana from us, and the Mauri won't want anything to do with them. The Franks may be barbarians to us, but to the Mauri they are just a different kind of Roman. The Mauri want all their lands back. These Franks will end up as our allies against the Mauri. That is what I wrote in my letter to Nova Carthago, and I suspect they will see it our way."

"Well argued, sir" said Fabius.

The two Franks had been quietly arguing for several minutes, and they had come to a conclusion. Both returned to rejoin the Romans.

Alberic slowly drew his sword and turned the handle toward Marcus. "We submit," he said quietly.

Marcus took the sword and handed it to Flavius. "I will ask all of you to swear a sacramentum to our Emperor Augustus Gaius Messius Quintus Decius. You will instruct your men to place their arms, including armor, in the plaza by the Praetorian Tower. You may keep your knives. You will follow the instructions of the head douviri Fabius Porcius in all matters."

Alberic nodded his assent. Hildebold slowly drew his sword as well and handed it to Marcus, who passed it on to Flavius. "Welcome to the Empire," said the duoviri.

XXXVI

Demaratus, Cassius, Coventina, and Flavius sat around a small table set outside a taverna not far from the docks, which were now crowded with Franks loading ships or carrying supplies down to the mole. A jug of wine sat on the table, which was spread with various small dishes filled with olives, oil, and small, salty fish. A basket filled with flatbread sat at the center.

They had spent the last hour exchanging stories and consuming a great deal of wine.

The first topic had been the "triumph." The city had insisted on giving Marcus, the VII Legion, and the auxiliaries a "triumphant march," with horns, rose petals, representatives of the city's merchants and veteran's organizations. Vipsania and her "Legion of Tarraco" marched just behind Vallerius, Demaratus, and the veterans who had fought near the tower. Coventina initially resisted marching with the "Legion," but Valeria pleaded for her to join them. It had been Valeria who had struck the Frank in the market and freed Coventina.

The triumph was delayed when Marcus refused to give up his horse and replace it with a huge charger that the head duoviri insisted would be a better representation than Marcus's slow, fat, unattractive horse. Fabius suggested that the legate ride on a chariot, but Marcus was as hostile to chariots as he was to horses. "I will walk," he announced.

But that would never do. "Sir, no Roman general has ever walked in a triumph," the head douviri pointed out.

"There is a first time for everything," replied Marcus. "In any case, it is a city triumph, not one declared by the Senate."

It was finally decided that if Marcus wanted to ride his fat, ugly horse, that was his business, and so the triumphant general rode into Tarraco on his ponderous steed, while crowds lined the streets and cheered.

Cheer they did, and throw flowers, even coins, and, as the day progressed and the wine stores were liberated, the triumph became quite jolly. The whole thing embarrassed Coventina, but the "Legion" was cheered as lustily as was Marcus and the real legions. Since the Franks had surrendered as part of a negotiated peace, they were not forced to march in chains. A good time was had by all.

The procession ended up at the top of the city at the Temple of Zeus, where people made speeches and drank more wine. Finally, the celebration wound down, with the crowds scattering to their homes and Marcus retiring to the VII Legion's headquarters just off the plaza.

Demaratus and Coventina sought out Flavius and Cassius and suggested they meet up at a small taverna, which is why they were still drinking hours after the celebrations were over.

Flavius had just finished relating the details of the battle at the bridge, with Cassius offering the cavalryman's view of the fight. Demaratus had already filled them in on what had happened with him and Coventina. Normally, it would have been awkward with three men and a woman, but Cassius and Flavius had been so taken with her story that they had begun to think of her as one of their own.

"How is our commander?" asked Demaratus.

"A natural legate, that's our Marcus," said Flavius. "Of course, he listens a lot to me," a remark that drew groans from Demaratus and Cassius.

"What happens now?" asked Coventina, dipping a piece of bread into her wine cup and eating it.

"I am not sure of the details, but apparently Nova Carthago saw things Marcus's way and agreed to let the Franks go to Tingitana," said Flavius, pouring a cup of wine.

Coventina crossed her arms, her face clouding over. Demaratus slipped an arm around her. Cassius and Flavius looked uncomfortable. "My love is not sure the debt has been repaid," he said quietly.

"Two dead Franks, another cut up, a riot, and stealing a bunch of ships," said Flavius, "that seems like a pretty good settling of the score. In fact, remind me not to get on your bad side."

Coventina smiled in spite of herself and the frozen moment thawed.

"What now, brother?" asked Flavius of Demaratus.

"Coventina and I have decided to be married," said Demaratus, setting off a round of congratulations and more wine.

When that had run its course, Cassius announced that he was heading back to Corduba with enough horses to satisfy even a Lusitanian. That meant a new jug of wine and another round of drinks.

"And you, brother?" asked Demaratus of Flavius.

"Oh, I will keep the VII Legion together and Marcus upright," he said.

Cassius stood, swayed a bit and put his hands on the table. "Brothers, Coventina, I must be going."

"Try to ride a horse in that condition and you'll end up in a thorn bush like Marcus," laughed Flavius, a remark that drew another short toast, after which Cassius attempted a salute, failed, wove his way around several tables, and drifted across the plaza, tipping slightly to his right.

Flavius pushed himself to his feet. "Well, comrade, I also have things to do. I await the details of your coming nuptials, and I will tell Marcus that you will be back on the job by tomorrow." He gave Coventina a little bow and strode off toward the docks.

Coventina squeezed Demaratus' arm. "I like them," she said.

He turned and stroked her cheek. "We will be seeing a lot of them, my love."

Flavius was drunk, but he had learned how to appear sober as long as the ground was not too uneven. He made his way toward the docks, all the while scanning the crowds of Franks, looking for someone in particular. He was about ready to give up when the familiar figure of Hildebold strode out of a warehouse and started back toward the city's center.

The optio caught up to him. "You, Frank. A moment."

Hildebold whirled and glowered at Flavius. "What do you want, Roman?" he asked.

"Not ending up on the wrong side of a sword certainly hasn't improved your disposition, Frank," glowered Flavius back. "You don't have anything I might want. But I thought there was something you ought to know about where you are going."

Suspicion and interest warred visibly on Hildebold's face. He had not, at first, recognized Flavius, who was not wearing a helmet as he had been during the negotiations between the commander of the VII Legion and Alberic. But the optio's smashed nose and stocky build jarred his memory. Flavius was also a reminder that the Franks had been defeated. Still, he knew the Romans had recently been in Tingitana. He took a deep breath and made himself relax. He even managed a stiff smile.

"I am Hildebold," he said. "I believe you are called Flavius. I would appreciate your views on our destination."

Flavius nodded in the direction of a deserted section of the docks and indicated that Hildebold should go in front of him. The two strode across the mole until people coming and going no longer surrounded them. Hildebold stopped, turned and waited for Flavius to talk.

"Where are you headed?" asked Flavius.

"Tingis," answered Hildebold.

"You might want to re-think that," said Flavius.

"Why?" asked the Frank.

"Do you know much about where you're going and who's who in Mauretania?" asked Flavius.

Hildebold shook his head. "No. We knew there was no legion and that there was supposed to be land, but that is all we knew."

"The governor's name is Domitius Antonius, and if a poisonous snake bit him, the snake would curl up and die," said Flavius.

Hildebold laughed. It was the first time Flavius had seen the man do anything but glower, and he grudgingly started to like the short Frank.

"If you have anything to do with him, you'll all end up being slaves and most likely sent south," said Flavius.

Hildebold stopped laughing. "What choice do we have?"

"Don't go to Tingis," said Flavius. "Go through the pillars of Hercules and turn south. There is a big cape that juts out and a channel that runs north up its other side. You can't miss it. It is about a day's sail south. There's a beach where you can land."

"But what do we do?" asked Hildebold.

Flavius glanced around to be sure no one was listening. "Look, try to have anything to do with that governor and you're dead. What you need are some allies, and I have a suggestion."

Hildebold blinked. Flavius was pretty close to treason. "Yes?" he asked.

"Tingitana isn't of much concern to Rome," said Flavius. "She produces some slaves and animals for the games, but that's about it. Most of the Romans live up north on the coast. There is a town near the beach called Sala, but it's not much and doesn't have anyone who can cause you trouble. The trouble will come from the Mauri, and they are major trouble. We were lucky to get out alive the last time we tangled with them."

Hildebold shook his head confusedly. "So, what are you suggesting? We fight the Mauri to avoid fighting the governor? We don't have weapons to fight any of them."

"A lot of your weapons were brought into the city and stored. I can arrange for them to end up on your ships, at least swords and such. I can't manage armor or shields, although I might be able to get some spears," said Flavius.

Hildebold also glanced around and then whispered, "You would do this? How?"

"A number of the lads who went to Tingitana with us last year would like to put a spear up that Governor's ass, and they would be more than willing to help out if it means trouble for the son of a bitch. He double-crossed us and nearly got a lot of them killed," said Flavius.

Hildebold decided that Roman revenge was in a category by itself, and something one should try to avoid in life.

"But if you had a bad time with the Mauri, why do you think we can handle them?" asked Hildebold.

"First, there are a lot more of you. We were a single cohort," answered Flavius, "and second, you don't want to fight the Mauri, you want to talk to them."

"They would be interested?" asked Hildebold doubtfully.

"Listen, the Mauri are the best horsemen in the Empire. They can run rings around these Lusitanians, who are about as good as I have encountered. But they don't know anything about infantry. They used Libyans against us, but they didn't have a lot of them, and I think they were fighting just for pay," said Flavius. "You want a place to settle. I figure you perform a service for the Mauri, they give you some land."

"You think this might work?" asked Hildebold dropping all reserve.

Flavius shrugged. "I know if you go to Tingis, you'll end up slaves. I don't know what the Mauri want. They might only want to kill you. But it is the best bet you have."

Hildebold gave him a considered look. "How do you know we won't try to take over the province?"

"Go ahead, but I doubt you can do it. And if you tried, you would be fighting both the Governor and the Mauri, and together they would make short work of you. No, the only chance you have is to cut a deal with the Mauri and hire out as infantry," said Flavius. "Anyhow, that's the deal. You want those weapons?"

"Yes," answered Hildebold. "We are in your debt, Flavius."

"You are, Frank. You can repay it by making that bastard who calls himself governor unhappy. If you can kill him, all the better," said Flavius. "I'll arrange things. Keep this quiet."

Hildebold extended his hand. "I honor you, Flavius. You have given us back our lives."

Flavius nodded. "Give me revenge on the governor, Frank." He grasped Hildebold's hand, then abruptly turned and walked away.

Hildebold watched him go. I will never be able to figure them out, he thought; Romans are simply different than other people.

Marcus contemplated a table he had turned into a desk at the spacious headquarters of the 10th Cohort's Third Century. It was piled with requests, requisitions, wax tables, and scrolls. A small cloud of clerks came and went, adding more to the piles. Demaratus, who would usually take control of the matter, sorting things out, would not be back until tomorrow. Marcus' head hurt from too much wine, and he was feeling tired, crabby and sorry for himself.

He defeats a Frankish army, and they plague him with requests for olive oil, bread, mules, and an endless list of things that he had no control over. He decided that being a victorious general consisted mainly a being a clerk. He poked at one pile, which spilled over onto another.

The outer office was crowded with petitioners for everything from compensation for the Frankish invasion to requests to open businesses. There were 10 marriage proposals. Just as he was thinking of sneaking out the back and heading for the baths, Flavius strolled in.

"Well, it is about time, optio," grouched Marcus.

"Sorry, sir. I needed to take care of some matters concerning the Franks. Shall I begin sorting out that crowd in the outer office?" asked Flavius.

Marcus poked again at the mounds of scrolls. "What about all this?"

"Oh, leave that, sir. Demaratus will be back tomorrow, and he'll take care of it. I think I can clear out a lot of the people waiting to see you as well, sir. You do need to meet with the two duoviri, and Cassius would like to get started south. I'll have some food sent in." He rummaged around the table for a moment, then seized on a wax tablet. "Here is Cassius's request, sir. You can just make a mark, and I'll see he gets it."

Marcus relaxed. He had defeated an army. He had liberated the oldest Roman city in Hispania (and without an enormous butcher bill). He had been given a triumph, and he was a hero. And now that Flavius was here (and the redoubtable Greek, Demaratus, would sort this all out tomorrow), he didn't have to clutter up his life with minutiae, he could accept some accolades, and maybe even have a bath before long.

Life was good.

Glossary and Notes

Acetum. Sour wine, the standard drink of soldiers.

Ala. Auxiliary cavalry unit, roughly the size of a infantry cohort.

Alae. A cavalry wing.

Century. Basic administrative and military unit of a legion.

Cohort. Basic tactical unit of the legion.

Centurion. Commander of a century.

Cornus. Roman war horn.

Contubernium. The smallest unit in a century.

Dolabra. Basic infantry entrenching tool, a sort of pick-axe.

Domus. House.

Gladius. Short stabbing sword of the Roman infantry.

Intervallum. Border inside of a fort or marching camp.

Legate. Commands a legion.

Librarius. Junior clerk at army headquarters.

Liburna. A light, swift Roman warship.

Optio. Second in command of a century.

Pilum. Heavy spear of the Roman army (pl. pila).

Praetorians. Emperor's personal legion, the only legion allowed in Rome.

Prefect. Third in command of a legion.

Principia. Army headquarters.

Pugio. Short dagger.

Quingeniaery. Cavalry unit. It is composed of 16 *turmae* of 30 men each, normally from 480 to 500 men.

Quinquereme. Heavy Roman warship. Its name means "five," the basic team of rowers. It had three banks of oars.

Sacramentum. Oath of loyalty to the Emperor.

Sagum. Cloak used by soldiers, fastened at the right shoulder.

Scutum. The basic rectangle shield of a legionnaire. It was 4 ft long, 2' 6" wide, and curved to deflect blows.

Signaculum. Lead identification tags, the Roman Army equivalent of dog tags.

Signifer. Officer who carries the century standard, and also oversees the unit's books and the men's pay.

Signum. A century's standard.

Spatha. Long sword used by Roman cavalry.

Taberna. Tavern.

Tesserarius. Most junior officer in a century, oversees assigning guard duty.

Testudo. "The tortoise," an infantry maneuver that forms a wall and roof of shields. It is effective for sieging towns and to protect against archers.

Tribune. Senior staff officer in a legion.

Trireme. Basic warship of the ancient Greeks, also used as a light ship by the Romans. It means "three," referring to its three banks of oars, each rowed by a single rower.

Turmae. Basic cavalry unit, normally 30 men.

Valetudinarium. Hospital.

Vexilla. A detachment of troops operating away from their parent body.

Vigiles. Served as police and firemen in cities.

The Structure of a Roman Legion

A Roman legion was designed to be a tactically flexible fighting force. To enhance that flexibility, it was divided into discrete units. In that way, a legion resembled a modern infantry division, which is divided into brigades, battalions, regiments, companies and squads. The legion's units could act independently of one another so that they could reinforce a unit that was in trouble, exploit a weakness in the enemy's line, or block an attempt to out-flank the legion. Mobility was the essence of a legion's tactics and made it virtually invincible for almost 700 years. Modern armies owe much of their organizational structure to the Roman legion.

A legion was constructed as follows:

Contubernium: An eight-man squad, the smallest unit in a legion.

Century: Comprising 10 contuberniums. A century is normally 80 men, commanded by a centurion.

Cohort (regular): Composed of six centuries, approximately 480 men.

First Cohort: Composed of five centuries, but each century has160 men. A First Cohort would be approximately 800 men.

Legion: Made up of 10 cohorts normally deployed in three lines. When Headquarters units, plus specialists, are included, a legion would be approximately 5,400 men.

Legate: Legion commander.

Tribune: Senior legion staff officer (normally three per legion).

Prefect (Praefectus castrorum): Third-in-command.

The Structure of a Century

The century was the smallest tactical unit in a legion. That is, it was the smallest unit capable of fighting on its own. It was closest to a modern infantry company, although smaller. In the case of a century from the first cohort, however, it was somewhat larger than a modern infantry company.

A century had four officers:

Centurion: Commander.

Optio: Second-in-command.

Signifer: Holds century standard during battle and keeps the unit's books.

Tesserarius: Junior officer, who also sets sentry duty and oversees camp construction.

Centurions, in order of seniority:

First Cohort
Primus Pilus
Princeps
Princeps Posterior
Hastatus
Hastatus Posterior
Hastatus Posterior
(The five centurions

of the First Cohort
make up the *Primi Ordines*,
a group of the most senior
centurions)

Regular Cohort
Pilus Prior
Pilus Posterior
Princeps Prior
Princeps Posterior
Hastatus

Place Names

Tarraco Names/ Modern names
Augustobriga/ Talavera la Vieja
Barcino/ Barcelona
Brigantium/ La Coruna
Carthago Nova/ Cartagena
Caesaraugusta/ Zaragoza
Clunia/ Coruna del Conde
Corduba/ Cordoba
Emporiae/ Ampurias
Gades/ Cadiz
Gaul/ France
Ilerda/ Lerida
Legio/ Leon
Lugdunum Convenarum/ St. Bertrand de Comminges
Mauretania Caesarienis/ Algeria
Mauretania Tingitana/ Morocco
Namausus/ Nimes
Narbo/ Narbonne
Norba / Caceres
Osca/ Huesca
Rhodus/ Rhode
Tarraco/ Tarragona
Tortosa/ Tortosa
Valentia/ Valencia

Rivers and Seas

Anas River/ Guadiana River

Baetis River/ Guadalquiver River

Duris River/ Duro River

Iberus River/ Ebro River

Bibliography

Adkins, Lesley and Roy A. Adkins. *Handbook to Life in Ancient Rome*, Oxford University Press, 1994.

Appian. *Wars of the Romans in Iberia*. Translated by J.S. Richardson, Aris & Phillips LTD, 2000.

Breem, Wallace. *Eagle in the Snow*, Rugged Land, 2004.

Campbell, Brian. *War and Society in Imperial Rome: 31 BC-284 AD*, Routledge, 2002.

Casson, Lionell. *Ships and Seafaring in Ancient Times*, University of Texas Press, 1994.

Goldsworthy, Adrian. *The Complete Roman Army*, Thames & Hudson, 2003. Southern, Pat. *The Roman Empire: From Severus to Constantine*, Routledge, 2001.

Grant, Michael. *The Army ,of the Caesars*, Charles Scribner's Sons, 1974.

Griess, Thomas E. *Ancient and Medieval Warfare: The West Point Military History Series*, Avery Publishing Group, Inc., 1984.

Hadas, Moses. *Imperial Rome*, Time-Life Books, 1965.

Hamey, L.A. and J.A. Hamey. *The Roman Engineers*, Cambridge University Press, 1981.

Hopkins, Keith. *A World Full of Gods: The Strange Triumph of Christianity*, The Free Press, 1999.

Keppie, Lawrence. *The Making of the Roman Army: From Republic to Empire*, University of Oklahoma Press, 1984.

Le Glay, Marcel, Jean-Louis Voisin and Yann Le Bohec. *A History of Rome*, Blackwell, 2001.

Lewis, Jon E., editor. *The Mammoth Book of Eyewitness Ancient Rome*, Carrol & Graff Publishers, 2003.

Luttwak, Edward N. *The Grand Strategy of the Roman Empire: From the First Century AD to the Third*, Johns Hopkins University Press, 1979.

MacMullen, Ramsay. *Roman Social Relations*, Yale University Press, 1974.

Richardson, John S. *The Romans in Spain*, Blackwell, 1998.

Scarre, Chris. *The Penguin Historical Atlas of Ancient Rome*, Penguin, 1995.

Strauss, Barry. *The Battle of Salamis*, Simon & Schuster, 2004.

Wells, Peter. *The Barbarians Speak: How the Conquered Peoples Shaped Roman Europe*, Princeton University Press, 1999.

Acknowledgments

This book could not have been written without the careful copy editing of Anne Bernstein, Betsy Wootten, John Isbister and Roz Spafford, as well as their critiques and suggestions. Danny Hallinan was the book's historical editor and Jack Radey gave valuable advice on the Roman Army and ancient warfare. I am deeply grateful to readers like Susan Watrous, Antonio Hallinan, Danny Beagle and Linda Williams who gave me practical suggestions on how to make the book better, plus invaluable encouragement. My thanks go to Ann Higgins for the cover design and to Caroline Jennings for interior formatting and final editing.

Conn M. Hallinan was a long-time columnist for Foreign Policy in Focus, "A Think Tank Without Walls," and an independent journalist. He holds a PhD in Anthropology from the University of California, Berkeley. For 23 years he oversaw the journalism program at the University of California at Santa Cruz, where he won the UCSC Alumni Association's Distinguished Teaching Award, as well as UCSC's Innovations in Teaching Award and its Excellence in Teaching Award. He also served as Provost at Kresge College of UCSC, retiring in 2004. He is a winner of a Project Censored "Real News Award," and lives in Berkeley, California. The Middle Empire books are his first works of fiction.